CURB APPEAL

Book One of *The Shaker Protocol*

A Novel

KEN KONET & Ibrahim Roble

Humbolton Press

Copyright

CURB APPEAL
Book One of The Shaker Protocol

Published by Humbolton Press
Texas, United States of America
www.humbolton.com

First Edition: April 2026

ISBN (Paperback): 978-1-966703-36-5

For permissions inquiries, bulk orders, foreign rights, film/television rights, or media requests, contact:
permissions@humbolton.com

Editorial: Humbolton Press

Set in Bookman Old Style.
Printed in the United States of America.

10 9 8 7 6 5 4 3 2 1

Abstract

Theo Novak is a corporate instructional designer in Cleveland, Ohio. On a Sunday afternoon in August of 1996, he stops his Jeep at a curb in Shaker Heights and takes a bronze sculpture from a free pile in front of a house being emptied by an estate company. He believes, at the time, that he is making out very well. Inside the sculpture, he will find a brass key, a sealed envelope, and a typed page of seven names. Within a week, his apartment will be tossed, his girlfriend will be taken, and he will be sitting across from an FBI agent in a kitchen in Cedar-Fairmount, agreeing to do something he is not qualified to do, in a building he has been to as a tourist, in a city he thought he understood.

This is the story of that week. It is told, years later, by Theo himself. Some of it is told by Frankie. Some of it should not be told at all.

The Shaker Protocol is a four-book sequence about a small group of unremarkable people who, between August of 1996 and the spring of the following year, walked into a residual Cold War operation and did not walk back out the same.
Curb Appeal is Book One.

Table of Contents

ONE: *The Pickup*

Sunday, August 18, 1996, 2:47 PM.

The thing about garbage picking in Shaker Heights is that you have to act like you belong. You can't creep. You can't slow-roll with the window down like some kind of vulture. You pull up confidently, like you're a contractor, like you're there on business, like the three-and-a-half-pound bronze sculpture on the tree lawn is something your client specifically asked you to come get.

My client had not specifically asked me to come get the sculpture.

My client was a compliance training module for TRW Systems Division, seventy-one slides on the handling of classified documents under the new Executive Order 12958, and it was due at 9 AM Wednesday, and at this specific moment on this specific Sunday in this specific August it did not even know I existed.

But the sculpture was beautiful. In an ugly way. A good ugly. The kind of ugly that costs a lot.

I pulled the Jeep up, popped the hatch, and hauled it into the back like I was moving a body, which — as it turned out — was not the worst metaphor I could have picked.

I had been cutting through Shaker to avoid the Cedar Road construction, which had been dragging on since Memorial Day. South Park Boulevard ran along the upper Shaker Lakes, the water flashing between trees. I was doing maybe twenty, with the light that slow golden color the sky gets when it has decided to stop pretending, listening to Ben Folds Five on the tape deck because my car radio had stopped picking up anything except WMJI, and WMJI was doing a seventies block party that morning that I was not in the mood for. The houses were too big for the trees, or the trees were too big for the houses — I could never decide which. Old money. Quiet money. The kind of money that does not need to tell you about itself.

The U-Haul was the first thing I noticed.

Twenty-six-footer, parked at the curb in front of a long Tudor Revival with a green slate roof. Not a mid-century modern — I would misremember that later, for years, in the telling. The house was older than that. Thirties. Heavy black shutters. A wrought-iron address plate that read *2341 South Park* in the kind of ornamental script you paid somebody in 1935 to design for you once and never thought about again.

The free pile was the second thing I noticed.

It filled the tree lawn. Two chairs. A brass floor lamp. Three or four packing boxes with their lids thrown open, overflowing. A tangle of stereo equipment. And on top of a wooden crate, sitting slightly off-center like somebody had set it down mid-argument, a small dark bronze sculpture.

I took my foot off the gas and coasted for a second.

There's a specific feeling to finding something good on a curb, and I have been trying to describe it to Frankie for two years. It is not greed, exactly. It is closer to the feeling of spotting the one good cookie on the tray of mostly bad cookies at a wedding reception. It is a brief private joy, followed almost immediately by a brief private shame that you are thinking about cookies at a wedding. You want the thing. You want the thing very much. But you also know, at a level just under your conscience, that you are about to go briefly feral in public.

I put the Jeep in reverse.

Two people were standing by the back of the U-Haul: a man my age, maybe a little older, in Dockers and a rumpled polo shirt, and a woman with her hair up in the kind of ponytail people do when they are not thinking about their hair. They were sweating. They were arguing, quietly, the way people argue in front of strangers — with their eyes mostly, and with their shoulders. The woman pointed at one of the boxes. The man sighed and dragged a hand down his face.

They were tired. They were done.

I pulled in behind the U-Haul and got out.

I had learned the hard way, over a decade of committed garbage picking across three neighborhoods of Cleveland, that the only thing that mattered in this moment was confidence. You had to walk like a person who had a specific reason to be there. You had to not hunch. You could not mumble. You had to wave, make eye contact, and say something that sounded normal.

I waved. I made eye contact. I said, "Mind if I take a look?"

The man — I could see now that his eyes were red, that he was not just tired, he was *tired* — looked at me like I had just asked him the time in Portuguese.

"Take whatever you want," he said.

"You sure?"

"We're putting it out for the trash tomorrow anyway."

"I'll —"

"Take it," he said. "Please."

He said *please* with a particular weight. I have thought about that *please* a hundred times since. At the moment I read it as *please stop making me engage with the contents of my dead parents' house for one more second.* That was the right reading. I was just missing everything that was in its shadow.

I said thank you. I meant it.

Then I started picking.

I am not going to pretend I did this gracefully. The truth is I went a little fast, because the longer I spent on the curb of a stranger's house sorting through a dead person's life, the more I was going to feel like the specific kind of man I did not want to be. I pulled the sculpture off the crate first. Heavier than it looked. Smaller than it had seemed from the street — maybe eight inches tall. Dense. Cold. The color of wet chocolate. It had a roughness in some places and a silken patina in others, and the whole thing was shaped into what I thought might be a woman, bent, with something like a second figure reclining below her. Or a woman and a landscape. Or a hat and a shoe. I couldn't quite tell, which I took as a good sign. Good art takes a minute to tell you what it is.

I put the sculpture in the back of the Jeep.

Next, from one of the open boxes, I pulled two small oil paintings. Both canvas, both unframed, both of yellow flowers. Not professional yellow flowers — not a gallery piece. Closer to the work of someone with real craft who had nonetheless painted these for themselves, probably on a Sunday afternoon with a glass of something white. I liked them. They had a soft, confident quality that made me want to put one on the wall above our stairs and one above the stove. I took both.

At the bottom of one of the packing boxes, under a tangled silver tea set and three broken picture frames, I found a wooden cigar box. Empty. Cedar inside, dark mahogany outside, with a gold-leaf label that had been rubbed away until only the word *Habana* remained. I took that too, because I am a cigar-box guy. My grandfather had been a cigar-box guy. I used to store baseball cards in the ones he gave me. You can make a whole personality out of having a cigar box, in my experience.

I loaded everything into the back of the Jeep. I closed the hatch.

The man and the woman were staring at me, but not unkindly. I waved again. The woman gave me the kind of half-smile people give to a neighbor's dog when the neighbor has briefly lost control of it.

"Sorry for your loss," I said. It came out before I could talk myself out of it.

The man nodded. "Thank you."

"What's in the U-Haul?"

"Everything else."

He said it flatly, like a punchline he had run out of energy for. Then he turned and walked back to the house, and the woman followed him, and I got in the Jeep and drove away.

I did not look in the rearview.

It is one of the small regrets of my life that I did not look in the rearview.

Cleveland Heights was a fifteen-minute drive from Shaker, north and slightly west, through streets I knew well enough to drive on autopilot. Cedar-Fairmount was one of the small commercial nodes where the Heights leaned into its old bones — a stretch of brick storefronts built in 1920, a bakery that had been there in some form since my grandmother's childhood, a used bookstore, a diner, a bank branch, a Rite Aid, and a very specific population of shaggy Case Western grad students with too many opinions about jazz. Frankie and I rented the upstairs unit of a brick half-double on Cedar, three blocks from the intersection. The downstairs unit was occupied by a professor of mathematical logic named Dr. Anselmi who rarely came out during daylight hours and who had, I was certain, at least three cats that were not supposed to be there. We had an informal agreement. He did not mention our cat. We did not mention his cats. The landlord, who lived in Arizona and only visited in the spring, had never caught on to either of us.

I pulled up behind Frankie's truck — a 1989 Ford F-150 in the exact shade of faded red that construction sites had collectively agreed on at some point — and killed the engine. For a moment I sat there.

The bronze was, for some reason, already pulling at me.

I got out. Walked around to the back. Popped the hatch.

The sculpture was lying on its side in the bed. A little awkward. I rolled it upright and picked it up with both hands. It was, I now thought, maybe three and a half pounds, which was startlingly heavy for its size. You think something is eight inches tall and you expect it to weigh less than a book. This did not.

I carried it up the stairs.

Frankie was on the back porch.

Our back porch was a small wooden structure, original to the house, that had been slowly tilting toward the driveway for about six years. Frankie had decided — without consulting me, which was not unusual for her, though she was perfectly happy to *inform* me — that we were rebuilding it this summer. She had drawn plans. She had sourced reclaimed cedar from a tear-down in Ohio City. She had borrowed a compound miter saw from a guy named Mario I had never met. On this specific Sunday afternoon, she was kneeling in the center of the porch frame in cutoff jeans and a tank top that had probably been white once, hammering a joist into true with the calm fury of somebody who had been at this problem since breakfast.

She looked up when I came through the gate.

Francesca Russo was a specific kind of beautiful I had, in two years of dating her, decided not to try to describe, because every time I tried I embarrassed myself. She was five-foot-nine. She was tanned in a way that was clearly the result of working outdoors and clearly had a hard border at mid-bicep. Her hair was dark, thick, and always escaping whatever she had tied it back with that morning, and today's version was a bandana that had once been red and was now a kind of apocalyptic orange. Her shoulders were the shoulders of a person who lifted things for a living. Her hands were her grandfather's hands. She was wiping her face with the back of her wrist, and she was looking at me with the specific expression she wore when she had decided in advance I was about to bring her a small problem.

"You found something," she said.

"How do you know."

"Because you look like a Labrador who just found a dead bird."

I held up the sculpture.

Frankie set the hammer down. She climbed off the porch. She walked toward me across the yard with that long stride of hers and stopped about three feet away and crossed her arms.

"Oh," she said. "Oh no."

"It's art."

"Babe."

"It's *art.*"

"It looks like my aunt after a bad divorce."

I laughed. I couldn't help it.

"Give it here," she said, and she took it from me, and she turned it in her hands with real care. Frankie knew about objects. She could tell at one glance how old a thing was and how it had been made. Watching her assess something I had just dragged home was one of the pleasures of my life. She tilted the sculpture. She checked the underside. She ran a thumbnail along one of the edges.

"Cast bronze," she said.

"Yeah."

"Hollow. Sand mold, maybe. Not a commercial pour."

"It's good, right?"

She frowned. "It's *interesting.* It's not terrible. I would not have paid a dollar for it."

"I didn't pay a dollar for it."

"That tracks."

"Somebody made this with their hands," I said, "and somebody else threw it away on a tree lawn, and I think that's a minor tragedy, and I think we owe the maker something, and I propose we put it on the shelf above the TV."

Frankie looked at the bronze. Then she looked at me. Then she looked at the shelf above the TV, which she could see through the back door.

"Top shelf," she said. "Behind the plant. Where nobody has to make eye contact with it."

"Deal."

She handed the sculpture back.

"What else you get?"

"Two paintings. A cigar box."

"The paintings good?"

"You're going to love the paintings."

"Then we're going to put the paintings in the kitchen. And we're going to put the cigar box on my tool shelf, because you already have three of them. And we are going to *consider*, over dinner, whether the statue goes in the basement."

"It's not going in the basement."

"It is extremely going in the basement."

"I love you," I said.

"I know," she said. She kissed me on the top of the head. She always kissed me on the top of the head when she wanted me to feel short, which was — and I understood this intellectually — not the same as wanting me to feel *less*. She walked past me back toward the porch. "Help me with this joist before dinner. I can't get the left side to square."

"Okay."

I carried the sculpture inside.

I put the paintings on the kitchen counter, leaned against the tile backsplash. I put the cigar box on the breakfast table. I set the sculpture on the top shelf of the living-room built-in, behind a pothos plant that had been alive longer than our relationship and seemed determined to remain so. I stepped back.

From across the room, with the plant partially obscuring it, the sculpture looked smaller than it had in the Jeep. It looked, oddly, at home.

I picked it back up. I turned it over, the way Frankie had. Cast bronze, hollow, sand mold maybe. I held it with the base toward me. There was a disk of dense wool felt covering the underside, glued on, neat as a kitchen tile. Factory-standard. The kind of felt bronze sculptures come with from the foundry so they do not scratch your furniture.

On the lower edge of the base, just beside the felt, somebody had stamped two small letters into the metal.

**M.O.*

They were sans-serif. A little crooked, like they had been tapped in by hand with a jeweler's punch. About the size of my pinky nail each. They looked like a signature — *the* signature — which would explain why the piece was not signed more prominently on the front.

M. O.

I ran my thumb over them. I wondered who M. O. was. I wondered if they were still alive, and if they knew that one of their pieces had just been thrown on a curb in Shaker Heights. I wondered, for a moment, whether I should try to find out.

I put the sculpture back on the shelf.

Monday was going to be a long day. I had a module to finish.

I went to help Frankie with the joist.

TWO: *Monday at TRW*

The TRW Systems Division campus was in Lyndhurst, which was the kind of close-in suburb that was trying to pretend it was country. It sat on Richmond Road, with a long curving driveway that looped through a landscaped berm designed to keep passersby from seeing what was inside, and with a security gate that was very polite and very fast. The main building was a low, wide, dark-glass thing that looked less like a corporate headquarters than like a cruise ship that had been beached.

I worked in the Training and Development group. Eighth floor, south wing. My cubicle was one of thirty-two in a room that had the same beige carpet as every other cubicle room in America and the exact same smell — coffee, printer toner, and a faint undercurrent of somebody's leftover Arby's. I had decorated mine with a framed postcard of the Cedar Point Gemini rollercoaster (we had taken a long weekend there in June), a calendar from the Cleveland Museum of Natural History, and a Polaroid of Frankie on the porch of a house in Euclid, smiling through a haze of sawdust.

I had been at TRW for three and a half years. It was the longest I had ever held a job. Most of what I did on any given day was read specifications from engineers whose native language was a dialect of technical English I had spent four years learning to reverse-engineer, and then translate those specifications into training modules that other engineers could consume in ninety minutes without actively wanting to die. It was not glamorous work. It was the opposite of glamorous work. But I was good at it. I was good at it in the specific way that certain kinds of teachers are good at it — I was patient, I was observant, and I knew that the smartest people in any room are almost always the ones who remember how to sound like a beginner.

Also, I liked money.

Monday morning I pulled into the garage at 7:48, swiped my badge twice because the reader was in a bad mood, and took the elevator to eight. Our admin, Doreen, was already at her desk eating a cinnamon roll from the Bob Evans near her house. Doreen ate a cinnamon roll from the Bob Evans near her house every Monday. It was one of the few reliable facts of my life.

"How was the weekend, doll?"

"Good. I drew seven more slides on Saturday."

"You're a machine."

"I'm on track to hate my life by Wednesday."

"You say that every week."

"It comes true every week."

She waved me on. I went to my cubicle. I turned on my IBM PS/2. I pulled up the compliance module in PowerPoint. I read the slide I had ended on Friday, which was slide forty-two, titled LEARNING OBJECTIVE 4.2: IDENTIFY APPROPRIATE SAFEGUARDS FOR CLASSIFIED MATERIAL IN AN OPEN-OFFICE ENVIRONMENT.

I stared at it for a while.

The thing about designing learning for adults — which I will spare you, mostly — is that you have to make peace with a central paradox of the job, which is that adults almost never want to be taught anything. Kids are used to being taught things. Adults find it undignified. The only way to get an adult to absorb information is to phrase it as something they already suspected. You have to meet them in the state of already being smart. You have to make the lesson into a confirmation.

This was my strategy for the module. It was also my strategy for marriage, for traffic, and for most of my conversations with my mother.

I typed a bullet point. I deleted it. I typed it again.

Visual separation of classified material from the workstation at all times, even during short absences (e.g., bathroom breaks, meetings with coworkers).

I stared at this. I changed *even during short absences* to *especially during short absences.* I read it again. I changed it back. I typed another bullet.

Awareness of line-of-sight angles from unsecured workspaces (e.g., open doorways, shared monitors).

This was better. This was the kind of thing a defense engineer would read and nod at. *Oh, yes. Line-of-sight angles. That is the real issue.* They would not notice that I had, in my entire professional life, never personally handled a classified document, or that I was making up the specific vocabulary of compliance as I went along. They would read the line-of-sight angles bullet and feel that their instincts had been confirmed. This was my art.

I worked for two hours. I got through three more slides. At 10:12 I went to refill my coffee in the break room.

Galen Brennan was already there.

Galen was sixty-one years old, six-foot-two, with the specific shambling posture of a tall man who had decided early in life not to apologize for it. He had a silver crewcut, a face like a kind bulldog, and the soft brown eyes of somebody who had been the smartest kid in every room he had ever walked into and had responded by becoming the calmest one. He was a senior propulsion engineer, with twenty-eight years at TRW and three patents to his name, and he was one of three people on the eighth floor I would have called a friend.

He had met Frankie twice. He liked her. Frankie had deemed him, after their second meeting, "one of the good ones, babe, he's got kind hands."

"Novak," he said. "You look like you're already three days behind."

"I am three days behind. I am one day behind and also in the future."

"That's not a calendar problem, that's a physics problem. You want to talk about it?"

"Not unless you want to write the slides for me."

"I cannot write the slides for you."

"Then no."

I poured coffee. I dumped in creamer. I watched him pour his own, which was black. He was not looking at me. He was looking at the coffee like it was a test.

"Hey," I said. "Speaking of physics problems. Question for Meg."

"Shoot."

"We got a sculpture off a free pile yesterday. Small bronze. I think it's interesting. I can't find a signature. Mind asking Meg if she has any idea?"

Meg was Galen's wife. Meg restored antique furniture as a hobby and had contacts in the Cleveland art scene that went back to the late sixties. If anybody could glance at a small bronze and tell me who made it, it was Meg.

"Sure," Galen said. "You got a picture?"

"I've got a Polaroid in my wallet."

I fished it out. I had taken the picture Sunday evening, on the shelf, with the plant moved aside. The flash had washed out some of the detail, but you could see the shape of it, and you could make out the M.O. mark if you knew where to look.

I handed it to him.

Galen took the Polaroid. He smiled at it. Then he stopped smiling.

It was quick. You could have missed it. Almost — but not quite. His face went through two expressions in under a second, and the second one was a bad expression, and then it was gone again, and he was smiling the old smile, and handing the Polaroid back.

"Huh," he said. "I'll ask Meg."

"You all right?"

"Yeah. Just — you know. Interesting piece."

"Yeah?"

"Yeah."

He was holding the coffee. He was holding the coffee the way people hold coffee when they have forgotten they were holding coffee.

"I gotta make a call," he said. "Thanks, Theo. I'll get back to you on the sculpture."

He left.

I stood in the break room for a full minute after he had gone, holding my own coffee, looking at the door he had just walked out of. Something had happened. I did not know what something. Galen had been on the way into the break room when I arrived, to refill his coffee. Now his coffee was on the counter, and his coffee was still full, and Galen was gone.

I told myself I was being paranoid.

I went back to my cubicle.

I worked for three more hours. I did not see Galen again that morning. I did not see him again that afternoon, either.

I did not see Galen again for six days.

What I did not know at the time — what I would not learn until a week later, when Claire Mwangi sat me down at her kitchen table with a cup of coffee and a manila folder and walked me through a reconstructed timeline — was that Galen Brennan, at 10:47 that morning, walked out the south entrance of the TRW campus, got in his 1993 Ford Taurus station wagon, and drove exactly one mile south on Richmond Road to the BP station at the corner of Mayfield.

He parked at the edge of the lot. He went to the payphone by the ice chest. He fed four quarters into it. He dialed a number he had been told never to write down.

When the man who answered said one word in Russian, Galen said, in plain English: "The package is moving. I have seen it in Lyndhurst. I need instructions."

The voice on the other end — it was not the voice Galen had expected, but he did not know that yet — said, in careful English: "Describe it."

Galen described it.

The voice was silent for a beat. Then it said, "Stay where you are. We will call you back at this number in eight minutes."

Galen hung up. He stood by the payphone. He checked his watch. He had made this call, under one version or another, on two previous occasions in his life, and each time it had been with a sum and a deliberation that had not served him well. A woman came up to use the phone. He told her, apologetically, that he was waiting on a call. She moved along. Eight minutes crawled past. The phone rang. Galen answered.

A different voice this time. Same careful English.

"Continue your normal routine. Do not initiate contact with the new party. You will be instructed. Your coworker's name."

"Novak. Theodore Novak. Instructional designer."

"Spell it."

Galen spelled it.

"Address."

Galen gave it. He had been to my apartment for a small dinner in March. Meg had brought a cheesecake.

"Continue normal routine. End."

The line went dead.

Galen walked back to the Taurus. He sat in the driver's seat for a long time with his hands on the wheel. He thought about calling Meg. He did not call Meg. He drove back to TRW. He did not come up to the eighth floor. He sat in his ground-floor office with the door closed from 11:21 to 4:45 PM, and he did not come out.

I would learn all of this later. At the moment, I was in my cubicle, writing bullet points about line-of-sight angles, and Galen was a small worry I was choosing to set down and come back to in the morning.

I did not know that the man on the other end of the first call had been the wrong man.

I left TRW at 5:22 PM.

The parking garage was a four-level structure attached to the main building by an enclosed walkway, and my Jeep was on the third level, near the west stairs. I walked out into the garage the way I walked out every evening — keys out, laptop bag over my shoulder, thinking about what we had in the fridge. I was maybe twenty yards from the Jeep when I noticed the grey Buick Century.

It was parked four spaces down from mine. It had not been there when I came in that morning — my memory for the third level of the garage is embarrassingly detailed because I look at it a lot — and the man sitting in the driver's seat was reading a newspaper.

This was not strange. The third level of a corporate parking garage has, at any given time, three or four people sitting in their cars doing tax returns, eating sandwiches, making calls, crying, or napping. I was not alarmed by a man reading a newspaper in his car. You see men reading newspapers in cars all the time in Cleveland. It is one of the three or four things that hold the city together.

I just happened to glance over as I approached my Jeep.

The newspaper was upside down.

I kept walking. I opened the Jeep. I got in. I sat for a second, engine off, and I looked at him in the mirror.

He was still holding the newspaper. He was still not turning the page.

I told myself: the world is full of idiots. I told myself: he is probably just spaced out. I told myself: maybe he is left-handed and he's working some kind of backward crossword puzzle that I am too tired to imagine.

I started the Jeep. I backed out. I drove away.

I did not look in the mirror again.

That turned out not to be a pattern I could sustain.

THREE: *Research*

Tuesday afternoon I left TRW at 4:45 — I had permission to leave early for class — and drove south to Case Western.

I was three semesters into an MBA I did not especially need and did not especially want but had started taking in a fit of career pique in 1995 and had not yet been able to justify quitting. My program met on Tuesday nights at the Weatherhead School of Management, seven to nine-thirty. That evening's seminar was on operations management — the one where we read cases about how a bakery in Boston had optimized the order in which its bakers stacked loaves — and I had scheduled my arrival in University Circle deliberately early so I could spend some time in Kelvin Smith Library beforehand.

I had not stopped thinking about Galen in the break room.

I had not stopped thinking about the man with the upside-down newspaper.

I had, of course, told Frankie about both. Over dinner Monday night, she had listened carefully, with the particular stillness she wore when she was taking something seriously. She had asked me three specific questions. Did Galen actually say anything about the sculpture? (No, he had said he would ask Meg.) Had I ever seen the Buick before? (No.) Was I sure the newspaper was upside down, or was it possible I had misread a Cyrillic or an Arabic paper? (I was sure. *Plain Dealer.* Sports section. The Browns helmet was upside down.) She had listened to my answers and she had said, calmly: *Let's see what tomorrow brings.*

Frankie did not get agitated about small things. It was one of the reasons I loved her. She had a threshold. If a thing did not cross the threshold, she would not spend energy on it.

I was trying to honor her threshold.

I was not succeeding.

The sculpture was part of it, if I am being honest.

I had moved it twice since Sunday — once to look at the M.O. stamp again, for no reason I could explain, and once because Frankie had to say my name twice from the kitchen before I remembered I was supposed to be doing something else. I did not know what I was looking for. I just knew the thing kept pulling me back to the same room.

Kelvin Smith Library at Case Western was built in 1971 out of what appeared to be a single eight-hundred-ton block of sand-cast concrete. It was the kind of seventies university building that looked like it had been designed by somebody who had visited Lincoln Center once and misinterpreted it. From the outside it announced that the people inside were serious. From the inside it confirmed this, but also made the point that they were not having any fun.

I swiped in at the gate with my continuing-ed card. I rode the elevator to the third floor, where the reference desk was, and where the Fine Arts librarians kept office hours until eight on weeknights during the fall semester.

The librarian on duty was a woman I did not know. She was maybe my age, with very straight black hair and no-nonsense glasses and a small enameled pin on her cardigan lapel that said, in two lines, CASE / RUSSIAN STUDIES. I did not see the pin at first. I would see it later. She had a name tag that said OLENA, which I also did not register the implications of at the time.

I asked if I could get some help with a sculptor. Cleveland School, probably, maybe mid-century. Just initials. M period, O period.

She said, "We can try. Come with me."

We went to a small workstation along the wall. She pulled up three databases in sequence. *AskArt. The Smithsonian Archives of American Art.* A reference CD-ROM of Ohio artists, exhibitions, and collections, 1900–1990. In each one she typed in various versions of the initials — M.O., M. O., MO, O.M. — and various combinations with *Cleveland, Ohio, sculpture,* and *bronze.*

She got seven results, total. All of them were wrong. Three were a twentieth-century sculptor named Morris Olinsky, who had worked in stone, not bronze, and who had died in Brooklyn in 1973. Two were the wife of a collector named Margaret Olds, who had never made any art that anyone knew of, but was mentioned in a footnote to a gallery catalogue. One was a Cleveland ceramicist named Millicent Owsley, who had been active in the fifties and sixties but had worked exclusively in earthenware. One was a scan of a museum acquisition card from 1965 that listed an artist as *M.O. (?)* and had a question mark after the name. Nothing fit.

"I'm sorry," she said. "It's not coming up. Is it possible the initials are something else? Some artists use a monogram that *looks* like initials but is actually stylized in a different way."

"It's pretty clear. M period. O period. Like a punch stamp."

"Hm."

She thought.

"What does the piece look like?"

I told her. Small modernist bronze. Figurative abstract. Cast hollow. Female form, maybe.

"And where did you get it?"

I hesitated for half a second. Then I said, "I bought it at an estate sale."

I have no idea why I lied. I have thought about that half-second of hesitation a lot. Frankie's threshold, maybe. Something at the low level of me saying *do not volunteer Shaker Heights and free pile and tree lawn and the specific address to a stranger.* Later, I would think: maybe I already knew something was off. Maybe I had already flagged that I was not telling the whole story even to myself.

The librarian said, "Huh. Okay. If you want, we can come back to it. Try another angle."

"Can I look up obituaries?"

"You can. They're on microfilm, second floor, readers along the back wall. The *Plain Dealer* is fully indexed through July of this year — we have the August index coming in next month but it's not on the shelf yet. Do you have a specific date range?"

"Last six months."

"Should be easy. Do you know how to run the reader?"

"Yes."

"Good luck."

I thanked her. I went downstairs.

I had been coming to this library for three semesters and I had not been on the second floor in at least a year. The microfilm readers were lined up along the back wall. Three of the eight were occupied by grad students, all of them wearing the expression of people who had missed something in a primary source and were now paying for it. I loaded a spool of *Plain Dealer* obituaries from April 1996. I spun the crank.

I did not, at this moment, actually know why I was looking.

The Ostrowskis had not been in my head when I left TRW. I had been thinking about the sculpture, and about Galen. But it was the *kind of house* that was bothering me. The kind of house with a U-Haul out front on a Sunday in August and two exhausted adult children. The kind of house that had been lived in by people who had accumulated something specific enough to fill a U-Haul. I wanted to know who those people had been.

I started at the date of the pickup and spun backward.

Elena Ostrowski was on July 29, 1996. A half-column obituary with a photograph — a small black-and-white square of a smiling woman in her sixties with her hair up, standing in front of a painting. *Elena Bellavita Ostrowski, 56, of Shaker Heights, passed away July 26 after a brief illness. A native of Milan, Italy, she was the founder and owner of Bellavita Fine Art at Shaker Square, which she operated from 1978 to 1995. Mrs. Ostrowski was a member of the Cleveland Museum of Art's Women's Council and served on the board of the Italian American Society of Cleveland. She is survived by her husband, Mikael Ostrowski, a son, Jonathan of Boston, and a daughter, Sarah of Seattle.*

The photograph was nice. I stared at it a while.

Her husband, *Mikael,* I found six pages back. April 23, 1996. *Mikael Ostrowski, 58, of Shaker Heights, died suddenly on April 19 of a heart attack at the Cleveland Clinic. A native of Kraków, Poland, Mr. Ostrowski immigrated to the United States in 1969 and had resided in Shaker Heights since 1973. He was the principal of Ostrowski International Trade Consulting. He is survived by his wife, Elena Bellavita Ostrowski, his son Jonathan, and his daughter Sarah. A private service will be held. In lieu of flowers, the family asks that donations be made to the Cleveland Public Library Foundation.*

I sat with these two notices for a while.

It was — I could not articulate this yet — a specific kind of sad. Two people had died within four months of each other. Her of something brief. Him of a heart attack I could not help reading as an adjunct to her illness, even though he had actually died first. The obituaries did not say that. But obituaries have a shape. You read a lot of them and you develop an ear for the shape. Theirs had the shape of a couple.

I printed both. I put the printouts in my laptop bag.

I sat at the reader for another minute.

Then I rewound the spool, signed out of the workstation, and went back upstairs.

The Fine Arts librarian was still at the reference desk. I thanked her for her help. I told her I had struck out on the sculpture but that I had a lead and would be back.

I was zipping up my bag to leave when she reached into her cardigan pocket and took out a scrap of receipt paper and a pen and wrote something on it, quickly, without making eye contact, and pushed it across the desk to me, and kept her finger on it until I looked up at her.

She was staring at me.

Her pin was right under her chin. CASE / RUSSIAN STUDIES.

The scrap said:

Dr. Lorraine Hayes

216-555-0194

Call her. Not from here.

I looked at the librarian.

The librarian did not move.

"Who —"

"Please don't ask me any questions," she said. Quietly. Very quietly. "Please just take the paper and put it in your pocket and go to your class."

I put the paper in my pocket.

I went to my class.

I did not hear a single word of the operations management seminar that evening. The professor said something about loaves of bread. He said something else about cycle time. He said something I think was a joke but that I did not parse at all. At one point a woman across the seminar table said my name three times before I realized she had a question for me, and I apologized, and I gave a functionally correct answer, and the rest of the seminar moved on while I sat there with my hand in my jacket pocket, moving the folded paper between my fingers.

When I got home at ten, I took the paper out of my jacket and put it on the kitchen counter and stared at it.

Frankie came up from the basement, where she had been wiring a new outlet in the laundry area. She had a screwdriver in her hand. She looked at my face. Then she looked at the paper.

She did not say anything.

She set the screwdriver down on the counter. She read the name and the number and the instruction. She picked up the paper. She turned it over. The back was blank.

She set the paper back down. She looked up at me.

"Okay," she said. "Tell me everything."

FOUR: *The First Visitor*

Wednesday morning I filed the compliance module thirty-one minutes late.

This is probably, when the actuaries run the numbers, the smallest consequence of the events of the preceding four days — a filing that was thirty-one minutes late to a client who had already extended the deadline by two days — but it stayed with me. I had never filed a piece of work late at TRW. Not in three and a half years. I was the kind of person who got work in twenty minutes early and used the twenty minutes to re-read a final pass for typos.

On Wednesday morning I uploaded the module at 9:31 AM, with seven typos I had not yet caught, and I went to an 11 AM meeting, and I thought about the scrap of paper in my jacket pocket the entire time.

Frankie and I had, the night before, made a small and provisional plan.

The plan was: do not call the number from home. Do not call it from TRW. Do not call it from Kelvin Smith Library. Do not call it from Frankie's mobile, which was a bulky Motorola she used for her clients and which had her name on the bill. Go to a payphone. Somewhere not obvious. Make the call when we were both there. If the conversation went well, fine. If it did not go well, we would — Frankie said — *figure it out.* She had said this with a specific calm I had found reassuring at the time and would in retrospect recognize as the calm of a person who had been in difficult rooms before.

We had decided to make the call Thursday evening, after she finished her job in Lakewood.

Wednesday was supposed to be a day of not thinking about it.

I was bad at that.

I came home at 6:17. Frankie's truck was in its spot. I could hear her through the open window of our apartment — she was upstairs on the phone, talking to a supply company about cedar, in a voice that was dangerously close to the voice she used just before somebody had a bad week. I came up the stairs. I did not interrupt. I put my bag on the chair by the door. I started water for pasta.

The knock came at 6:42.

It was a light knock. A business knock. Two quick taps with a knuckle, the kind of knock a salesman gives — enough to be heard, not enough to be rude.

I went to the door.

The man on the landing was in his mid-fifties, on the shorter side of average, with neatly combed grey hair and a tweed sport coat I would have admired in any other context. He had a pleasant face. He was holding a business card between his index and middle finger the way magicians hold playing cards, which is a way professional people do not normally hold business cards unless they are trying to perform a specific effect.

He had come up two flights of stairs to my front door. He was not winded. He was not even breathing hard. That was, I realized later, the first thing.

"Good evening," he said. "I am so sorry to disturb you. I wonder if I might have a moment of your time."

He had a British accent.

It was not a good British accent.

Do not misunderstand me. It was not a *bad* British accent. He was not doing Dick Van Dyke. It was a British accent that sat in the *almost* — it had the right vowels, it had most of the rhythms, and it had small moments that caught in the wrong places. The word *evening* had come out very slightly too crisp. The word *moment* had been pronounced with a clarity Americans only ever give to it when they are trying not to swallow the T. If you had asked me in that moment whether this man was British, I would have said — yes, probably. But something in my gut was already taking notes.

I am not, for the record, trained in dialect. I had just, as it happened, spent six weeks in the summer of 1988 in Oxford on a cheap study-abroad program. I had kissed a woman named Helen from Leeds and I had drunk several warm pints in several cold pubs and I had talked to enough real British people that my ear had, on a low background level, a sense of what the performance was supposed to sound like. This man did not quite land it.

I said, "Can I help you?"

"I do hope so. My name is Edmund Holloway, I am an independent fine-art appraiser" — he extended the card, and I took it, out of reflex, though I had not yet decided to — "and I have been engaged by a client, a private collector, who has asked me to inquire after a number of pieces that may have emerged from the estate of Mikael and Elena Ostrowski of Shaker Heights. The family has been rather — disorganized — in their disposal, and my client is concerned that several items of consequence may have been dispersed in ways that could be, shall we say, regrettable."

I did not say anything.

"May I ask — have you, by any chance, come into possession of any pieces from the estate?"

"Who told you I had."

"I beg your pardon?"

"Who told you I had anything from that house."

His face did a very small thing. A microexpression. The kind of thing that happens when somebody is running a script and the next line of the script is not the next line of the conversation. It lasted a quarter of a second. He recovered smoothly. His expression went back to warm. He chuckled, which was a move I associated with cruise-ship magicians and certain television pastors.

"Forgive me," he said. "I should have been clearer. We have been in contact with a number of antique-resale establishments in the area, and several private parties have mentioned a gentleman matching your general description purchasing items from the Ostrowski estate. Nothing untoward. Simply a process of canvassing. I had hoped to reach you at home in the evening in the hope that you might have a moment."

I looked at the business card.

EDMUND HOLLOWAY / FINE ART APPRAISAL & ADVISORY / LONDON · NEW YORK

No Cleveland address. A 212 phone number. No email.

"What are you looking for, exactly?"

"Several pieces. A pair of oil paintings of flowers by Mrs. Ostrowski herself — she painted, you know, a fine amateur, her still lifes are of real interest to the family. And a small bronze. Approximately eight inches tall. Modernist in style. The artist is unknown. The family is — quite insistent — that it be returned."

I did not react.

I think I was proud of myself for not reacting.

"A bronze?" I said. "A woman?"

"A figure. Yes."

"By a known artist?"

"No, as I said. Unsigned, I believe. Or nearly so. A small stamp, perhaps. Unidentified artist."

He was watching my face.

I said: "I don't have anything from that estate, Mr. Holloway."

"You're quite certain."

"Yes."

"Not even a canvas? Flowers, you know? Quite charming pieces. You may not have noticed they were hers."

"I've never been to the Ostrowski house. I don't know the family. I'm sorry to have wasted your time."

"Not at all, not at all." He paused. He let the pause go maybe one beat longer than it should have. Then: "You are quite sure, Mr. — I don't believe I caught your name."

"I didn't give it."

Something behind me moved.

Frankie had come down the hall. She had finished her phone call. She had heard me open the door and she had heard my voice tighten and she had pulled on the boots she kept by the kitchen and she had walked down the hall quietly, and now she was behind me in the doorway with her framing hammer still hanging from the loop on her tool belt.

"Hey, babe, who is it?"

Frankie does a voice when she is being deliberately non-threatening. It is not her voice. Her voice is lower and dryer than that. The voice she does when she is being deliberately non-threatening is a pitch-up of her real voice by about one half-step, and it is the most terrifying voice I have ever heard in my life, because I can tell she is doing it, and because anyone paying attention can tell that she is doing it, and this man, I could tell immediately, was paying attention.

She stepped into the doorway beside me. She was taller than he was by an inch and a half. She crossed her arms over her chest, which was a gesture she had a trick with where she could make her shoulders look wider. I had never asked her about it.

The hammer swung on her belt.

Edmund Holloway's eyes went to the hammer. Then to Frankie's face. Then to her shoulders. Then back to the hammer.

The British accent did not survive this traverse. When he next spoke, it was still recognizably the performance he had walked in with, but the vowels had lost a quarter of their starch. Something underneath had come up briefly to take a breath.

"I — I do apologize for the intrusion."

"No trouble," Frankie said, in the voice.

"I was just making an inquiry. If your husband has —"

"He's not my husband."

"— if your partner, rather, has nothing from the Ostrowski estate, I shall simply —"

"He said he doesn't."

"Yes. Yes, quite. Well."

"Was there something else?"

"No. No, I think we are — all set. I do apologize. I'll see myself out."

He turned. He went down the stairs.

I noticed, watching him go, that he did not hold the railing. He descended the full two flights quickly, with an economy of motion, without once reaching out to steady himself. That was, I realized, the second thing. The first had been that he had not been winded coming up.

I closed the door.

I locked it.

I turned around.

Frankie was looking at the business card, which was still in my hand. She took it. She turned it over. She held it up to the light. She looked at it for a long time.

"It's a real card," she said. "The print is embossed. Not laser. Expensive."

"Yeah."

"That guy was running a script."

"Maybe he's just — you know. Maybe he really is an appraiser, and he's not very good at the door-knocking part. The art world's got plenty of weirdos."

Frankie looked at me.

"He's not an appraiser."

"How do you know."

"I just know, Theo."

"That's not helpful."

"It's going to have to be."

She walked to the living room. She walked to the shelf above the TV. She moved the pothos plant aside. She picked up the sculpture and she turned it over in her hands and she looked at the M.O. stamp on the edge of the base.

"Theo," she said.

"Yeah."

"We need to not put this down for a while."

"Yeah."

"And we need to make that phone call tomorrow."

"Yeah."

"Do not take the sculpture out of the apartment."

"I won't."

"And do not open the door tonight. For anybody."

"I won't."

She set the sculpture back on the shelf. She moved the plant back into place. She walked over to me. She was standing very close. She was looking down at me by a clear three inches.

"Eat your pasta," she said.

"Are you going to eat?"

"Yeah. I'm going to eat."

She leaned down. She kissed me on the top of the head.

She did not say the thing about the aunt.

We ate the pasta.

Frankie set an aluminum Louisville Slugger under her side of the bed that night. I had never seen this bat before. I asked her where it had come from. She said *my trunk*. I asked her why it had been in her trunk. She said *for moments when there is a bat in my trunk*. I did not press.

I lay awake past three.

Through the window, the streetlight made a soft grey rectangle on the ceiling. Ramona was at the foot of the bed, heavy and warm on my ankle. Frankie was breathing beside me — the slow, regular breathing of a person who has decided she is going to sleep, and therefore she is going to sleep. I envied it. I envied it bitterly.

I thought about the sculpture on the shelf in the other room.

I thought about the M.O. stamp.

I thought about the librarian's pin — CASE / RUSSIAN STUDIES — and about her finger pressing down on the scrap of paper, and about Galen's two expressions in one second, and about the British accent that had not quite been a British accent, and about the upside-down newspaper.

I thought about a U-Haul at the curb and a man in Dockers, too tired to talk, saying *please, take it.*

I had not kept anything. I could tell Holloway the truth tomorrow if he came back. I could hand him the sculpture. I could hand him the paintings. I could hand him the cigar box. I could open the door and say *here, these are yours.*

Except I had, at some point in the last ninety minutes — without quite naming it — decided that I was not going to do that.

I did not know why.

I did not yet know the M.O. on the base of the sculpture was not the signature of an unknown Cleveland artist.

I did not yet know I had intercepted something.

I did not yet know Dr. Lorraine Hayes, or her cat-filled bungalow on Lee Road. I did not yet know my girlfriend had lived two years of a life she had never told me about. I did not yet know a man named Rook was already in Cleveland. I did not yet know Galen had made a phone call from a BP station. I did not yet know that on Saturday, at Jacobs Field, during a rain delay in the seventh inning, somebody was going to walk through our apartment without making a sound.

I did not yet know any of it.

I just knew the sculpture was on the shelf in the other room, and that I was not going to sleep tonight, and that when Frankie reached across in her sleep and found my hand and laced her fingers through mine, I held on a little tighter than usual.

Outside, on Cedar Road, a car passed.

I counted six seconds before I heard the next one.

I was, for the first time in my adult life, counting seconds between cars.

I closed my eyes.

FIVE: *The Ransack*

Thursday came and went.

This fact — that we made it through an entire Thursday without anything happening — was, I realize in retrospect, the exact kind of thing we should not have let reassure us. I would later spend a lot of time thinking about the mechanics of fear: how it spikes, how it plateaus, how it quietly falls off when nothing happens for twenty-four hours, and how that fall-off is itself a design feature that the people who engineer fear rely on.

Thursday morning I got to work at 7:48. I worked on the next module, because I had nothing else to work on. Doreen brought me a cinnamon roll she had picked up for herself and had decided, for no reason, to give me. I ate it. I thought about the scrap of paper.

I did not see Galen.

At lunch I walked the third floor of the parking garage to see whether the grey Buick was there. It was not. I walked past my Jeep twice, at a casual pace, and checked every row. No Buick. No Crown Vic. No one in any of the cars. Just the usual sad lunch eaters and one woman doing her lipstick in a visor mirror with real commitment.

Thursday evening I came home at 6:10. Frankie was upstairs, painting the hall baseboard, which she had torn out on Wednesday night and reinstalled that morning because she had been too wired to sit still. She looked up at me. Her hands were covered in white trim paint. Her hair had paint in it.

"Anything," she said.

"Nothing."

"Hm."

We ate leftover pasta. We did not talk much. At 8:40 she set down her fork and said, "I want to hold off on the call."

"What?"

"I want to hold off. One more night. If nothing happens tonight or tomorrow, we call Saturday. If something happens, we call immediately."

"Why."

She chewed. She swallowed. She did the thing where she took a long drink of water before answering, which meant the answer was going to have shape to it.

"Because right now," she said, "the only people who know we have this sculpture are the three kids who threw it on the curb, Galen, whoever Galen called, and Edmund Holloway. Plus that librarian. When we call the number on that scrap, we add another person to the list. I want to know more before we do that. I want to see if anything else shakes out of the trees."

"What do you think is going to shake out."

"I don't know, Theo. That's the point. Let's just — let's just watch for one more day."

I did not like it. But I did not argue.

I slept well Thursday night, which was the first lie fear told me.

Friday at work was Friday at work. I saw Galen in the hall once, around 11. He waved. He did not stop. He kept walking, and his walk was the walk of a man going somewhere on purpose, which was not the usual Galen walk. The usual Galen walk was a shambling mosey. Friday's walk was a walk. He did not look at the Polaroid on my desk.

Friday evening I drove home. Frankie met me at the door with two slips of paper in her hand.

I said, "What."

"Your Indians tickets."

I had forgotten. I had completely forgotten. Frankie's brother Vinny worked for Jacobs Field security and occasionally gave us a pair of comp tickets as a thank-you for Frankie having installed, two summers ago, a complicated railing on Vinny's mother-in-law's front porch. He had dropped them off at our door Tuesday evening in an envelope with *ENJOY ASSHOLES* written on the front, in what Vinny thought was a charming note. They were good seats. Lower deck. Section 118, first-base side.

Tribe vs White Sox. 7:05.

"I'll trade them," I said. "Vinny can give them to somebody."

"Absolutely not."

"Frankie."

"Theo. Absolutely not. If we sit in this apartment for a fourth straight night we are both going to lose our minds. We are going to the game."

I looked at her.

"Also," she said, "Belle's batting third tonight. I'm not missing Belle."

"Yeah."

"Grab your hat."

Jacobs Field was only two years old in 1996 and it still had the smell new stadiums have — the specific combination of concrete that has not yet absorbed its first decade of beer, and the hot-dog cart smell in the concourses, and the clean astringent of the bathrooms before they have been properly broken in. We parked in a garage at the Tower City end and walked east through downtown in the dusk. Frankie held my hand the entire way. She had left the hammer at home. I did not know, but I suspected, that she had something under her jacket — there was a slight asymmetry to the way the denim hung. I did not ask.

The game started on time. Orel Hershiser was on the mound. He was thirty-seven years old that year and still had the control of a surgeon. He retired the White Sox in order in the first and by the third the Tribe had a 2–0 lead on a Jim Thome home run that

I only saw because Frankie grabbed my arm and said *Theo,* and I looked up from my hot dog.

Belle came up in the bottom of the fourth.

Frankie and I had, across our two years together, developed a specific ritual for Albert Belle at-bats. Frankie did not believe in cheering when Belle was at the plate. Frankie believed that cheering Belle was redundant. Her position was that Belle did not need encouragement and that it was impolite to yell at a man with Belle's focus. So we sat. We held our breath. We watched. It was a thing we did. Other people in section 118 yelled. We did not.

Belle took the first pitch for a ball.

He fouled off the second.

He singled sharply to left on a hanging slider, and the runner on second scored, and Frankie grabbed my thigh hard enough to leave a fingerprint bruise.

"*There* he is," she whispered.

In the top of the fifth, the sky started to darken.

I do not mean that the sun set. Sunset at Jacobs Field in August is a slow brass drape that descends over the city over the course of an hour. This was not that. This was the specific fast darkening of a Midwestern sky deciding to rain. The clouds moved in from the west, low and black, with the lake-affected weight they sometimes had, and by the time Hershiser got the third out of the fifth the umpires were looking up.

In the bottom of the fifth the grounds crew started moving toward the tarp.

In the top of the sixth, with the White Sox batting, play was suspended and the tarp went on.

We sat through the delay. We ate Cracker Jack. Frankie went to get us beers. I watched the dugouts. Around 9:20 the umpires announced they were going to try to resume. The tarp came off. The grounds crew swept. Play resumed at 9:34. By the top of the seventh it was raining again, harder this time, and Frankie looked at me and said, "Let's go."

I did not argue.

We walked to Tower City under a golf umbrella Frankie had produced from her jacket with the air of a woman who had known it was going to rain since Tuesday. The umbrella was red. We were both mostly wet by the time we got to the garage.

We drove east on Carnegie, then north up Cedar, then through Cedar-Fairmount to our block. It was 10:18 when we pulled up to the house. The rain had briefly lightened, then picked up again. I parked behind Frankie's truck. We ran up the walk with our jackets over our heads. Frankie had the key.

She put the key in the door.

She stopped.

"Theo."

"What."

"Back up."

"What."

"*Back up.*"

She was in front of me. She was holding me with her left hand flat against my chest, pushing me back, and I was backing up because in two years of dating her I had learned the specific weight of her voice when she said *back up* that way.

"What is it," I said.

"The door is already unlocked."

"I don't —"

"I locked it, Theo. I locked it when we left. The deadbolt. I checked it twice."

"Maybe —"

"It didn't."

She stepped back off the porch. She pulled me with her. She scanned the sidewalk in both directions. The block was quiet. A few porches had lights on. The rain was drumming steadily on the step.

"Is there anyone still inside?" I whispered.

"I don't know. Probably not. But we're going to stand on this sidewalk for two minutes and watch the house before we go in."

"Frankie."

"Two minutes."

We stood on the sidewalk in the rain for two minutes. Her left hand was still on my chest. Her right was inside her jacket, and when I looked at her face I understood, fully and for the first time, that she was *listening.* Not in the sense of *listening carefully.* In the sense of *listening for a specific sound she had been trained to listen for.*

After two minutes she said, "Okay. I go first. You stay behind me. If I tell you to go, you go. You run back to the Jeep and you drive to a payphone and you call 911 and you do not come back."

"Frankie —"

"Theo. If I tell you to go, you go."

"Okay."

"I love you. I need you to say okay."

"I said okay."

We went up the steps.

She opened the door.

The apartment had been turned over.

I do not use that phrase the way real-estate brokers do. I mean the apartment had been physically, systematically, purposefully ransacked. Every drawer in the kitchen was open. The silverware was on the counter. The contents of the refrigerator were on the kitchen table. The cushions of the couch were slit along their long seams and the stuffing had been pulled out in handfuls. The bookshelves were empty; every book was on the floor, pages up. The rug was rolled up against the far wall. In the bedroom, the mattress was off the frame, leaning against the closet door. The closet was empty; everything that had been in it was on the bed frame. The floorboards in two places had been pried up, and a putty knife had been left on the ground beside them, which was the single most galling detail of the whole thing — they had brought their own tool, or they had used one of Frankie's.

Ramona was under the bed.

I got down on my hands and knees and I said her name and she looked at me with the specific offended dignity of a cat who has been wronged, and she came out, and I picked her up, and I held her, and I did not cry, but it was close.

Frankie was walking the apartment with a discipline I had never seen in a civilian. She moved through each room in a specific pattern — clockwise, walls first, then floors, then obvious hiding spots. She did not touch anything. She did not exclaim. She was making a mental catalogue. I watched her from the bedroom doorway with Ramona in my arms and I understood that I did not know the person I lived with.

Actually — that is not quite right.

I knew her. I knew everything about her. I knew that she put vinegar on her fries. I knew that she slept on her right side and rolled onto her back around 3 AM. I knew the names of her six cousins and the order they had been born in. I knew that when she was angry she got very quiet, and when she was afraid she got very practical. I knew her.

What I did not know was *what* she was.

She came back to the bedroom doorway. Her face was neutral. It was the kind of neutral that was, I understood, a deliberate choice.

"The sculpture's still on the shelf."

"Okay."

"The paintings are on the kitchen counter."

"Okay."

"The cigar box is on the floor but it's whole. They opened it, looked inside, didn't keep it."

"Okay."

"Your laptop's on the desk. My tools are in the basement. The emergency cash is still in the sock drawer, under the socks where I put it, and they moved the socks but they didn't take the cash."

"Okay."

"Theo."

"Yeah."

"They didn't find what they wanted."

She said it flatly, without looking at me. She was looking at the wall behind me. She was still cataloguing.

I said: "What do they think we have?"

She turned her eyes to me then.

"I don't know, babe. But we need to find it before they come back."

She walked past me into the living room. She moved the pothos aside. She took the sculpture down from the top shelf and held it in both hands. She stood there for a long moment, looking at it.

"Pack a bag," she said. "We're not sleeping here tonight."

"Where are we going?"

"We're going to sit in my truck in a parking lot until sunrise, and then we are going to find a motel, and then we are going to figure out what this thing actually is."

"Frankie —"

"Pack a bag, Theo."

I packed a bag.

We left the apartment at 10:52. Frankie took the sculpture and the two paintings and the cigar box. I took my laptop bag and a duffel of clothes and Ramona in a carrier. She insisted I carry the sculpture with me once we were in the truck. *Do not put it down.* She said this twice.

We drove to a Denny's on Mayfield. She parked at the back of the lot, facing out, under a sodium light that made everything the color of overcooked egg yolk. She killed the engine. She put her hands in her lap.

"I have to tell you something," she said.

"Okay."

"Not now. In the morning. When we have coffee. I need a few hours first."

"Okay."

"You're going to be mad."

"Okay."

"I love you."

"I love you too."

She reached over and took my hand. She held it on the console between us. She watched the parking lot. Somewhere, over on Mayfield, a siren went by. Ramona yowled in the carrier.

We sat in the Denny's lot until dawn.

SIX: *The Felt*

At 6:42 AM on Saturday morning we checked into a Motel 6 on Chagrin Boulevard in Beachwood.

The choice had been Frankie's. She had explained it to me while we were driving there from Denny's, with the specific calm of someone teaching a child to tie shoes. Beachwood was close enough that Frankie could get back to any of her ongoing jobsites in under twenty minutes. It was far enough from Cleveland Heights that nobody who had turned over our apartment was going to casually stumble on us. It was a motel that took cash. It was on a main commercial strip, which meant we were visible — she specifically wanted visible, she explained, because the people we were hiding from wanted *not visible,* and what they wanted and what we wanted were going to be opposites for a while.

I was listening to her and nodding and thinking *she has done this before.*

The clerk did not ask why we were checking in at 6:42 AM. He was a teenager with a faceful of acne who was watching *Saved by the Bell: The College Years* on a little TV behind the desk. He gave us a room key without looking at us. Frankie paid cash. We put Ramona in the bathroom with her carrier door open and a bowl of water. We put the sculpture and the paintings on the bed. We sat on the other bed and looked at them.

"I need coffee," I said.

"There's a Bob Evans across the street."

"I need a shower first."

"Take one. I'll get the coffee."

"Don't —"

"I'll be ten minutes."

"Frankie."

"Theo, if somebody was able to follow us here from Denny's, we are already dead, and a Bob Evans coffee is the least of our problems."

"That's not reassuring."

"It's not meant to be."

She left. I sat on the bed. I looked at the sculpture.

When she came back, twelve minutes later, she had two large coffees and two styrofoam boxes of eggs and a plastic bag from the CVS next door containing, when she dumped it out on the table, a pair of latex gloves, a pack of double-sided tape, a flashlight, a small magnifying lens, two Sharpies, and a dental pick.

"You got all that at a CVS?"

"The dental pick was at the pharmacy counter. You need a pharmacy card for them, but I have my grandma's."

"Your grandma is dead."

"Yes."

I ate. I drank the coffee. I was too tired to argue with her about fraud.

While I ate, Frankie put on the gloves and moved the sculpture and the paintings to the little table under the window. She set the flashlight beside them. She cleared space on the bed for the cigar box. She stood for a moment with her hands on her hips, looking at everything.

"We are going to go through every one of these objects," she said. "Slowly. With our eyes. Do not touch anything with your bare hands."

"Am I also putting on gloves?"

"Yes."

She handed me the other pair of gloves. They were too big.

We started with the paintings.

They were small. Nine inches by eleven, maybe. Oil on stretched canvas. Both were of yellow flowers in clear glass vases. Both were in the same hand.

Both had, I could now see in better light, the same distinctive thumbprint in one lower corner — not a literal thumbprint, but a kind of repeated small brushwork that functioned as a signature. They were good. They were private-good. They had been painted by someone who had never tried to sell a painting, because they did not need to.

Frankie turned them over. She examined the stretcher bars. She pressed, gently, along the seams where the canvas was folded. She held them up to the window. She shone the flashlight through them. She set them down.

"Nothing in the paintings," she said.

"You mean —"

"No compartments. No papers taped behind the canvas. No hollow stretcher bars. Just paintings."

"Okay."

The cigar box came next. Cedar inside, dark mahogany outside, the gold-leaf *Habana* rubbed to a ghost. Frankie opened it. Empty. She held it upside down and shook. She held it to the window and shone the flashlight in. She tapped the bottom. She tapped the sides.

"Solid," she said. "No compartment. Just a cigar box."

"Hmph."

"The cigar box is the cigar box."

"Which leaves —"

"Yeah."

She picked up the sculpture.

She sat down at the edge of the bed, with the sculpture in her lap. She did not say anything for a while. She turned it in her hands. She was not looking at me. She was going through what I would later come to recognize as a specific set of checks — a protocol, something she had been trained to do and had not done in six years and was remembering in real time.

She ran her thumb around the edge of the base where the felt bottom met the bronze. She frowned.

"Theo."

"Yeah."

"Look at this."

I got up and came around. I bent down. She was holding the sculpture upside down in her lap, with the flashlight pointed at the felt. On one corner — the back left, from the sculpture's perspective — the edge of the felt had separated slightly from the bronze. It was maybe a millimeter. You could not see it in ordinary light. But under the flashlight, at an angle, you could see that the adhesive had dried. The felt was lifting.

"That's not factory," she said.

"How do you know."

"Because factory felt is glued with a thin even layer of contact cement. This one is glued with something else. Something that separates over time. Like a rubber cement or a craft glue."

"Maybe —"

"Theo. Factory felt does not come up in thirty years. Factory felt is on there forever. This felt has been replaced."

I did not say anything.

She took the dental pick out of its package. She slid the tip under the lifted corner of the felt. Very slowly. Very carefully. She worked it along the seam. The felt came up in a single intact disk with almost no resistance, which told her — and told me, now that I was learning her language — that the glue had indeed dried and that the disk had been meant to come up one day.

Under the felt there was a thin circle of black foam.

Under the black foam there was a shallow rectangular cavity set into the interior of the hollow base.

Inside the cavity were three things.

One: a small sealed envelope of silver Mylar, about the size of a playing card, with a transparent strip down one edge through which you could see a tightly rolled cylinder of film.

Two: a small brass key, maybe an inch and a half long, flat on one side, with three tiny numerals stamped into it. I could not read the number without picking it up.

Three: a single sheet of onionskin paper, folded twice, tucked against the far wall of the cavity.

Frankie did not touch any of them.

She sat back. She let out a breath I had not realized she had been holding.

"Okay," she said, quietly. "This is a problem."

"What is it."

"I don't know, Theo."

"That's microfiche, right?"

"Looks like microfiche."

"And a key."

"Yeah."

"And a letter."

"Some kind of paper. Not a letter. The shape's wrong for a letter."

"What's the shape for, then."

"I don't know."

I sat down next to her on the bed. We both looked at the cavity. Outside, on Chagrin Boulevard, a truck went past. The Motel 6 shook slightly. Ramona made a small noise in the bathroom.

"Frankie."

"Yeah."

"What were you going to tell me at Denny's."

She did not answer right away. She set the sculpture down on the table, very gently, with the cavity open to the ceiling. She peeled off the gloves. She walked to the little coffee maker on the dresser and she started it running. She stood with her back to me while it hissed.

"Frankie."

"Eggs first," she said.

"Frankie."

"We eat our eggs. We drink our coffee. Then I'll tell you. Then we'll figure out what to do with these three things. I need fifteen minutes, Theo."

"Okay."

She turned around. She was crying, which was a thing she almost never did, and had not done in front of me in a year. Two tears. She wiped them on the back of her wrist.

"Fifteen minutes," she said.

"Okay."

We ate our eggs.

She washed her plate. She washed mine. She poured both of us a second cup of coffee. She sat down across from me on the other bed, with the sculpture between us on the little table.

"Okay," she said.

"Okay."

"I was in the Army."

I did not say anything.

"1988 to 1990. Two years. Active duty. I enlisted at nineteen. I got out at twenty-one."

"What did you do."

"Signals intelligence. Attached unit. I can't tell you the specifics, Theo. Not because I'm being mysterious. Because it doesn't matter right now, and because I don't want to tell you the full version in a Motel 6 on Chagrin Boulevard. You are going to get the full version. But I need you to not ask me right now."

"Okay."

"What matters right now is: I was trained to handle objects like this. I was trained to do the kind of walking I did through the apartment last night. I was trained not to pick up microfiche with my bare hands. I am not guessing any of this. I know it."

"Okay."

"I should have told you a long time ago. I know that. I thought it didn't matter. I thought — honestly, I thought it was going to be more interesting than it was, and then less interesting than it was, and then I didn't know how to bring it up. And then I loved you, and telling you felt like it would change something. And I did not want to change anything."

"Frankie."

"Yeah."

"I love you."

"I know."

"I am not mad."

"You might be later. That's okay. It's an earned mad."

"I am not mad now."

"Okay."

We were both quiet for a minute. I reached across and I took her hand.

"Okay," I said. "So what do we do with the microfiche."

She squeezed my hand. She smiled at me for the first time since Denny's.

"Now," she said, "we figure out who Dr. Lorraine Hayes is."

SEVEN: *Not the Cops*

My first instinct was the police.

I said this out loud, over the dregs of the coffee, and Frankie let me say it, which was a thing she did when she wanted me to hear my own argument and reconsider it without her having to tell me to. She did not interrupt. She did not make faces. She sat across from me on the bed with her hands folded around the paper coffee cup and she listened.

I had a lot to say.

I said that we were civilians. I said that what was in the bronze was clearly not our problem. I said that the police had procedures for exactly this kind of thing — found objects, potential evidence, cooperation with federal agencies. I said that Cleveland Heights had a small, competent force that I had twice seen handle situations on our block with quiet professionalism. I said that we had broken no laws. I said that calling the number on the scrap of paper would, by definition, mean calling a stranger, and that a stranger was a stranger regardless of what a frightened librarian had written on the scrap. I said that the correct move — the legally safest move, the morally cleanest move, the one our parents would have told us to make — was to walk into a Cleveland Heights police station, set the sculpture on a table, and say, *we found this in our apartment, and our apartment was broken into last night.*

I said it all. It took about four minutes. I felt better for having said it.

Frankie waited until I was finished. Then she said, "Okay. Let's war-game it."

"Okay."

"We walk into CHPD. Sergeant on duty. What do we tell him?"

"Exactly what I just said."

"And what do we put on the table."

"The sculpture. The microfiche. The key. The paper."

"And what do we say about the break-in."

"We say our apartment was broken into last night."

"And they say — did you report it last night?"

"No."

"And we say — no, we slept in the Jeep at a Denny's and then checked into a Motel 6 because my girlfriend thought that was safer."

"Yes."

"And they say — and why did you think the break-in was about the sculpture?"

"Because of the appraiser."

"And they say — okay, do you have the appraiser's contact information?"

"Yes. A business card with a New York number."

"And they call the number."

"Yes."

"And the number is either a dead line, or it rings at a mail-drop, or it rings at Edmund Holloway's actual office in London, where a very nice woman answers and says yes, Mr. Holloway does inquire about estate pieces routinely, and she has no record of a Cleveland Heights visit this week, and she'd like to know more about the allegations. And the police thank her and hang up and look at us."

"Frankie."

"And then they ask us why we think a piece of microfiche we found in a sculpture we grabbed from a curb is worth breaking into our apartment over."

I did not say anything.

"And we say *we don't know,* because we don't. We don't know what's on the microfiche. We don't know what the key opens. We don't know what's on the onionskin. And the police say, *can we have the microfiche and the other items while we sort this out.* And we say, *yes, of course.* And they take them. And they put them in an evidence locker. And by Tuesday, someone who should not have access to that evidence locker has accessed that evidence locker, and we are back where we started, except we no longer have the microfiche."

"Frankie —"

"I am not saying this to be paranoid. I am saying this because this is exactly what I was trained not to do in exactly this kind of situation. You do not hand unknown intelligence material to the first institutional authority you encounter. You figure out what you have first. Then you figure out who needs it. Then you figure out which door you walk it through."

"You were *trained* for this kind of situation."

"Theo."

"Sorry. I'm sorry."

"I know."

"I'm sorry. I am processing."

"I know you are."

"So what do we do."

"We call the number."

"The number on the scrap."

"Yes."

"From a payphone."

"Yes."

"Not a Motel 6 phone."

"Absolutely not."

"You trust her."

"I trust the librarian who gave us the number. That is *not* the same as trusting the number. But the librarian looked at you — at *you*, Theo, at your face — and made a decision to break protocol and give you a name. Librarians are careful people. They do not do that casually. Somebody on that phone number knows what's happening, and somebody on that phone number knows why the librarian was willing to stick her neck out to connect us to them."

"Okay."

"We call. We listen. We decide."

"Okay."

"And for the record — I will also be willing to call the cops. At some point. When we understand what we have and we know who to give it to."

"Okay."

I stood up.

"Let's call," I said.

We left the Motel 6 at 11:04 AM. We took the sculpture and the microfiche and the key and the onionskin with us, wrapped in a towel, in Frankie's tool bag. We took my laptop bag. We took Ramona.

We drove south on Chagrin. Frankie spotted the payphone first — outside a CVS at the corner of Chagrin and Richmond. The kind of payphone that had clearly been installed in 1983 and forgotten. It had a half-torn sticker on the handset that said, for some reason, FREE AOL 100 HOURS. Frankie pulled into the far end of the lot, facing out. She killed the engine. She did not get out.

"I'll go," she said.

"No."

"Theo."

"No. It's my scrap. It's my sculpture. I'll go."

She looked at me for a long moment. She nodded.

"Ten feet from the phone, I want you to look at me before you dial. If I'm scratching my nose, you do not dial, you come back to the truck. If I'm touching my hair, you dial."

"What if —"

"I won't be scratching my nose. But I want you to look before you dial, as a discipline."

"Got it."

"And keep it under two minutes. Give her the information. Listen. Hang up. We get out of this lot."

"Got it."

"I love you."

"I love you."

I got out of the truck. I walked across the lot. Ten feet from the payphone, I turned. Frankie was in the driver's seat, one hand on the wheel, the other playing with the end of her ponytail. Hair. Not nose. Dial.

I fed the phone three quarters. I dialed the number.

It rang once.

A woman's voice said, "Address."

That was the whole greeting. One word. *Address.*

I said, "2341 South Park Boulevard, Shaker Heights."

There was a pause. It was not a long pause, but it was a considering one. The woman on the line had, I could tell, not been expecting that address.

"No," she said. "Your address."

"Oh."

I gave her our address on Cedar.

"Were you there last night between 7 and 10 PM."

"No. We were at a ballgame."

"When did you return."

"10:18."

"What did you find."

"The apartment was turned over."

There was another pause.

"What was taken."

"Nothing."

"Say that again, please."

"Nothing was taken. Everything was searched. Nothing was taken."

The pause this time was longer.

"Are you at your address right now."

"No."

"Good. Where are you."

"A payphone in Beachwood."

"Good. Do not return to your address. Do not go to your place of work. Do not tell anyone you know. Are you with anyone."

"My girlfriend."

"She can come. Tomorrow morning, four AM. Service entrance, south side of Kelvin Smith Library. Park in the lot on Euclid, walk from there. Bring the item. Bring anything you found with the item. Do not tell anyone where you are going."

"Who are you."

"Tomorrow morning."

"Why not today."

"Because I need tonight."

"Okay."

"One more thing."

"Yes."

"Do you have somewhere safe to stay tonight."

"I think so."

"Think harder."

"I'm in a Motel 6. Cash."

"Which one."

"Chagrin."

"Check out. Drive west to Lakewood, not east. Stay at a different motel, not a chain. I can suggest one if you need."

"We'll figure it out."

"Four AM. South entrance. Kelvin Smith."

"Yes."

She hung up.

I stood there for a second with the dead line against my ear. Then I set the handset back into the cradle and I walked back across the parking lot to the truck. Frankie had the engine running.

I got in.

"Four AM tomorrow, Kelvin Smith basement," I said. "Different motel tonight. Lakewood."

Frankie put the truck in gear.

"Lakewood it is," she said.

EIGHT: *The Basement Reader*

We spent Saturday night at the Westerly Inn on Detroit Avenue in Lakewood.

It was a two-story motor court from 1952 that had survived exactly the way motor courts survive — by not changing anything. The neon sign out front still said VACANCY in red cursive. The rooms had chenille bedspreads. The floor was linoleum. The lock was a single Schlage deadbolt with a key you could have copied at a Home Depot in six minutes. Frankie had picked it precisely because it was not on any chain-hotel registry. She paid cash. She gave a fake name. She did not look at me when she signed the register, which was how I knew the name was fake.

We ate at a diner on Madison called Rosie's. We did not talk much. We were both running on very little sleep. Frankie had me order the meatloaf because, she said, "You're going to need the protein," which was the kind of sentence she never said and which I did not challenge.

We went back to the motel at 8 PM. Frankie lay down on top of the bedspread fully dressed. She said, "I need three hours."

"Sleep."

"Wake me at 11."

"Okay."

She slept. She slept immediately. It was a thing she could do that I could not. I sat on the other bed with Ramona in my lap and I listened to her breathe and I thought about the fact that I did not know anything, and that I had an appointment at 4 AM with a woman whose name was all I knew about her, and that the floor of my life had dropped a story without warning and the ceiling had, in its place, gotten lower.

I did not sleep.

I woke Frankie at 11. We got coffee from a gas station at 11:30. We drove east on Detroit, then south on 117th, then east again along Clifton, and we got to University Circle at 1:10 AM. We parked in a small lot on Euclid across from the Allen Memorial Art Museum. Frankie killed the engine. We sat in the truck.

It was Sunday morning and University Circle was dead. An ambulance went by once. A security vehicle from Case Western crept along East Boulevard. Nobody else.

At 3:45 AM, Frankie said, "Let's walk."

We got out. Frankie carried the tool bag with the sculpture and the envelope and the key and the onionskin wrapped in the towel. I carried nothing, which made me feel useless, but which was the job she had given me. *You carry nothing. Your hands stay free. If anything happens, you run.*

We walked west along Euclid in the dark. Kelvin Smith Library was a block over. We went around the south side of the building, along a brick service path I had never noticed, past a loading dock and a bank of dumpsters, to a small metal door marked SERVICE — NO ENTRY.

At 3:59 AM the door opened.

The man who opened it was in his fifties. Thin, wiry, wearing a grey Case Western sweatshirt that had clearly been washed eight hundred times. He had the specific paleness of a person who worked nights. He had small wire-rimmed glasses and an expression that was not welcoming but was, I could tell, deliberate — a man who was choosing not to react to us because reacting would be expensive.

"Inside," he said. "Quickly."

We went in.

He closed the door. He locked it. He led us down a narrow concrete stairway — two flights, fluorescent lights, the specific smell of university basements everywhere, which is cleaning-product over concrete with an undercurrent of the exhausted air of the people who had to be there. At the bottom of the stairs he led us through a corridor and through another locked door and into a small, brightly lit room that had once been a microfiche viewing room and was now, from the look of it, used mostly as a technician's office. There was a desk. There was a coffee maker. There were three microfiche readers along one wall. There was a large metal cabinet with a humming fan that I recognized, after a moment, as an archival temperature-controlled storage unit. Somewhere, a dehumidifier was running.

He turned to us.

"My name is Oleg," he said. His accent was faint. A long vowel in *name* and a flattened *g* at the end. "I am a microfilm preservation technician. I am doing you no favor. I am doing a favor for a person I owe a favor to. Do you understand."

"Yes," I said.

"What do you have."

Frankie took the Mylar envelope out of the tool bag. She handed it to him.

He took it with the care of a man handling a live bird. He walked to one of the readers. He sat down. He opened the envelope with a small tool from a desk drawer — not his fingers, the tool. He threaded the film onto the reader with unhurried precision. He flicked the reader on.

He advanced to the first frame.

He read.

I was watching his face. It was a face that had seen a lot. It had almost certainly seen more microfiche than any other face I would ever meet. It was a face that, in the course of its professional life, had been trained not to react to the content of whatever was on the screen in front of it.

It reacted.

The reaction lasted less than a second. The man who had told us he was doing us no favor, that he was doing a favor for someone else, went grey. Not pale. Grey. His jaw set. His hands, which had been relaxed on the edge of the reader, tightened once and then relaxed again with visible effort.

He advanced to the second frame.

He read it.

He did not advance to the third frame.

He reached up and he switched the reader off. He rewound the film manually. He unthreaded it. He put it back in the Mylar envelope. He walked back across the room and he handed the envelope to Frankie, because he was not willing, I noticed, to put it back in my hand.

"I did not see that," he said.

"What is it," I said.

"Mr. Novak."

"What."

"I do not know what this is."

"That's not true."

"Mr. Novak. I am saying this carefully. I do not know what this is. I have not read it. I have not read it, because reading it would mean I would have to do something about it, and I cannot do something about it. I am a microfilm technician. I have a wife and a daughter. My daughter is in the second year of a biology program at this university. I pay for that program. I intend to keep paying for it. I cannot know what this is."

"Okay."

"You understand."

"Yes."

"You have never been here."

"Yes."

"I have never been here."

"Yes."

Frankie said, "You called Lorraine."

"Yes."

"When."

"Three hours ago."

"And?"

"She will see you at seven this morning. Shaker Lakes Nature Center, the north lot off South Park. She will be on the east bench by the pond. She will be in running clothes. She will look like a woman who has finished her morning run. Do not approach her if there is anybody else in sight. Walk past her. Walk around the pond. Come back when she is alone. She will not signal you. She will simply be there."

"Seven AM. North lot. East bench."

"Correct."

"How will we know her."

"You will know her. She is the only Black woman in her seventies who will be sitting on a bench at the Shaker Lakes at seven AM on a Sunday in running clothes. This is not a populous demographic."

"Thank you."

"Please do not thank me. Please do not come back. Please do not ever refer to me by name again. If you meet me on the street, you do not know me. I do not know you."

"Yes."

He walked us to the service door. He unlocked it. He held it open. He did not look at us as we passed. He closed it behind us. I heard the deadbolt engage.

We walked back along the brick path, past the dumpsters, past the loading dock, out onto Euclid. The sky was still black. The streetlights were still on.

Frankie said, "Whatever's on there is worse than we thought."

"Yeah."

"We are way out of our depth."

"Yeah."

"We're going to see her at seven."

"Yeah."

She put her arm around my shoulders as we walked. She did not kiss the top of my head.

She did not say the thing about the aunt.

It was 4:17 AM. Sunday, August 25, 1996. The first light was not going to come up over Lake Erie for another hour and forty minutes. We walked back to the truck along University Circle with the envelope wrapped in a towel at the bottom of Frankie's tool bag, and I thought about what Oleg had told us, and what he had *not* told us, and which of those two was larger.

I thought: whatever is on that film, it is the kind of thing that made a man with a daughter in a biology program decide he had never seen it.

I was beginning, for the first time, to be afraid of the sculpture itself.

NINE: *The Bench*

We killed time until seven AM.

Killing time in Cleveland in the pre-dawn of a Sunday in August is a specific experience. There are very few places open. There are very few people. The city has the quality of a stage set that has not yet been lit. We drove from University Circle along Cedar, east into Cleveland Heights, and we stopped at a 24-hour Dunkin Donuts on Lee where we bought two large coffees and two plain glazed donuts and where I noticed, for the first time, that Frankie's hand was shaking slightly as she paid. I did not mention this. She held the coffee cup with both hands in the truck and she did not drink it for twenty minutes.

At 5:40 we drove south on Lee, then east on Shaker Boulevard to the Shaker Lakes.

The Shaker Lakes were two small ponds connected by a creek, nestled into a nature preserve on the border between Shaker Heights and Cleveland Heights. The preserve had footpaths and wooden bridges and a small educational center that would not be open at this hour. It was the kind of place that felt, on a Sunday morning, like somebody's private backyard that had been accidentally enlarged. Old trees. Stone markers from the 1930s. Signs warning about the coyotes that had, apparently, become a regional problem.

Frankie parked the truck in the north lot off South Park. The lot was empty except for one blue Volvo station wagon that had been backed in against the fence. Frankie noted the Volvo. She made me note it. She spent maybe forty seconds looking at it from the driver's seat, committing the plate to memory — 1FVO, something — and then she said, "Probably an early birder. Probably fine."

It was 5:52.

We sat in the truck.

At 6:48, a thin woman in running gear jogged past the lot entrance. She did not look in. She continued down the path into the preserve.

At 6:59, Frankie said, "Let's walk."

The east bench was maybe two hundred yards along the path from the north lot, past the smaller pond and over a wooden footbridge. The bench sat on the far side of the larger pond, angled so that whoever sat on it was looking back across the water toward the lot. I understood, as we walked toward it, that this was not a casual choice of bench. This bench had excellent sight lines on everything that approached it.

Dr. Lorraine Hayes was sitting on the bench.

She was, as Oleg had said, the only person at the Shaker Lakes at seven AM on a Sunday in running clothes. She was small — five-three, maybe five-four, compact, with the specific shoulder set of a woman who ran long distances on purpose. She was in her early seventies. Her hair was short, grey with a steel-wool quality, cut plainly. She was wearing a navy blue zip-up running jacket, black running tights, and a pair of Asics that had seen serious mileage. A small hydration belt was clipped around her waist. Her face was sweaty. She had run. She was in the recovery phase of her morning, which she had apparently been having at this bench for, I would later learn, eleven years.

She did not turn to look at us as we approached.

Frankie said, quietly, "Good morning."

"Sit down," Dr. Hayes said.

We sat.

She did not look at either of us. She was looking at the pond. The morning light was still low — the sun had come up maybe an hour ago — and the water was gold-grey in a way that I would, in any other circumstance, have appreciated.

"Mr. Novak," she said.

"Yes."

"I am going to ask you some questions. You are going to answer them in as few words as possible. You will not ask me anything in return, yet. We will get to your questions. But for the next five minutes I need facts. Is that all right."

"Yes."

"How old is the microfiche."

"I don't know. It was in the sculpture I found nine days ago."

"Where did you find the sculpture."

"Tree lawn, 2341 South Park Boulevard."

"When."

"August 18th. Two forty-seven in the afternoon."

"How do you remember the time."

"I looked at the clock in the Jeep when I parked."

"Hm. Good. Were there other people present."

"A man and a woman. Mid-thirties, both. Dockers. Ponytail. They were loading a U-Haul. They seemed to be the adult children of the house."

"Were they."

"Yes. The obituaries confirmed it."

"You read the obituaries."

"Tuesday night. At Kelvin Smith."

"Who helped you."

"A Fine Arts librarian. Olena. I did not get a last name."

"You don't need a last name. Continue. When did the break-in occur."

"Friday night between 7 and 10 PM."

"Describe the search pattern."

"Professional. Systematic. Everything opened. Floorboards pried. Nothing stolen."

"Who knew you had the sculpture."

"My girlfriend" — I glanced at Frankie — "my coworker, Galen Brennan. An appraiser who came to the door Wednesday evening, British accent, calling himself Edmund Holloway. A private collector, he said. Asked about bronzes specifically."

Dr. Hayes did not react to the name.

She did not react to *Galen Brennan* either.

"Did you tell anyone else."

"The librarian. Olena. When I came in to ask about M. O."

"The initials on the base."

"Yes."

"All right. Mr. Novak, if you would give me the envelope."

Frankie hesitated. She looked at me. I nodded. She took the Mylar envelope out of her tool bag and handed it across the bench to Dr. Hayes.

Dr. Hayes reached into her hydration belt and took out a small black jeweler's loupe.

She did not unroll the film. She held the envelope up against the pond light. She looked at the first visible frame through the transparent strip, using the loupe. She shifted it slightly. She looked at the second visible frame. She did not look at the third.

She folded the loupe and put it back in her belt.

She handed the envelope to Frankie.

She was quiet for a long moment.

Then she said: "How long have you had this."

"Nine days."

She nodded slowly.

"Then we have about seventy-two hours before you're dead."

Frankie said, "Okay."

That was all Frankie said. She did not say *how do you know,* or *what do you mean,* or *who's going to kill us.* She said *okay,* and she said it with the specific flatness of a person receiving a piece of information they had already suspected was true and were now filing.

Dr. Hayes looked at Frankie for the first time.

"Miss — I'm sorry, I don't know your name."

"Francesca Russo. Frankie."

"You have done this kind of work before."

"1988 to 1990. Army signals. Attached unit."

"Which one."

"Wiesbaden."

The two women looked at each other.

Something passed between them. I would spend a long time trying to decide what it was. It was not quite recognition, and it was not quite suspicion. It was closer to the way chess players look at each other across a board when the game has opened and each has realized that the other one is real.

Dr. Hayes said, "Wiesbaden."

"Yes."

"What year specifically."

"Arrived late 1988. Left early 1990."

"Were you at Lindsey."

"Yes."

"Do you know what Lindsey was."

"Yes."

"Tell me what Lindsey was."

"Forward signals collection. Cross-border intercepts. We did not acknowledge the existence of the building."

Dr. Hayes nodded once.

"Miss Russo, I am going to trust you to a specific extent based on what you just said. I would like you to do the same with me. Is that acceptable."

"Yes."

"Thank you."

Dr. Hayes turned back to me.

"Mr. Novak. What you have in that envelope is of very serious consequence. I cannot tell you the specifics here. The specifics require a different venue. I need to take a look at the full film, and I need coffee, and I need to sit down in a room I control. I would like to take both of you to my home. I would like to do so in a way that makes it extremely unlikely anyone is following us. It will require about an hour of what Miss Russo will recognize as dry-cleaning. Are you willing."

"Yes."

"Good. Miss Russo, you will drive. Mr. Novak, passenger seat. I will sit in the rear. We will not speak while in the vehicle. I will instruct you on the route. The dry cleaning will take us west, south, east, north, and then west again, and we will end at my home on Lee Road. I will tell you one turn at a time. Clear."

"Clear."

She stood.

She was no taller than Frankie's chin. She was, visibly, not a large woman. But she had the specific physical compactness of a person who had never, in her adult life, let her body be something other than hers to direct. She put the jeweler's loupe back in her belt. She zipped the belt closed. She looked at me one more time.

"Mr. Novak," she said.

"Yes."

"I am very sorry."

She walked ahead of us along the path.

Frankie and I looked at each other.

Frankie said, in the same flat voice she had used to say *okay:* "Let's go."

We followed Dr. Hayes to the lot.

TEN: *The Briefing*

The dry cleaning took fifty-four minutes.

I will not describe all of it, because most of it was uneventful in a way that was specifically the point. We drove west on Fairmount, then south on Lee, then east on Chagrin, then north on Warrensville Center, then back west on Cedar, then south on Green, then east on Larchmere, then through a small neighborhood north of Shaker Square I had never had reason to drive through before, then back up Lee Road, then across Lee into the low residential streets of Cleveland Heights west of the Shaker border. Dr. Hayes gave each instruction about thirty seconds before we needed it. She watched the side mirrors the entire time. At two points she said, "Pull over. We are waiting ninety seconds." We pulled over. We waited. At another point she said, "Run this yellow." Frankie ran it. At a fourth point Dr. Hayes made us drive a full circle around an elementary school block, twice, in opposite directions.

By the end of it Frankie was driving with the specific calm of a person who had been asked to do the thing she was best at. Her hands were no longer shaking.

At 7:54 AM we pulled into a driveway on Lee Road.

The house was a small brick bungalow, exactly as Oleg had described it. Blue siding where the brick ended. White trim around the windows. A green front door. A wide front porch with a porch swing and two metal folding chairs that did not match each other or the porch. A brown cat was asleep on the swing.

"That cat is not mine," Dr. Hayes said, climbing out. "He belongs to the woman across the street. He sleeps here for reasons of his own."

We went inside.

The inside of Dr. Hayes's bungalow was the inside of a person's life.

I mean that in the specific way a house reveals the person who has lived in it for decades. Every inch of wall that was not a doorway was bookshelves. Every bookshelf was full. Books were wedged in behind other books. Books sat in stacks on the floor in front of the shelves. There was a leather armchair by a front window, a small table beside it with a pair of reading glasses and a lamp and a stack of what looked like mail, three coffee cups of varying ages, and a small brass bowl of paper clips. There was a rug that had once been red and had been walked on for so long by the same person along the same routes that it had two specific paths worn into it — from the front door to the kitchen, and from the armchair to the hallway. There were photographs on one wall. A man, not young, not old, smiling in a black-and-white. A younger woman in a graduation gown. A wedding photograph. Then an empty frame, which I did not know how to read.

Three cats emerged from three different rooms when the front door closed. A large grey one from the hallway. A small black one from behind the couch. A very old tabby from a sunbeam in the kitchen. They all looked at us with the cool evaluative stare of animals who knew exactly who belonged and who did not.

"Alexei, Pushkin, Mrs. Nabokov," Dr. Hayes said, gesturing at each in turn. "Do not try to pet Mrs. Nabokov. She will bite you."

"Noted," Frankie said.

Dr. Hayes went into the kitchen. We followed. She put a kettle on. She gestured at a small round oak table with four mismatched chairs. She said, "Sit. I will make coffee. You will both drink one cup before we speak. I will not begin until you have finished the first cup."

Frankie and I sat.

We drank. Frankie was faster than I was. I was drinking it too hot. I burned my tongue. Nobody said anything.

When the cups were empty, Dr. Hayes poured three more, sat down across from us, put the envelope between us on the table, and folded her hands.

"All right," she said. "What do you want to know first."

I did not know what to ask first.

Frankie said, "What's on the microfiche."

Dr. Hayes nodded.

"A list. Forty-seven names, though I have only confirmed two so far, through the loupe at the bench. I believe I recognize the format. I will need a proper reader to confirm the rest."

"Names of who."

"American citizens in classified or semi-classified positions who have, over the last two to three decades, accepted payment from Soviet and subsequently Russian intelligence services in exchange for the transmission of information useful to those services."

"Spies."

"Assets."

"Russian spies."

"American spies working for the Russians. There is a distinction, but the distinction is not important for our conversation. Yes."

"And this is that list."

"One of them."

I said, "One of them?"

Dr. Hayes looked at me carefully.

"Mr. Novak, there are — in the world — a small number of these lists. They are compiled by handlers on one side of a conflict as personal insurance, or by case officers on the other side of the conflict as operational records. They are extremely rare. They are extremely consequential. A list like this — the two names I saw on the loupe suggest this particular one, specifically — has been a rumored object of interest in certain professional circles for some years."

"Rumored."

"Rumored. Now located."

"Who put it in the sculpture."

"A man named Mikael Ostrowski. Born Michał Ostrowski in Kraków, Poland, in 1938. Immigrated to the United States in 1969 under what his passport called a business visa and what was in fact an arrangement with the Central Intelligence Agency. He moved to Shaker Heights in 1973 with his wife Elena. He operated, under the cover of a trade consultancy, a network of CIA case officers and assets across the American Midwest for twenty-three years. He intended to retire this year. He died on April 19th."

"Of a heart attack."

"Of a potassium chloride injection administered during a routine cardiac workup at the Cleveland Clinic."

Frankie made a small sound.

Dr. Hayes continued.

"His wife Elena was his partner in the operation, both professionally and after 1976 romantically. Her gallery at Shaker Square — Bellavita Fine Art — was the cover for the network's international travel and customs infrastructure. She died of pancreatic cancer in July. Her cancer was real. It is one of the few things in this conversation that is not a euphemism. She received a diagnosis in March, outlived the statistical median by six weeks, and died at home on July 26th. Mikael outlived her by three weeks, at which point he was, in my professional reading, no longer working to stay alive."

"And the sculpture."

"The sculpture was his operational legacy. The contents of the sculpture — the film, the key, and the page of cipher — constitute what is called a cache. It was meant to be transferred in person to his successor on his retirement. The successor would receive the sculpture through a rendezvous that would have happened, if Mikael had lived, sometime between late spring and early summer of 1997. The successor would, on receiving it, know to examine the base. The successor would know because Mikael would have told him in person."

"But Mikael was killed."

"On April 19th, three months before he would have even begun the preliminary contacts for the handoff. The cache remained in his home. His wife was already unwell at that point. When she also died in July, the cache remained with the estate. When the children — who did not know the house contained anything unusual — came to clean out the house in August, they threw the cache into a pile at the curb."

"And I picked it up."

"And you picked it up, Mr. Novak, yes. From an operational perspective, what you have accomplished over the last nine days is an accidental interception. From a moral perspective, what you have accomplished is roughly what somebody would accomplish if, through no effort of their own, they wandered onto the site of an in-progress bank robbery and found that they were now holding the money."

Frankie said, "Jesus Christ."

Dr. Hayes reached across the table for the sculpture.

She had asked for it at the bench. Frankie had kept it in the tool bag through the drive. Now

Frankie took it out and set it on the table in front of Dr. Hayes. Dr. Hayes did not pick it up at first. She looked at it for a long moment. Then she turned it over.

She pointed at the small stamp on the edge of the base.

"Mr. Novak."

"Yes."

"The initials on the base. You have been assuming those are the artist's."

"Yes."

"They aren't."

I did not say anything.

"They are Mikael's. M. O. Mikael Ostrowski. He stamped his own initials into the base of the sculpture in the early 1980s, after he had the cavity cut and the felt replaced by a machinist in Slavic Village. He stamped them adjacent to the original artist's mark, in the same style, so that the casual eye would not distinguish the two. It was a recognition signal. When his successor walked into the Ostrowski home on the day of the handoff, Mikael would gesture at the sculpture. The successor would turn it over. The successor would see the two marks, next to each other, and would know: *this is the object*. You have been calling it *M.O.* because you did not know what the second signature was. The second signature is the piece's operational designation."

She set the sculpture down on the table, gently.

"You did not garbage-pick a sculpture, Mr. Novak. You intercepted a dead drop that was supposed to be passed to a CIA officer at a retirement party. You did it three days before Mikael intended to make his first outreach to that officer, because Mikael did not get three days. You have been carrying that intercept around for nine days, partly on a shelf in an apartment that was turned over last night by people looking for exactly what you have, and partly in a truck with your girlfriend. The people who want this do not know who you are by name yet. They know only that a man with a Jeep took items from the curb in front of 2341 South Park Boulevard on a Sunday afternoon. It is a matter of hours, at most, before they know your name. It is a matter of, I believe, between twenty-four and seventy-two additional hours before they have come to the conclusion that the cleanest solution to their problem is to kill you both and remove the cache from your effects."

I sat down in the chair I was already sitting in.

I do not know how to describe this. The chair, I am aware, was underneath me. My body was sitting on it. But something in me — the specific animal underneath the specific man — sat *down* in the chair a second time, from the inside. I felt like I had, in the preceding ninety seconds, dropped through two more stories of my life.

Frankie's hand was on my knee under the table.

Dr. Hayes was watching me with a kindness that she had not, until this moment, demonstrated.

"You will get through this," she said.

"Okay."

"Both of you. I will make sure of that."

"Okay."

"But you are going to have to do exactly what I tell you to do for the next two weeks, and you are going to have to do it without asking a great many questions. Some of the questions I cannot answer. Some of them I will answer when you need to know. Some of them you will never need to know the answer to. Is that acceptable."

Frankie said, "Yes."

I said, "Yes."

"Good."

She pulled the envelope toward her across the table. She set it on top of the sculpture. She took her glasses off and cleaned them with the hem of her jacket and put them back on.

"Now," she said, "let's begin."

ELEVEN: *Going Dark*

The first hour was logistics.

Dr. Hayes did not believe in spending emotional energy on a task that could be solved procedurally. As soon as I said *yes* to doing what she told me to do, she opened a drawer in her kitchen — the drawer next to the silverware drawer — and took out a spiral-bound notebook with a faded red cover and a mechanical pencil. She wrote, in a hand so precise it could have been typed, a list of twelve tasks. She numbered them. She underlined the ones she wanted done before noon.

She read them off.

- Do not go home.
- Do not call work.
- Burner phones.
- Cash, not cards.
- New clothing: one change each, bought with cash at two different stores, neither in Cleveland Heights, Shaker Heights, University Circle, or Lyndhurst.
- Safe place to sleep tonight.
- Cover story for employer.
- Cover story for family.
- Notify no one.
- All four of us meet here at 6 PM Monday.
- Bring the sculpture, the key, the envelope, and the page.
- Bring the cat.

"Four of us," I said.

"I anticipate a fourth party by Monday evening. I will handle that. Do not concern yourself with item ten, only with items one through nine and item twelve."

"The cat."

"Mr. Novak, you cannot go home. If you cannot go home, your cat cannot go home. Your cat must eat. Your cat must drink. We will accommodate your cat."

"Okay."

"We will return to item ten when it is time. Now. Item one is already handled. You are not at home. Item two —"

"Wait. I can't just not go to work. It's Monday morning tomorrow."

"Item two is item seven. You are going to call your manager at TRW first thing Monday morning and you are going to tell him you have a family emergency of indeterminate duration, that you will be unavailable by phone or email for at least ten business days, and that you will be in touch when you are able. Your manager is named —"

"Kevin."

"Kevin. Yes. Does Kevin strike you as a problem about this."

"No. Kevin is — Kevin's fine. He'll be annoyed but he'll be fine."

"Good. Then item two and item seven are resolved. Do you have any current work product that absolutely must be delivered before your return."

"I turned a module in on Wednesday. There's another draft due the fifteenth of September."

"You are going to go back to work on the fifteenth of September and you are going to deliver it as if nothing has occurred. Is that acceptable."

"Yes."

"Good. Item three. Miss Russo."

Frankie, who had been listening with the particular stillness of a student who was paying attention in a way she had not paid attention in years, said, "I have three Nokia 2110s in my truck under the passenger seat."

I looked at Frankie.

Dr. Hayes did not look at Frankie. She was writing something in her notebook.

"Pre-paid?"

"Yes."

"Not registered to you in any form."

"No."

"How long have you had them."

"Four months."

"Why."

"Because sometimes I have them."

"That is an acceptable answer."

I said, "Frankie — why —"

"Theo. Not right now."

"Okay."

Dr. Hayes wrote another line in her notebook.

"Miss Russo. Keep one. Give one to Mr. Novak. Give one to me. We will use these and no other phones for the remainder of this operation. Do not use the phones to contact anyone other than each other and me. Do not bring your personal mobile phone to any meeting. Do not use the phones in moving vehicles, because the cell tower handoff produces a useful record. Do not use them in your truck, which is a cell tower amplifier with wheels. Park the truck. Walk a block. Make the call. Is this clear."

"Yes."

"Item four. Cash. How much do you have between you."

Frankie said, "Eight hundred at the house. Two hundred in the truck. Maybe another three hundred in my tool bag. I can get another thousand from my bank by Monday without raising a flag."

"Good. I will provide an additional two thousand for the operation from my own resources. That is not a loan. That is an operational disbursement and you will not reimburse me. Do not argue with me about this; it is not negotiable."

Frankie said, "Understood."

Dr. Hayes wrote another line.

"Item five. New clothing. I want you both in different outfits than what you wore to University Circle this morning. Buy cheap. Buy practical. Both of you need to be able to run in what you're wearing, which I will note, Mr. Novak, you currently cannot."

I looked down at myself. I was wearing loafers.

"Yes," I said.

"Mr. Novak, before noon tomorrow, you will be wearing running shoes. Not athletic sneakers. Running shoes. Please accept this as an operational requirement and not a judgment."

"Yes."

"Item six. Safe place to sleep tonight."

Frankie said, "I have a vacant rental on Forest Hill."

Dr. Hayes looked up from the notebook.

"Tell me about it."

"Bungalow. 1923. I've been restoring it since May for a client whose mother died. She lives in Portland and has not been to Cleveland since April. She will not be here again until next spring. The house has electricity, working plumbing, and heat. There is no furniture other than a mattress on the floor in the upstairs bedroom, which I put there because I was sometimes working late and needed somewhere to take a nap. There is no phone. Nothing is registered to us. My work truck has been parked at the house on and off for four months and nobody in the neighborhood will think anything of seeing it there. The neighbors, in fact, think the house belongs to me."

"Why do they think that."

"Because they asked me once whether I was the owner and I did not correct them, because the actual owner had asked me not to draw attention to the fact that the house was empty."

"Miss Russo."

"Yes."

"You did not plan this."

"No."

"You did not plan to have a safe house four months before you needed one."

"No."

"And yet you do."

"Yes."

Dr. Hayes looked at Frankie over the top of her glasses for a long moment.

"Miss Russo, you are going to be an asset in this operation beyond what I had expected. I apologize for underestimating you."

Frankie said, "You didn't."

Dr. Hayes smiled, for the first time. It was small, and it was dry, and it was a real smile.

"No," she said. "I did not."

She wrote another line in the notebook.

"Item seven is resolved. Item eight. Cover story for family."

"My parents are in Arizona," I said. "Frankie's family is all here. They'll notice."

"What do they notice."

"Frankie and I usually do Sunday dinner at her mother's house. Collinwood. Every other week. Last Sunday we skipped because I was at TRW. This Sunday we were expected."

"Today is Sunday."

"Yes."

"And you are expected at Collinwood when."

"Three PM."

"At what address."

Frankie gave the address.

"At that address will you be expected to eat a full dinner."

Frankie said, "Dr. Hayes, we will be expected to eat two full dinners."

Dr. Hayes wrote *DINNER @ RUSSO 3 PM* in the notebook, underlined it twice, and then said, "You will go."

I said, "What?"

"You will go. You will be seen. You will act normally. You will eat two dinners. You will leave at a reasonable hour. You will not go back to your apartment. You will drive to the Forest Hill rental. You will sleep there. Meeting is here at 6 PM Monday."

"We can't go to Frankie's mom's house, we're —"

"Mr. Novak."

"Yes."

"What did Ms. Russo tell you last night she had been trained to do in exactly this kind of situation."

"To figure out what she has before she does anything else."

"And what have we just finished doing."

"Figured out what we have."

"And part of what we have is a family in Collinwood that is going to *notice* if you do not show up, and is going to start asking questions of everyone they know, including your mother in Arizona, who is going to start asking questions of the friends you and she have in common. Is that what you want."

"No."

"Then go to Collinwood."

"Okay."

She wrote another line. She put the pencil down.

"Items nine, eleven, and twelve are self-explanatory. We are, for the moment, complete. Miss Russo, I would like five minutes of your time before you leave."

Frankie nodded.

Dr. Hayes turned to me.

"Mr. Novak. There is a green armchair in the front room. Please sit in it for a moment. Alexei, the grey cat, will come and sit on your lap. You will let him.

You will breathe. I need to speak with Miss Russo privately."

"Okay."

"Thank you."

I got up. I went to the green armchair. Alexei came. He sat on my lap.

I breathed.

Frankie and Dr. Hayes spoke in the kitchen for eight minutes. I could hear the timbre of their voices but not the words. At the end of eight minutes, Frankie came into the front room and put her hand on my shoulder and said, "Let's go."

Alexei did not move.

I stood up. Alexei slid off my lap with the specific offended dignity of a large grey cat being dispossessed. I apologized to him. He did not accept my apology.

Dr. Hayes walked us to the door.

"Six PM tomorrow," she said.

"Yes," Frankie said.

"Mr. Novak."

"Yes."

"Running shoes."

"Yes."

She closed the door.

We bought the new clothing at a Burlington Coat Factory in Willoughby and an Old Navy in Mentor, two separate trips. We bought running shoes for me at a Sports Authority in Eastlake, which was, I realized halfway through trying on the third pair, the first time I had been to an Eastlake Sports Authority in my adult life. I paid cash. The clerk did not ask for identification. I walked out in the shoes.

We had Sunday dinner at Frankie's mother's house in Collinwood.

We arrived at 3:04 PM. Frankie's mother, Angela — who was a fraction of Frankie's height, spoke four different languages in rapid succession while she cooked, and did not, in my two years of dating her daughter, seem to have aged by a single day — met me at the door with her usual assessment, which was that I was too thin. She kissed me on both cheeks. She took the small cake Frankie had bought at a bakery on Mayfield on the way over as if we had baked it ourselves. She directed us into the dining room. There were nine other people there. I was, over the course of the next three hours, embraced by a total of six of them, corrected on a point of Italian grammar by one, offered a cigarette by a great-uncle who was ninety-one, and fed, as predicted, two full dinners with a half plate of antipasto in the gap between them.

We did not mention the microfiche.

We did not mention the break-in.

We laughed at the right jokes. We answered the right questions. Frankie held my hand under the table once, for a long moment, and I understood that she was telling me: *we can still do this. We can still do our regular lives. We can still hold on to this.*

We left at 7:40 PM.

We drove to the Forest Hill rental.

The rental was a small brick bungalow with a front porch and a stone path and a pair of hostas on either side of the stoop. Frankie let us in with her copy of the key. The house had the specific emptiness of a house in the middle of being restored — drop cloths, a compound miter saw in the dining room, a stack of baseboard trim against the living room wall, a single mattress on the floor of the upstairs bedroom, a kitchen with a working fridge and a kettle and nothing else.

I released Ramona from the carrier in the kitchen. She walked around the perimeter of the room twice, looking up at me resentfully, and then she walked up the stairs with great dignity and she did not come down until morning.

Frankie and I sat on the mattress in the upstairs bedroom with the light off. The window looked out onto Forest Hill Boulevard. The streetlight outside the window made a soft grey rectangle on the floor. The house was very quiet.

"I'm tired," I said.

"Yeah."

"How are you this calm."

"I'm not calm, Theo. I'm just not showing you the not-calm."

"Oh."

"I will show you the not-calm when we are somewhere where showing you the not-calm is not going to get us killed. Right now that means — not now."

"Okay."

"Okay."

She lay down. I lay down. We did not get under any covers. We did not have any covers. We slept in our clothes.

I did not dream.

I woke up at 4:37 AM.

I lay there in the dark and I watched the grey rectangle on the floor and I listened to Frankie breathing. Ramona came into the room at some point and curled up between us. The rectangle on the floor shifted shape slowly as the moon moved.

I thought about Mikael Ostrowski.

I thought about a man who had been killed three days before he was going to retire. I thought about a man who had spent twenty-three years running a CIA network out of a Tudor in Shaker Heights, who had built a cache of forty-seven names as his final act, who had bought a small bronze sculpture at an art show in 1981 and paid a machinist in Slavic Village to cut a hidden compartment into its base, who had stamped his own initials next to the artist's because he had wanted his successor to find it. I thought about a man who had an identity and a marriage and two children and a gallery and a business and a network, and who was also an operational officer of the CIA, and who died with both the operational and the personal intact in the same body on the same day.

I thought about the fact that he had died on a Friday.

I thought about the fact that I was lying on a mattress on a floor in a house I did not own because a man I had never met had decided, in 1981, to hide a list inside a statue.

I thought about how thin the thread was that had connected his decision to mine.

I did not sleep again.

At 6:15 the light came up. I got dressed.

Monday.

TWELVE: *Galen*

Monday morning I had to call Kevin.

This was item seven on Hayes's list, and it was overdue. Kevin was my manager at TRW. Kevin was fifty-three years old, had two kids in high school, liked golf, liked college football, liked his job but had stopped pretending, some years ago, that he liked it *a lot.* Kevin was, in all the ways that mattered, a decent man. He had told me once, after I had delivered a difficult module early, that I could take an afternoon off whenever I wanted. I had never taken him up on it. I was now, at just past eight on Monday morning, August 26th, cashing the check.

I had the Nokia in my hand.

Hayes had told me to make this call. She had not specified which phone to make it from — her list said *cover story for employer* and nothing else. I had two options. The home landline was at the apartment I was not going back to. The Nokia was what I had.

The Nokia was also, I understood, the only number Kevin could call back.

I had been thinking about this since I woke up. If something happened — if Kevin needed to reach me, or if someone at TRW asked questions that Kevin felt I should know about — he would need a number. My home number was tapped, maybe, or at least exposed. The Nokia was clean. If I called Kevin from the Nokia, he would see the number on his display and he would have it, and he could use it if he needed to.

I dialed Kevin from the Nokia at 8:09 AM.

"Kevin, it's Theo."

"Theo! How's it — are you okay? You sound weird."

"Family emergency. I need to take some time."

"Oh no. What's going on."

"It's — it's my mother." I closed my eyes. My mother was in Arizona. My mother was fine. My mother was going to be fine. "It's — I can't really talk about it yet. I'm not ready to. But I need a couple of weeks."

"Oh, Theo. Oh God. Okay. You take what you need. Do you want me to call Janice in HR, or —"

"If you could. I'll check in with her when — when things settle."

"Oh, absolutely. Take care of yourself. And listen — if there's anything we can do, will you let me know? The whole team —"

"Kevin. Thank you. I will."

"Call me if you need anything."

"Yeah."

"Seriously."

"Yeah."

I hung up.

I sat on the mattress on the floor of the upstairs bedroom of a bungalow that did not belong to me, and I watched the dust motes in the pale morning sun coming through the window, and I hated myself for ten seconds for lying to Kevin about my mother. Then I stopped. Then I accepted that I was going to do worse things than that in the next two weeks. Then I accepted that the Nokia number was now in Kevin's display, which was the reason I had used it, and that Kevin would use it only if he needed to, and that Kevin was the kind of person who understood, even without being told, what *only if you need to* meant.

Then I put the Nokia on the floor next to me.

Frankie was downstairs making coffee on a camp stove she had pulled from her truck.

I went down.

We drank the coffee. We ate bagels Frankie had bought at a Dunkin. We did not discuss the day. Frankie had a list of her own. She was going to, this morning, visit three of her ongoing jobsites, in a very specific order, and tell each of her clients she was going to have to push the timeline by a week. She would do it in person. She would do it with the right expression. She would not draw attention. She would be back at the bungalow by 3 PM so we could drive to Dr. Hayes's together at 5:30.

She left at 9:15.

I sat with the Nokia on the kitchen counter and I worked through the yellow legal pad Hayes had told me to get. I wrote down the route from the Forest Hill bungalow to the Cedar-Fairmount half-double — the route I was not going to take, and the alley entrance I was. I wrote down Kevin's name and the time I had called him. I wrote down the things I needed to do this week, in order, the way I had learned to write them from three and a half years of designing adult learning modules: sequenced, specific, with the dependencies marked.

At 11:03 the Nokia rang.

I looked at it.

Frankie was at her jobsites. Dr. Hayes wouldn't call this early without a reason. I had given the number to one other person this morning, and Kevin calling back three hours after I had called him meant Kevin had a reason.

I picked it up.

"Theo."

"Kevin. What is it."

"You called me on this number this morning. I'm calling you back on it. Is that — is that okay."

"Yes. What happened."

"Galen came by my office about an hour ago. He was asking about you."

I did not say anything.

"He said he hadn't heard from you in a few days and he wanted to check in. He asked if I had a home number for you, or a pager, or anything. I told him you'd called out. He asked what the emergency was. I told him I didn't have details. He asked if you had

— Theo, he asked if you had a way I could reach you this week. I told him I didn't have a cell. Then he gave me a number. He asked me to pass it to you if I heard from you. He said it was important. He said he wanted to grab lunch."

"Okay."

"Theo. I know it's none of my business. I don't know what's going on. But Galen seemed — he seemed off."

"What do you mean."

"I mean he was — he was nervous. He was — he's a guy who doesn't get nervous. You know what I mean."

"Yeah."

"You want the number."

"Yeah."

Kevin read the number. I wrote it on my palm in ink from a pen Frankie had left on the kitchen counter.

"Theo."

"Yeah."

"Take care of yourself."

"I will, Kevin. Thank you."

"Be careful."

He hung up.

I stood in the kitchen of the Forest Hill bungalow and looked at the number on my palm. I looked at it for a long time.

Frankie came in from the porch.

"Who was that."

"Kevin."

"Everything all right."

"Galen wants to have lunch."

She did not say anything for a second.

Then she said, "Huh."

I called Dr. Hayes.

I walked two blocks from the bungalow first. I stopped on the corner of a residential street I had never set foot on before and I dialed the Nokia number she had given me. She picked up on the second ring.

"Yes."

"Galen Brennan wants to have lunch with me."

A pause. She was thinking.

"How did he contact you."

"Through Kevin, my manager. Kevin called me on the Nokia. He gave me a number Galen left with him."

"Did Galen have the Nokia number himself."

"No."

"Good."

"Should I do it."

"Yes."

"I thought you'd say no."

"Mr. Novak, I need information about Mr. Brennan that I do not currently have. You are going to go to lunch with him. You are going to be a man who is having a difficult week because his mother is ill, and you are going to be *not quite the same* as your coworker remembers you. You are going to be vague in small ways. You are going to answer questions you are asked with a short sentence and then a change of subject. You are going to pay close attention to what he asks. Especially the order he asks it in."

"Okay."

"Do you have a pocket recorder."

"No."

"Are you comfortable not having one."

"I — yes."

"You are a corporate instructional designer, Mr. Novak. What you do for a living is watch people absorb information badly and then rewrite the information until they absorb it. You have trained yourself for a decade to remember what people said and how they said it. You do not need a recorder. You will recall the conversation in detail this evening for me. Word for word, as close as you can get. Do you hear me."

"Yes."

"Pick a restaurant. Not near his home. Not near your home. Not in Lyndhurst."

"There's a diner on Chagrin I know. The Lucky Star."

"Know it. It's fine. Public. Well-lit. Neighboring tables. Ask him to meet you at noon. Eat a full meal. Leave at one."

"Okay."

"One more thing."

"Yes."

"Miss Russo does not go with you."

"She's going to want to."

"I am aware. You will tell her I said so. She is going to be approximately one block away in her truck, because I cannot stop her from being approximately one block away in her truck, but she will not be in the restaurant. Is that clear."

"Yes."

"Call me after."

She hung up.

I called the number Galen had left. Galen picked up on the first ring.

"Hello."

"Galen, it's Theo."

"Theo. Hey. Thanks for calling back."

"Yeah. Kevin said you were looking for me."

"Yeah. Yeah. Look — I heard about your mom. I'm really sorry. If there's anything Meg and I can do — anything at all —"

"I appreciate that."

"I was just wondering — look, I know this might be a weird time, but I wanted to catch up. I have some — I wanted to just check in. Can we grab lunch today. I can drive wherever."

"Sure. Lucky Star on Chagrin, noon?"

"Yeah. Yeah, perfect. I'll see you there."

"See you there."

I hung up.

I stood on the corner in the Forest Hill neighborhood with the sun starting to climb over the trees behind me. A bird was making the specific three-note call I have never been able to identify. I could hear a lawnmower several streets away.

I walked back to the bungalow.

The Lucky Star Diner had been on Chagrin Boulevard since 1963. It had a Formica counter, vinyl booths the color of unripe avocado, a jukebox that still worked, and a waitress named Doris who had been on shift during the first Bush administration and did not show any signs of leaving. I had eaten at the Lucky Star probably two dozen times in my life. It was, as Dr. Hayes had noted, public and well-lit. It was also, for the specific purpose I needed, full of the wrong kind of noise — a constant background of dishes, small talk, jukebox, and Doris calling orders through the service window — which would make it hard for anybody beyond my own table to hear what was said at it.

I sat in a booth by the window at 11:52.

Galen came in at 12:03.

He was in khakis and a golf shirt. His silver crewcut was freshly cut. He had circles under his eyes I had not noticed in the break room, which meant either they were new or I had not been looking properly. He saw me. He walked over. He slid into the opposite side of the booth.

"Theo."

"Galen."

"How's your mom."

"She's — we're hoping."

"I'm sorry."

"Thank you."

Doris came. We ordered. Galen ordered the Reuben. I ordered a grilled cheese, because I was not hungry and because grilled cheese is the order of a person who is not pretending. Galen got coffee. I got a Coke.

Doris went away.

Galen put his hands on the table. He looked at them.

"Theo," he said. "Listen. I wanted — I wanted to check in. And — look. I don't know what's going on. I don't. But I've got a — I've got a bad feeling."

"About my mom."

"About you."

I did not say anything.

"Are you okay. I don't mean with your mom. I mean — are *you* okay."

"I'm tired, Galen."

"That thing you showed me last week."

"The sculpture."

"Yeah. Did you — did anything come of that."

"Meg didn't recognize it."

"She didn't. No. I'm asking because — because I'm curious. Any other leads on it."

"I don't — no. Nothing. It's just a thing on my shelf."

"It's on your shelf."

"Yeah."

A pause.

"Theo."

"Yeah."

"Be careful with that thing."

I waited.

"You know," he said. "Just — if it's a thing, get it appraised. Get it insured. I had a buddy once who —"

"Galen."

"Yeah."

"Is there something you want to tell me."

He looked up at me.

For a long moment his face was, specifically, his face. The face I knew. The face of the man who had sat across from me at dinner in his house in Euclid with his wife who had brought a cheesecake. The face of a man who had three patents and a silver crewcut and soft brown eyes and a grandson I had heard about. He was, for that moment, just Galen Brennan.

Then the face shifted. It went through one of those two-expression moves again — two micro-things in one second — and when it settled, it was the face of a man who had decided *no.*

"Theo, man," he said. "I'm just — I'm just checking in. That's all. Take care of your mom. Take care of yourself."

"Yeah."

"If you need anything."

"Yeah. Thanks, Galen."

Doris brought the food. Galen ate the Reuben. I ate about a third of the grilled cheese. We talked about the Indians. We talked about Kevin's upcoming golf vacation, which was apparently happening, which I had not known about. We talked about a new Cleveland Heights restaurant that had opened where an old Arabica used to be. We did not talk about the sculpture again.

At 12:58 Galen paid the check before I could reach for my wallet.

We stood in the parking lot.

"Take care of yourself, Theo."

"You too."

"Just — be careful, man."

He said *be careful* with too much weight.

He put his hand on my shoulder. He held it there for a second.

Then he got in his Taurus and drove away.

I stood in the parking lot.

Frankie's truck was parked down the block, pointing away from me. I walked to her. She was in the driver's seat with a pair of binoculars on the console, which I did not comment on. I got in.

"Was he clean."

"I don't know."

"What do you mean you don't know."

"I mean he said some things any coworker would say, and he said some things no coworker would say, and I don't know where the line between the two was. I don't know what he came to find out and I don't know whether he came to warn me."

"Theo."

"Yeah."

"Hayes will know."

"Yeah."

"Let's go."

We drove back to Forest Hill. I made two pages of notes on a yellow legal pad Frankie kept in her glove compartment. I wrote down every question Galen had asked me, in order, with the exact phrasing. I wrote down the words he had used that had not been normal coworker words. I wrote down *take care of that thing, get it appraised, get it insured.* I wrote down *be careful, man* twice, with a note about the weight. I wrote down the two micro-expressions.

I did not know what any of it meant.

But I understood, for the first time, what Dr. Hayes had meant at her kitchen table about my career.

I had spent a decade watching people absorb information and I had gotten good at knowing when they were performing.

Galen had been performing.

I did not yet know what role he had been assigned.

But he had been assigned one.

What I did not know, driving back to Forest Hill with my yellow legal pad on my lap, was that Galen Brennan, at 1:51 PM — fifty-three minutes after he had said *be careful, man* in the parking lot of the Lucky Star — walked back to a grey Taurus on

Chagrin Boulevard that was not his own grey Taurus, and got in.

I would learn the specifics of what followed much later, from Galen's own account, given to a federal prosecutor in Cleveland in the spring of the following year. He was, by then, a man who had decided that accuracy was the only currency he had left. He was specific, and complete, and he did not editorialize. I am going to tell it now the same way he did.

Martin Doyle had been parked on Chagrin for forty-three minutes when Galen arrived. He was in the driver's seat with a paper coffee cup in the cupholder and a notebook on the seat beside him. He was not performing the reasons for being in a parked car. He did not need to. He was the specific kind of person who could occupy a space without explaining himself to it, and who could do this for as long as the operation required.

Galen got in. He closed the door. He did not speak.

"Walk me through it," Doyle said.

Galen walked him through it. The sequence of the questions. Theo's answers. The two moments where the conversation had not gone the direction the script called for. Doyle listened with a stillness Galen had come to recognize over the preceding week as a professional technique — a completeness so total that the person talking tended to fill it with more than they had meant to say. Galen was aware of the technique. He did not say more than he meant to.

"Did he indicate where he's staying."

"No."

"Whether he still has the object."

"He said it was on his shelf."

"He was lying."

"I assumed so."

"Did he indicate who else he's been in contact with."

"No. He was vague. In a specific way. The way a person is vague when they've been told to be."

Doyle wrote something in the notebook. "He's been coached."

"Yes. I think so."

"By someone who knows what they're doing."

"He's different than he was." Galen paused. "Three weeks ago I would have known within five minutes of sitting across from him what was in his head. On Monday I couldn't read him."

Doyle capped the pen. "What you gave him was exactly right. He'll go to whoever is helping him and report that a worried colleague came to check in. That you meant well and offered nothing. That is the report we need him to make."

Galen nodded.

Through the windshield, a man in a hardware-store apron was changing the letters on a sandwich board outside a paint supply store. He made a change, stepped back, looked at the board, and appeared unsatisfied.

"What happens to him," Galen said.

"Novak."

"Yes."

Doyle set the notebook on the seat. He had the quality, in that moment, of a man giving an answer he had given before, in other contexts, about other people — not performed, exactly, but worn smooth. "He hands us the material and this is over for him. The Agency doesn't have an interest in an instructional designer. He goes back to his life. People forget. It takes time, but they do."

Galen looked at the sandwich board.

"He won't," he said.

"He'll have no choice."

"I know him. I've known him three years." He stopped. He started again. "He's the kind of person who notices things and doesn't stop noticing them. Whatever this is — it's already in him. It doesn't come out."

"That may be," Doyle said.

It was not a concession. It was punctuation. It meant: this part of the subject is not your responsibility.

Galen said, "What about the woman."

"She's not a concern."

She was his concern. She was the person Theo would push back for, and Galen knew it, and Doyle probably knew it, and what Galen did not say — what he sat with in the passenger seat of a grey Taurus on a Monday afternoon in August — was that six weeks ago, before the Polaroid and the appraiser and the Lucky Star, when Doyle had been a phone number at the end of a phone call from a BP station and not a man sitting eighteen inches away with very good posture, Galen had given that number Theo's address. His home number. The girlfriend's name. The cat. He had given all of it when it was still abstract. It was not abstract anymore.

He opened the door.

He crossed the parking lot to his own Taurus without looking back. He drove north on Chagrin. He was inside his house in Euclid before three. He sat at the kitchen table for a long time without doing anything. When Meg came home she said he looked tired and he said yes and she made spaghetti, and they ate it, and he helped her do the dishes, and he did not say a word about any of it. This was the choice he had been making for seven years. He had not stopped being able to make it. That was the specific thing he would have to live with.

Doyle sat in the parked car for eleven minutes after Galen left.

He thought, for all eleven of those minutes, about the one thing he had learned not to think about directly.

The list was real. He had known it was real since 1994, when the name MEADOWLARK had come to him through a channel that moved intelligence in one direction and personal exposure in another. Ostrowski had been thorough. Everyone said this about Ostrowski, in the specific tone people use to describe a quality they respect and fear in equal measure. He had been thorough in 1987 when the compilation began, and thorough every year since, and thorough enough that the record — if it still existed, which it did, which he now knew for certain it did — was almost certainly complete.

Doyle did not know which frame he was on.

He had been not-knowing this for eleven years. He had developed, over those years, a working theology: the past was not a debt until someone read it. As long as no one read it, the past was just the past. He had lived under this theology with a consistency he had come to regard as professional discipline, and it had served him, and it would serve him until Saturday.

He started the car.

He drove west on Chagrin toward the lake, and the lake was dark blue and flat at the end of Cedar, and he drove toward it with the specific forward motion of a man who has decided, a long time ago, that looking backward was a form of spending a resource he did not have.

He had work to do.

He drove.

THIRTEEN: *The Safe Channel*

We had arrived at Dr. Hayes's at 11:20.

Dr. Hayes read my notes on Galen for twenty-two minutes.

She did this with a specific method — in silence, without looking up, with a red pen in her right hand, marking each page as she went. She did not react at any specific moment. She did not nod. She did not grunt. She did not circle anything with urgency. Her red pen moved in short, quick flicks, the way a good editor marks. When she was finished she stacked the pages in a neat pile, set the pen on top of them, and looked up at me.

"You are very good at your job," she said.

"Thank you."

"Did he ask you about your home number."

"No."

"Did he ask you where you were staying."

"No."

"Did he ask you how long you would be out."

"No."

"Did he, at any point, try to determine your physical location."

"No."

"Did he, at any point, try to obtain a piece of information that would help somebody else determine your physical location."

"No."

"He did not come to you as a scout."

"That's what I thought. But I didn't have the language for it."

"He came to warn you."

"Yes. I think so. But I don't think the warning came out."

"No," Dr. Hayes said. "He was stopped halfway through it. He had come intending to say something that he then did not say."

"Who stops somebody halfway through a warning."

"His handler. Or his own fear. Probably both. Probably he was told very explicitly, before the lunch, that he was to determine whether you had something of value and to report back without alerting you, and that if he did anything other than that, he was going to have a problem. And probably, when he sat across from you, he looked at you and decided — for a minute — that he was going to warn you anyway. And then he thought about his wife. And then he thought about his daughter. And then he did not."

Frankie said, "Jesus."

"Yes."

"Can we — I don't know. Help him somehow."

Dr. Hayes looked at Frankie with a specific flatness.

"Miss Russo, our job in the next two weeks is to keep you and Mr. Novak alive and to get the cache to the right hands. Our job is not to save the forty-seven men and women on that list. Some of them will survive this. Most of them will not. A number of them do not deserve to. Mr. Brennan, whom I have now identified as one of the eleven names associated with TRW, sold classified propulsion research to the Soviet Union and subsequently to the Russian Federation for seven years beginning in 1989. He did it knowingly. He understood what he was doing. He was not coerced. He was paid. The reason he has a daughter in a biology program at Case Western — and, please note, the same biology program that Oleg's daughter is in, which is not a coincidence but is a conversation for another day — is that he sold the Americans out at a rate of approximately sixty thousand dollars a year."

Nobody said anything.

"Having said that," Dr. Hayes continued, "I will note that what Mr. Brennan did with his face at the

Lucky Star Diner, in the moment before he decided not to warn you, is one of the most sympathetic gestures a man in his position is capable of making. It does not redeem him. But it is worth noticing. And I am noticing."

"Okay."

Dr. Hayes set the pen aside.

"Now. The time has come to make a call that I have been putting off for about nine months."

"There is a woman in the FBI Cleveland field office," Dr. Hayes said, "whose name is Claire Mwangi. She is a counterintelligence agent. She is thirty-eight years old. She was born in Nairobi, raised in Silver Spring, educated at Georgetown Law. She has been in the Bureau for fourteen years. She is very good at her job, and she is one of the most honest federal employees I have ever worked with."

Frankie said, "You worked with her."

"Briefly. In 1988, on a joint NSA-FBI operation involving a Soviet defector at a ski resort in Colorado. The operation was — successful. Complicated. We each learned, in the process, that the other could be relied on at a specific level. I have not spoken to her in five years. But she will remember me. And she will, if I call her in the correct way, know what the call means."

"The correct way."

"There was a phrase we used in 1988. It meant: *this is Lorraine, this is not a routine contact, I need to speak to you immediately, do not discuss the call with anyone until we have spoken.* It is not a phrase you would ever say in any other context. If I say it on her voicemail tonight, she will know to return the call on the first safe line she can find tomorrow morning."

"What's the phrase."

Dr. Hayes smiled, the dry smile.

"The phrase is: *would you like to discuss the Heidelberg variant.*"

"Heidelberg variant of what."

"Nothing. Precisely nothing. There is no Heidelberg variant. That was the point of the phrase. There is, as far as the world is concerned, no such thing as a Heidelberg variant. Only Claire knows that. If anyone else ever heard my voicemail, they would think it was a wrong number."

She stood up. She went to the front hallway. There was an old black rotary telephone on a small table by the coat closet — the kind of phone that had outlived everything around it by sheer stubbornness. She picked up the handset. She dialed a number from memory. Seven digits — local. Cleveland.

She waited for the tone.

Her voice, when she spoke, was not her voice. It was pitched up a quarter-step and smoothed down — the voice of a friendly woman from a book club, a woman who had dialed the wrong number, a voice that did not carry any signal at all.

"Hi, this is Lorraine, I am just following up on our last conversation. I was hoping we could talk this week. Would you like to discuss the Heidelberg variant. I have some time Tuesday after three. Call me at home. Thank you, dear."

She hung up.

She stood for a second with her hand still on the handset.

"Now we wait," she said.

"How long."

"If she is in Cleveland and on duty, she will call back within twelve hours. If she is on assignment out of town, it could be twenty-four to thirty-six. If she does not call back within forty-eight, we assume something has gone wrong and we change course."

She did not call back within twelve hours.

She did not call back within twenty-four hours.

We slept Monday night at the Forest Hill bungalow. We drove back to Dr. Hayes's on Tuesday morning at ten, through two different dry-cleaning loops — one that Frankie designed, one that Dr. Hayes amended on the fly. We arrived at her house at 11:20. We sat in her kitchen for six hours. We drank a great deal of coffee. Ramona came with us, in her carrier, and after thirty minutes of suspicious exploration she settled into a specific armchair in the front room and had an uneasy truce with Alexei, who was willing to share his territory but did not intend to do so with any grace. Pushkin, the black one, did not appear. Mrs. Nabokov continued to bite.

Dr. Hayes did not do any work on the microfiche while we waited. She explained, carefully, that she did not want the film out of its envelope and on her microfiche reader while there was any possibility that someone would arrive at her house uninvited. The cedar closet stayed closed. The envelope sat on her kitchen counter in a small fireproof lockbox she had retrieved from her basement. The key to the lockbox sat in her front pants pocket.

At three PM on Tuesday she said, "I was expecting something by now."

At four, she said, "I am becoming concerned."

At five-thirty, she said, "The return call has been intercepted."

At five-fifty-two, there was a knock at the front door.

FOURTEEN: *Doyle*

I did not know, standing in the front room of Dr. Hayes's bungalow on that Tuesday evening, that the man who was about to knock had parked his rental car two blocks east and walked.

I would learn this later — from a surveillance note in Mwangi's file, and from Doyle himself, in a federal holding room in Quantico, in a debrief he gave in exchange for a cooperation agreement his attorney had negotiated down to something that might, in thirty years, be described as lenient. He described the walk on Lee Road with a precision that suggested it had stayed with him. I have thought about why it would have, and I believe I understand.

He parked on a side street east of Lee at 5:38 PM. He got out of the grey Taurus. He straightened his jacket. He picked up the leather portfolio. He walked.

Lee Road between Fairmount and the bungalow was residential in the specific way streets become residential when nobody is performing it — old maples over the sidewalk, front porches with metal chairs, a bicycle locked to a railing. He walked at the pace of a man who lived there. The portfolio was, as it had always been, the right prop. A man on a residential street in the evening with nothing in his hands was a man who could be asked what he was doing. A man with a portfolio was going to a meeting.

He was going to a meeting.

At 5:41 he could see the bungalow. Blue siding where the brick ended. White trim around the windows. Green front door. Through the front window, the specific interior of a person who has spent decades in the same house — bookshelves floor to ceiling, a reading lamp on, a leather armchair positioned at the angle of someone who had not moved it in twenty years. A brown cat asleep on the porch swing.

Hayes always had cats. He had known this about her. He knew a dozen things about Lorraine Hayes that were not in any file, because they were the kind of things you learned about a person in a ski resort in Colorado in 1988 when you were both there on the same operation and you spent eleven days eating breakfast across the same table and she was the only other person in the building who did not need something explained twice. She was formidable. She was honest in the specific way people were honest when they had decided, early in life, that dishonesty was expensive. She had been one of the four or five professionals he had encountered in twenty-three years whom he had allowed himself to genuinely respect.

He was going to lie to her completely.

This was not a conflict. He had been in this profession long enough that the recognition of worth and the management of a problem were not functions in competition with each other. They ran on different tracks. Lorraine Hayes was formidable. That was a problem to be managed. He would be warm. He would invoke the right names. He would give her exactly enough truth to borrow her caution for one more day, and in that day he would reach the channel he needed, and by Wednesday evening the cache would be in the right hands, and the problem that had been a debt for eleven years would resolve into the past, which was where it had always belonged.

He stopped on the front path.

The cat on the swing did not move.

Doyle looked at the green door.

He had been carrying a specific thing for eleven years. Not guilt — he had examined that question carefully, in the early years, and had arrived at a conclusion that was more technically honest than emotionally satisfying: he had not chosen the thing, not the first time, and by the time choice had become available to him the gap between what had already been done and what could be undone was too wide to cross. What he carried instead was the practical weight of a man who has built his professional position on top of a specific silence, and who understands that the silence must be maintained not out of fear but out of logic, because the alternative is a sequence of events that ends in a room not unlike the room in a federal building he had visited twice in the last decade to watch other people occupy.

He was not going to occupy that room.

He walked up the front path.

He raised his hand.

He knocked.

The man at the door was not Claire Mwangi.

The man at the door was six feet tall, in his early fifties, with silver hair cut with surgical precision and a navy sport coat over an open-collared white shirt. He had a square jaw, a suntan, and the specific kind of physical fitness you get from playing tennis on expensive courts. He was holding a leather portfolio. He was standing on Dr. Hayes's porch with the posture of a man who had rung doorbells at better houses than this one and had always been let in.

"Lorraine," he said warmly. "It's been too long."

Dr. Hayes — who had walked to the door with a specific slowness, as if she were fetching a neighbor's borrowed casserole dish — looked at him with an expression of mild, pleasant recognition.

"Martin."

"May I come in."

"Of course you may."

She stepped aside. He came in. He looked around the front room briefly — not surveying, exactly, but doing the kind of fast assessment a man in his profession did constantly, the way a fisherman looks at water. He clocked me. He clocked Frankie. He clocked the cats. He did not react to any of us.

"Martin," Dr. Hayes said, "this is Mr. Novak and Miss Russo. Theo, Frankie, this is Martin Doyle. He is with an agency I used to contract for. He and I worked together on some matters in the late eighties."

Doyle extended a hand. I took it. His grip was warm and exactly thc right firmness — the kind of handshake they teach you at good schools. He smiled at me. His smile was well-made.

"Theo. Pleasure."

"Hi."

"Frankie." He shook her hand too. Frankie's handshake was deliberately boneless, which was, I realized, a specific choice. Doyle registered the boneless handshake with a small flicker of something — amusement, possibly — and moved on.

"May we sit," he said. "I won't keep you long."

"Please," Dr. Hayes said, and she led us into the living room, where the armchair held Ramona and Alexei and where the rug under our feet had two worn paths in it. Dr. Hayes gestured at the couch. Doyle sat on one end of it. Dr. Hayes took the armchair beside him. Frankie and I sat on the couch on the far end from Doyle.

"Coffee?"

"Please."

Dr. Hayes went to the kitchen. She was gone for forty-five seconds. She came back with a single coffee cup on a saucer, which she set on the coffee table in front of Doyle. She did not offer coffee to Frankie or me. She did not take one for herself. She sat down in the armchair again.

Doyle picked up the coffee. He sipped it. He nodded.

"So," he said. "Lorraine. You called Claire."

"I left her a voicemail."

"She's in Chicago this week on a joint task force. She got the message, she recognized it, she flagged it to my office. She asked me to respond on her behalf."

Dr. Hayes said, "Hm."

This was, I thought, the specific *hm* she had used when Oleg said *I have never been here.* It was a sound that was not quite an affirmation and not quite a denial. It was a sound that bought her two seconds of thinking time and gave nothing away.

"Claire didn't mention this in her voicemail back to me," Dr. Hayes said.

"I don't believe Claire left a voicemail. She called the office directly. She had a sense of urgency and she wanted the right person on it. I'm the right person on it. I flew in this morning from Langley."

"And you drove here directly."

"I drove here directly from the field office on Lakeside, yes. It's about a nine-minute drive without traffic."

"In what vehicle."

"A Ford Taurus from the motor pool."

"What color."

Doyle smiled. "Grey."

"Where did you park."

"Two blocks east. I walked the rest. Assuming — correctly, I hope — that you would prefer I didn't advertise a federal vehicle on Lee Road."

"You were right."

Dr. Hayes had not smiled once since she had answered the door.

"Martin," she said, "Mr. Novak and Miss Russo are my house guests this evening. I am not going to ask them to leave. Anything you would discuss with me, you can discuss in front of them."

"Of course," Doyle said.

He set the coffee down. He opened the portfolio on his lap. Inside was a single manila folder, which he did not open.

"Lorraine," he said, "I understand you have come into possession of some material. I understand this material is of a classification level that should never have been held by anyone outside of a very small professional circle. I understand the material came to you via an unusual route, involving a civilian and a sculpture and an estate in Shaker Heights. I would like to help you with this. I would like to put the material in safe hands. I would like to do that tonight, if possible. I can write you a receipt, I can provide you with an operational assurance, and I can ensure that Mr. Novak and Miss Russo" — he glanced at us, warmly — "are not subject to any consequences for what has, obviously, been an accidental and inadvertent involvement."

Dr. Hayes said, "That's very generous, Martin."

"It is not generosity. It is simply the right sequence of actions."

"And who in particular, Martin, will hold the material after I give it to you tonight."

"The CI group at Cleveland station, on a temporary basis. Until it can be couriered to Langley, where — honestly, Lorraine, you know where it would go. You know the desk. You know the building."

"Do I know the analyst."

"You probably know the analyst by reputation. I can't share the name yet. Operational reasons, as you understand."

"Of course."

"May I see the material."

"You may not."

Doyle paused.

It was a small pause. The pause of a man who had not expected that specific answer in that specific cadence. He recovered.

"Lorraine —"

"Martin, you and I have known each other for twenty-one years. I respect your service and I respect your judgment. I am, however, not going to produce classified material in my living room tonight. I am going to take several hours to verify the chain of custody. I am going to reach Claire directly. I am going to confirm with her, in person, that she has in fact delegated this matter to you, and I am going to do this in a setting that is not a residential phone line."

"She is in Chicago."

"I have her home number."

"She's not *at* her home."

"I have her pager."

"Lorraine. Come on."

"Martin. Come on."

They looked at each other across the coffee table.

I was watching Doyle's hands.

I do not know why I was watching his hands. It was the hands that had caught my eye, though, and it was the hands that were going to matter later, when Dr. Hayes asked me for everything I had noticed. I was watching his hands because they had done something specific when Dr. Hayes said the word *pager.*

They had tightened on the leather portfolio. Just once. Just for a second. Then they had relaxed.

He had corrected himself quickly. But the grip had tightened.

A man whose chain of custody was genuine would not have grip-tightened at the word *pager.* A man who had flown in from Langley that morning to receive a delegation from Claire Mwangi would have been *reassured* by Dr. Hayes's reasonable offer to verify. That was a *good* move, operationally. An honest broker would have welcomed it.

Doyle had, for half a second, *hated* it.

I was sitting on a couch six feet away from this, and I was watching it happen, and I was understanding, for the first time since the Lucky Star Diner, what Dr. Hayes meant when she talked about the things you know that you do not know you know.

Doyle gathered himself. He smiled.

"That's your prerogative, Lorraine. I understand the caution. I'll go back to the field office and I'll try to reach Claire through her team. I'll call you tomorrow morning. Will nine be all right."

"Nine will be fine."

"In the meantime — the material."

"Stays here."

"Lorraine, at least let me —"

"Stays here, Martin."

A third pause.

Then he smiled again, stood up, picked up the portfolio, and offered his hand.

"Lorraine, as always, a pleasure."

"Goodbye, Martin."

He nodded at me. He nodded at Frankie. He walked to the front door. He let himself out.

Dr. Hayes did not move.

She sat in the armchair for a full minute, motionless, listening. Somewhere down the street a car door closed. An engine started. The engine faded away down Lee Road.

She waited another thirty seconds.

Then she said, "He's on the list."

"What."

"Mr. Novak, I don't know which name. I will know by tomorrow morning; I have two ways to check and I will use both of them tonight. But I know the face of a man who has been scared for eight years, and that is the face that man was wearing. Martin Doyle is on that microfiche. He came here tonight because he knew the list existed and he knew it had surfaced and he knew it had reached me, and he has been trying for twenty-four hours to intercept that channel. He reached Claire's voicemail. He erased it. He is operating on the assumption that Claire does not yet know I called, and he is going to make sure she continues not to know. He came here tonight to take the cache before Claire could be reached. He will come back tomorrow with more leverage."

Frankie said, "Wait. How did he know you had it."

Dr. Hayes's eyes went very narrow.

"That," she said, "is the question I'm going to spend tonight answering."

FIFTEEN: *The Swap Plan*

Dr. Hayes spent from eight PM until a little after one AM on the question of how Martin Doyle had known.

She did this in a specific way, from an armchair in her front room, with a legal pad on her lap and a pot of tea beside her. She made four phone calls. She did not tell us who they were to. She spoke in very short sentences. Two of them were in Russian. One of them was in what I later learned was the specific dialect of Finnish you get if you grew up speaking Ingrian Finnish north of St. Petersburg. The fourth was in English, with a woman whose voice, on Dr. Hayes's end of the conversation, sounded old and warm.

During the second Russian call — the shorter of the two, the one Hayes ended without a pause — I caught a word in the middle of a sentence I could not otherwise follow. It had the shape of a proper name. I am a person who writes down things he does not understand, on the theory that understanding sometimes follows, and I reached for the pen Hayes had left on the arm of the couch and wrote the word on my palm — the same way I had written Galen's number in the parking lot of the Lucky Star the day before — and I went on watching.

Yegorov.

I did not ask about it. I did not mention it.

At about eleven, Frankie went upstairs to sleep. Ramona went with her.

I stayed up.

Dr. Hayes did not seem to mind having me in the room. She did not talk to me. She did not look at me. She let me sit on the couch with my hands folded and watch her work, and I did, for five hours, and what I watched was the specific craft of a woman assembling a picture from the twenty-three corners of it she could see.

At 1:07 AM she set the pencil down.

"I have it," she said.

I said, "Yes."

"Claire was pulled off-duty Thursday morning of last week on an urgent CI matter in Chicago. The matter was manufactured. I do not yet know by whom. Her pager was issued a new number for the duration. The new number was routed through a CI switchboard in the Cleveland field office. Her voicemail at home is retrievable with a passcode she shared, years ago, with her then-supervisor — a man named Hal Rutkowski — who retired in 1994. That passcode was added, on Rutkowski's retirement, to a reference document for subsequent supervisors. Martin Doyle accessed that document yesterday morning. He retrieved my voicemail. He erased it. He flew in from Langley this morning on an unscheduled flight to respond to my message personally. He has been attempting, for the last ten days, to identify the asset who produced the microfiche we now hold — by which I mean he has been attempting to identify which of the forty-seven names compiled it, and he has been attempting to determine whether his own name appears on the compilation, which he does not yet know, because the list itself has not been in his hands at any point. He has used every resource he has been able to put a plausible cover on. He flew to Cleveland on the possibility that my voicemail might represent the break in the case. He arrived. He confirmed. Now he is going to go back to his hotel tonight and he is going to begin the work of ensuring this material never reaches anyone other than him."

"Wow."

"Yes."

"How do you know all that."

"I have spent thirty years cultivating a small number of relationships at other agencies and in other countries, most of whom owe me favors I have been holding for specific moments. I used five of those favors tonight. I will use three more tomorrow."

"And Mwangi."

"Is fine. Is in Chicago. Is genuinely on a manufactured task force. Is currently operating under the assumption that I have not yet attempted to contact her and that no contact has been made. Every channel I have is being watched. I will have to find a new one, and the new one will have to be a channel Doyle does not know exists. That is tomorrow's problem."

"We need her."

"Yes. We do. I will reach her, Mr. Novak. It will simply take longer than I had hoped."

"One more thing," she said.

She had not put the pencil down yet. She was looking at the legal pad — the last line she had written, I assumed, the line that had preceded *I have it*.

"Doyle has a handler. He has had one for some years. The handler knows his name is on the list. He has been protecting Doyle — not out of loyalty, I think, but because a compromised CIA officer is a functioning asset worth maintaining. Doyle almost certainly does not know how long the handler has been aware."

"Who is the handler."

"I have a name," she said. "I have not confirmed it. I will confirm it in the morning. Do not ask me again tonight."

She closed the legal pad.

"We will pick this up at seven AM," she said. "Go to bed, Mr. Novak."

"Yes."

I went upstairs. I slept four hours. I did not dream.

At seven AM on Wednesday morning, Dr. Hayes walked us to the hall closet.

It was a small closet — the kind of closet that houses, in most people's houses, coats and a vacuum and a shoebox of Christmas lights. This closet, when Dr. Hayes opened it, had none of those things. The interior walls were lined with cedar planks. A small track lighting strip ran along the top. Beneath it, on a built-in counter, sat a flat light box, two adjustable desk lamps, a laminating press, a spool of blank microfiche film in a brown cardboard canister, a pair of chemical trays, a pH-balanced rinse bottle, and a small machinist's vice that had been bolted to the counter in 1979 and had not, from the look of it, moved since.

The tools were old. They had been used well. Nothing in the closet was dusty.

Frankie and I stood in the hall and looked in at all of it.

Frankie said, "Dr. Hayes."

"Miss Russo."

"You can do that."

"Dear. I was building microdot propaganda when your parents were in middle school."

Frankie laughed. It was a short laugh. It was the first time I had heard her laugh since Monday morning.

Dr. Hayes stepped aside and gestured at the equipment with the same small proud hand movement with which a chef might gesture at a copper pan she had owned for thirty-five years.

"We are going to fabricate a decoy," she said. "It will be the same format as the original microfiche. It will contain forty-seven names. It will contain information that reads as plausible, compromising, and actionable at first pass. It will be old enough that at second pass, the names will look like they were compiled circa 1987. The handlers listed will be handlers who are dead or retired. The dead-drop locations will be locations that were surveilled and closed in the early nineties. The payment channels will be cutout accounts that were frozen in 1994. A serious cryptanalyst with three hours and a reference library can determine that the material is outdated and, upon deeper examination, was never active — though they will have to work to get there. A field officer in a hurry, reading by hand in an office on Carnegie, will see the top three names and will act on them before he looks at the fourth. Which is what we want."

"Why."

"Because if Doyle looks at the top three names and sees names that are real people who really took real money from the Soviets and are currently in positions of authority, he will conclude that he holds the authentic cache. He will go to Langley. He will move to burn the list. The first thing he will do is attempt to kill the top three names, to prevent them from surviving long enough to be usefully interviewed. The top three names are already dead. Therefore nothing happens. He believes he has neutralized the threat. He stands down."

"And by then —"

"By then the real list is with Agent Mwangi, and Doyle is a dead man walking."

"He's not —"

"He will be arrested within forty-eight hours, Miss Russo, on federal charges related to the manipulation of Agent Mwangi's pager routing. That charge is enough to hold him. The MEADOWLARK-related charges will follow."

"Meadowlark."

"That is the codename of the cache. I have not used it out loud until now. It is the operation's given name in its own compartment. It has been a rumored codename for the last six years."

“Meadowlark,” I said. “Why?”

Dr. Hayes looked at me for a beat.

“Because meadowlarks have a specific call that a naturalist can recognize from a mile away,” she said. “It is a call that cannot be confused with any other bird. Mikael thought of his network as birdsong. He thought of himself as the naturalist. He thought of the microfiche as the identification key. It was an affectation. He was in other ways a deeply unsentimental man. But he had this one.”

She fell silent.

I looked at the clock on the kitchen wall. It was 9:11 AM. The phone had not rung.

Hayes had not looked at the clock. She did not need to.

"He didn't call," I said.

"No."

"You told him nine would be fine."

"I told him nine would be fine because it was what the conversation required." Her voice was the same even register it always was, which was the register of a woman who had said this kind of thing before, in other rooms, about other men. "A man who intends to call at nine AM calls at nine AM. He didn't call because the call was never the point. He came last night to confirm that I had the cache. He confirmed it. Now he's building his next approach, and his next approach is not a phone call."

She picked up the pencil. She looked at it for a moment.

"That is the last thing we needed to verify. We've verified it."

She let out a breath.

“Let’s work,” she said.

The decoy took ten hours to fabricate.

We worked through Wednesday and into Wednesday night. Dr. Hayes did all of the precise work — the typing of the names on her Selectric II with a replaceable head she swapped out for one that had been used at Langley in 1987, the photographing of the typed pages on the light box, the chemical development, the trimming of the film. Frankie and I did the support work — holding lamps, running pages, standing where Dr. Hayes told us to stand, getting her fresh coffee.

Halfway through the afternoon, I understood that I was also learning.

Dr. Hayes was not teaching. She was doing. But she was doing it, deliberately, in a way that left me and Frankie free to watch. She explained each step only insofar as it affected the step before or after. She did not editorialize. She did not grandstand. She was a craftsman in her workshop, absorbed in her work, and the work was making a false document by hand in the back of a hall closet in a bungalow on Lee Road in Cleveland Heights in August of 1996.

At seven PM we broke for dinner. Frankie made pasta from the contents of Dr. Hayes's pantry, which was weirdly well-stocked with Italian ingredients for a woman who had told us twice that she did not cook.

Dr. Hayes explained, eating, that the pantry had been stocked by Elena Bellavita, who had insisted on sending over groceries twice a year for the last twelve years of her life.

"She thought I did not feed myself properly."

Frankie said, "Did you feed yourself properly."

Dr. Hayes thought about it.

"No," she said.

We all laughed.

It was the second laugh of the operation. The first had been Frankie's. This one went around the table.

We finished the decoy at 11:15 PM.

Dr. Hayes held the developed film up to a desk lamp. She examined it under the loupe. She checked it against a reference card of her own handwriting. She nodded.

“That is,” she said, “as good as anything the Agency ever produced. Better, in several respects.”

“Now what,” I said.

“Now we get the real microfiche to Claire Mwangi. And we arrange for Doyle to receive this one.”

“How.”

Dr. Hayes set the decoy down on the kitchen table.

“A donor preview at the Cleveland Museum of Art,” she said, “is scheduled for Saturday evening. I have received an invitation. I will be obtaining two more. We will pass the decoy to Doyle in one part of the museum. We will hand the real microfiche to Claire Mwangi in another part of the same museum, at approximately the same moment. There will, by then, be three federal agencies in the building and none of them will know about the others. Doyle will intercept the decoy and believe he has won. Mwangi will receive the real list and act accordingly.”

“Saturday.”

“Saturday.”

"That's — ten days."

"Ten days," she said.

"Use them."

“You still haven’t reached Mwangi.”

“No. I have not. But I will.”

I looked at Frankie.

Frankie looked at the decoy on the table.

Then she looked at me.

“Okay,” she said.

“Okay,” I said.

Dr. Hayes looked at us both.

“There is one thing between now and Saturday,” she said, “that I need.”

“Name it.”

“Pierogies.”

SIXTEEN: *West Side Market*

Dr. Hayes needed pierogies because Dr. Hayes was going to ask a fourth person into her house Friday evening, and the fourth person was someone she had known for forty-one years, and the fourth person had once made Dr. Hayes sauerkraut pierogies from a recipe that had been in their family since before the First World War, and Dr. Hayes had been intending, she said, to make pierogies in return for this person, as a gesture, for more than a decade. She had not done it. She was not going to do it now either, because she was terrible at pierogies. But she wanted pierogies, from the specific counter at the specific vendor at the specific market where this person's grandmother had bought her specific pierogies in the 1940s.

I was a little surprised, after seventy-two hours of watching her operate like a tactical machine, by how rigorously sentimental she turned out to be underneath.

She asked me to go.

She had selected me, she said, because Frankie needed to drop in on one of the Lakewood jobsites to maintain the cover that her business was continuing as normal, and Dr. Hayes herself needed the afternoon to make two more phone calls in pursuit of Agent Mwangi. That left me.

"West Side Market," she said. "West twenty-fifth at Lorain. You know it."

"Yes."

"You will go in at a specific time. You will not look like you are shopping. You will go directly to the Kaufman's stall. You will buy four dozen pierogies — two dozen sauerkraut, one dozen potato-cheddar, one dozen lamb-and-mint. Lamb-and-mint is my failing. Do not argue with me about pierogies."

"I would not dream of it."

"Good. You will also buy coffee at a stall three aisles east of Kaufman's. You will drink the coffee while you wait at Kaufman's. You will appear to be a man killing a lunch break. When you have the pierogies you will leave by the south entrance. Park on West twenty-fifth, north of Lorain. Walk in. Walk out. In and out under thirty minutes. Take the Cedar-Fairmount Rapid to get there and back."

"The Rapid."

"Yes. Not the truck. Not the Jeep. Public transit. Nobody watches public transit."

"Frankie is going to be uneasy about this."

"Miss Russo will be uneasy about this and she will tell you so, and you will tell her that I said so, and she will accept it, because she is a good operator and good operators accept directives they disagree with as long as the directives have been explained."

"Okay."

She gave me $25. She gave me her bag — a canvas tote that said, on the side, CASE WESTERN RESERVE UNIVERSITY RUSSIAN STUDIES DEPARTMENT, which seemed, under the circumstances, like a very Dr. Hayes accessory. I took it.

I left the bungalow at 1:10 PM on Thursday.

The Cedar-Fairmount Rapid was a specific Cleveland experience that you could not replicate anywhere else. The RTA Red Line ran from Tower City in downtown all the way out to Windermere in East Cleveland, and it stopped at Cedar-University, just east of University Circle, which was a twelve-minute walk from Dr. Hayes's bungalow. I had ridden the Rapid twice before in my life — once to an Indians game in 1994, once to Tower City to buy Frankie a birthday present at the Avenue food court. I had not really ever thought of it as transportation.

I walked to the station. I bought a round-trip ticket. I rode the Red Line west into the city —

through Little Italy, past the stadium, into the downtown tunnel — and transferred at Tower City to the Red Line west, which took me across the river to Ohio City and the West Side Market stop.

I arrived at 2:14 PM.

The West Side Market had been at West 25th and Lorain since 1912. It was a vast yellow-brick hall of food vendors, arranged in two big spaces connected by a passageway — the main interior hall, with its cathedral ceiling and hundred-odd stalls selling meat, cheese, bread, pastry, and prepared foods, and the outdoor produce arcade, open-air, with fruits and vegetables and flowers and the smell of the city rolling in off Lorain. My grandfather had brought me here the first Saturday of every October from the time I was seven until the time I was twelve. I knew the building.

I knew it well enough to find Kaufman's without thinking.

Kaufman's pierogi stall was in the interior hall, about halfway down the east aisle, in a spot between a Slovenian sausage butcher and a Hungarian pastry woman who sold dobos torte in a glass case. The stall had a hand-painted sign that had been repainted exactly seven times — you could count the layers by standing close — and was tended on Thursday afternoons, as it had been for thirty-one years, by a woman named Mrs. Kaufman, who was Mrs. Kaufman's daughter-in-law by a previous Mr. Kaufman.

I stepped up to the counter. I ordered the four dozen pierogies. Mrs. Kaufman nodded without looking at me. She began pulling pierogies from a warming tray and packaging them in deli paper with a speed that suggested she could have done it in her sleep.

I turned around while she worked.

I had planned to turn around because Dr. Hayes had told me to pay attention to everything in the hall while I waited. I had not planned to turn around because I expected to see anything.

I saw the man with the upside-down newspaper.

He was three stalls down.

He was not reading a newspaper. He was standing in front of a stall that sold seven kinds of olives, looking at the olives with the specific absorption of a person who had never bought olives in their life and was pretending otherwise. He was in a grey windbreaker over a grey henley. He was maybe thirty-eight. He was the exact same build as the man in the Buick Century in the TRW parking garage, and he had the exact same specific something about the way he held his shoulders — a low, balanced tension that I had registered unconsciously two weeks ago and had, apparently, filed.

I had not filed it consciously.

But the body that was now attached to my head recognized the body that was now attached to his head, and my stomach went cold.

He had not seen me yet. I was at an angle behind him. He was looking at olives.

I turned back to the Kaufman's counter with the specific slowness of a person choosing not to draw attention.

Mrs. Kaufman was finishing the last dozen.

"Two dozen sauerkraut, one potato-cheddar, one lamb-and-mint, ten dollars fifty," she said.

"Thank you."

I put twelve dollars on the counter. I took the bag. I did not wait for change.

I walked, not fast, toward the south entrance.

Dr. Hayes had walked me through a counter-surveillance route at her kitchen table two nights ago. She had done it in fifteen minutes, with a salt shaker and a pepper grinder and an assortment of coffee cups to represent pedestrians and cars. The principles were simple. Do not sprint. Do not make eye contact. Do not signal that you have seen him. Walk out of the venue in which you noticed him in a direction that is neither the direction he arrived from nor the direction a reasonable person in your position would depart in. Make three turns in four blocks. Enter a shop. Exit the shop through a back door. Walk one block parallel to your original path. Enter a second shop. Exit. Board transportation two stops earlier than you had planned, and in the opposite direction. Change trains twice before returning to your origin.

The goal, she had said, was not to escape. The goal was to force the tail to commit to visible decisions that you could observe, so that you could identify whether you were actually being followed. Nobody can follow a skilled counter-surveillance target without, at some point, doing something observable.

I walked out the south entrance of the West Side Market. I turned left on Lorain instead of right on West 25th. I walked two blocks. I turned right onto a residential street. I turned right again at the next corner. I walked past a row of brick duplexes with flower boxes. I entered a small corner bodega called Los Pobres with an awning that advertised TAMALES and LOTTO and PHONE CARDS in faded red. I bought a bottle of water. I asked the clerk if there was a back exit. He looked at me for a second, assessed me, and said, "Yeah, through the kitchen, it goes to the alley." I thanked him. I walked through the kitchen. I came out in the alley. I walked one block east. I emerged on Fulton. I turned south. I walked three blocks. I boarded a southbound bus on Fulton that I had not originally been planning to take.

I rode the bus for ten minutes, staring out the window.

The man in the grey windbreaker did not appear.

I did not see him again.

Which was not the same, as Dr. Hayes would carefully explain to me later, as *not being followed.*

It was only the same as *not being visibly followed.* A professional who recognized that he had been burned would not pursue. He would fall back. He would call. He would let me go. He would work on finding me again through other means.

I rode the bus to the Ohio City Rapid stop. I boarded an eastbound Red Line. I transferred at Tower City. I boarded an eastbound Red Line to University Circle. I got off at Cedar-University. I walked to Dr. Hayes's bungalow on Lee Road. I took two additional unnecessary turns on the walk back, which I would not have taken at 2:14 PM when I left.

I arrived at 4:32 PM.

I gave Dr. Hayes the pierogies.

She looked at me.

"Tell me," she said.

I told her.

She listened with the expression of a woman who was absorbing information and sorting it in real time.

When I was finished she said, "Good work. Two things."

"Yes."

"First, your recall of the route is excellent. I will ask you in a moment to draw it on a napkin for me. I will compare it against my own map of Ohio City and I will note the streets you took. Second, you are almost certainly correct that the man you saw at the olive stall was the man in the grey Buick. A coincidence of that order does not exist in this neighborhood on a Thursday afternoon. He is now aware that you were at the West Side Market this afternoon. He has probably alerted his handlers. This means you cannot return to the West Side Market, and it means we cannot return to any of the public venues he has likely surveilled."

"Which are."

"Any place you have gone in the last two years with any regularity."

"That's — a lot of places."

"Yes."

"What do we do."

"We move the operation forward. We hold for the museum. Saturday."

She opened the bag of pierogies. She set one on a paper plate. She picked it up. She ate it.

Then she said, "Pierogies are better when the people bringing them are not being followed. But these will do."

I would not learn any of what follows until months later — until Claire Mwangi sat me down at her kitchen table in Rocky River, in early November, with a cup of coffee and a manila folder and a transcript translated into English from a Russian-language audio intercept obtained, through means she did not specify, by a third agency.

At 9:47 PM on Thursday, August 29th, 1996, a man named Pavel Antonovich Yegorov was sitting at the small round table by the window of room 1447 of the Marriott Key Center on Lakeside Avenue downtown, eating from a foam container of room-service lasagna that he did not like but that he had ordered because the hotel room-service menu was, in his opinion, an insult to human civilization, and the lasagna had appeared to him to be the least offensive item on it.

He had been in Cleveland for sixteen days.

He was tired of the Marriott. He was tired of the Browns on the television in the lobby. He was tired of the weather, which, he had decided, had nothing on the weather of his own childhood in Kaliningrad but was nonetheless boring in a way he found personally insulting. He was tired of Americans. He was tired of the specific smell of American institutional carpeting.

He finished the lasagna.

He picked up the hotel phone. He dialed a number in Moscow that was routed, at two intermediate steps, through servers in Warsaw and in Helsinki.

He said, in Russian, "Report."

Someone in Moscow answered him.

He said, in Russian, "The target is more capable than the initial assessment indicated. He executed a counter-surveillance route this afternoon that was clean and that implies professional training. He is with a network. The network is older than the agents on our list. It has Eastern European origin. I will need additional time, additional resources, and a deployment authorization for permanent resolution of the civilian."

The person in Moscow considered.

The person in Moscow said, in Russian, "Requested. Approved. Timestamp for report — seventy-two hours."

Rook hung up the phone.

He stood. He walked to the window. He looked out at the dark water of Lake Erie, across the brightly-lit Browns Stadium that was being built on the site where the old stadium had been demolished. He put his hand on the glass. The glass was cold.

He was, that night, the only man in Cleveland who knew that Theo Novak had a wife and a mother and a cat, and that all three of those facts were operational data.

He did not know that Theo Novak did not have a wife.

He was working from imperfect intelligence.

He did not intend to remain in that condition.

SEVENTEEN: *The List*

Friday morning Dr. Hayes came out of her bedroom at 7:15 with the microfiche reader's carriage tray in her hand.

She had slept three hours. I could see the three hours on her face. She had that specific thinness under the eyes that comes from having willed yourself through a night. She was in a grey wool cardigan and a pair of pressed slacks that were the closest thing to a uniform I ever saw her wear during the operation.

She set the carriage tray on the kitchen table.

"Sit down," she said.

Frankie and I sat.

She went to the counter. She poured three cups from a pot she had evidently made at some point before seven. She set them down. She did not sit. She stood at the head of the table with her hands on the back of a chair, and she looked at us for a long moment.

"I finished the TRW section at three thirty this morning," she said.

Frankie said, "How many."

"Eleven names, as I had estimated. I know them all now. I can confirm for you what I suspected about Mr. Brennan."

She slid a piece of paper across the table.

It was not printed. It was written out in her neat, small hand. At the top of the page was a header that read, underlined: *TRW LYNDHURST, MEADOWLARK COMPILATION, CROSS-REFERENCE INCOMPLETE.* Below the header was a numbered list.

Name number twelve read:

BRENNAN, Galen Patrick. TRW Propulsion, Senior Engineer. Turned 1989 via Prague cutout (K. Novotný). Handler: KARPOV-7. Quarterly cash drops, Rocky River Reservation, southeast trail junction.

Last known drop: July 1996. Estimated lifetime disbursements: $420,000 USD.

I read it. I read it twice. Then I read the rest of the page.

Eleven names. Eleven TRW employees. I knew three of them. I had trained two of them. I had, on one specific afternoon in October of 1994, sat in a conference room with one of them and six others and walked them through a module on export-controlled information handling while they took notes with what I had assumed at the time to be polite interest. I had not known. There had been no reason to know. They had smiled at me at the break. They had thanked me at the end. One of them had mentioned his wife's garden.

His name was on the list.

Number seven. *ACHESON, Lawrence D. TRW Propulsion, Principal Engineer. Turned 1981 via East Berlin cutout (dec.). Handler: MARKOV-2. Semi-annual drops, Metroparks Zoo, mammal house.*

Larry Acheson.

Larry Acheson had, in the fall of 1994, walked me through his daughter's college application essay because he had wanted a second opinion from a man he had just described to his wife as "the teaching guy they hired, he seems sharp." His daughter had gotten into Case. Larry had sent me a bottle of Riesling at Christmas. I had sent him a thank-you note.

Larry Acheson had been selling classified propulsion research to the Soviets since 1981.

Larry Acheson was fifty-eight years old and his daughter was, as of today, a junior at Case Western, and he was number seven on a list of forty-seven that I had pulled off a tree lawn in Shaker Heights.

Dr. Hayes was watching me.

"Mr. Novak."

"Yes."

"Is this the moment you had when I first told you what the list contained."

"Not quite."

"Describe it to me."

"When you first told me — it was a category. Forty-seven names. Names. Abstract."

"Yes."

"Now it's — Larry Acheson sent me a bottle of Riesling."

"Yes."

"Galen — Galen's daughter —"

"Yes."

"Jesus Christ."

Dr. Hayes pulled out the chair at the head of the table and sat down. She did not pick up her coffee.

"This is the moment where you will feel, if you let yourself, that the forty-seven names on this list are human beings. That is a correct feeling. It is also a feeling that will get you killed in the next forty-eight hours if you do not put it away. You need to put it away, Mr. Novak. Do you understand."

"Yes."

"I am not unsympathetic. I am telling you the operational reality. Each of these men and women made a specific, repeated choice to sell their country out, and the consequence of that choice is now out of your hands, out of my hands, and out of theirs. What is in your hands is whether you and Miss Russo walk out of the Cleveland Museum of Art on Saturday night alive. Nothing else. Is that clear."

"Yes."

"Good."

Frankie said, "Saturday."

"Saturday next," Dr. Hayes said. "I received final confirmation at six this morning. The donor preview for the Van Gogh exhibition at the Cleveland Museum of Art is Saturday, September 7th, 6:45 PM. Invitations will be couriered here this afternoon. That gives us eight days."

"Eight days is a lot of days."

"Eight days is eight nights. Each of those nights is a night during which Martin Doyle — who knows this address, and who is deciding, at this moment, how hard to come back — is going to try to move against us. And Pavel Yegorov — I believe we have, in our conversation until now, been calling him the Buick driver — is going to try to find us as well. They are working toward the same object on different timelines, and I have now developed a reasonably good idea of how each of them is going to move."

"How."

"That, Mr. Novak, is what we are going to talk about this afternoon. This morning, I have one more thing to ask of you, and it requires some discussion."

She took a breath.

"I need you to go to TRW tonight."

I looked at her.

"Tonight."

"Yes."

"Why."

"Because, Mr. Novak, I have cross-referenced the MEADOWLARK list against every organizational chart I can build from open-source data, and the picture I have built is incomplete in one critical respect. It does not include the thirty-six names on the list who are *not* at TRW. To identify them I need the sort of information that lives in internal personnel databases. Specifically: I need the training and development records from your own office. Every module you have designed has a roster. Every roster has three hundred to a thousand names. Every name on a roster is cross-referenced to a department, a clearance level, and a physical location. I believe — I believe strongly — that if I can compare my thirty-six unplaced names against the aggregate of your roster database, I can place most of them within six hours."

"You think the thirty-six unplaced names are at *TRW*."

"No. I think fourteen or fifteen of them are. I think the remaining twenty-two are at Battelle, Rockwell, Wright-Pat, Lockheed Akron, and at one or two universities. Your roster database will not get me those names. But it will get me the TRW names I don't yet have, and the TRW names are the ones most likely to be in contact with Mr. Brennan, and Mr. Brennan is the one who is most likely to generate the specific event that will make the next eight days more dangerous than they need to be."

"What event."

"A tip. To his handler. About the possibility that you are the person who found the cache."

"You think Galen will tip on me."

"I think Galen *did* tip on you, Mr. Novak, on Tuesday of the week before last. From a BP station on Mayfield Road. I think he reported what he saw. I think he was told to observe without engaging. I think he complied. I think what we saw at the Lucky Star Diner was the operation of a man who had been reporting for two weeks and was now being asked to actively participate. He drew a line there. Admirable. But he did his damage in the earlier two weeks, and the damage is now a person named Pavel Yegorov standing at an olive stall at the West Side Market on a Thursday afternoon."

Frankie said, "What do you need Theo to do."

"There is a file cabinet in his office containing his training records from 1993 forward. There is also, I assume, a networked archive of the same records. I would prefer the physical files — they will be less scrutinized if they are found missing. The cabinet is typically locked; Mr. Novak presumably has a key. TRW's Lyndhurst campus is accessed on weekends by employee badge. Mr. Novak's badge is still active — nobody has deactivated it, because Mr. Novak is on a family leave, not a termination."

"How do you know my badge is still active."

"I have a friend at TRW Security. She is not on the list. She is a fifty-seven-year-old receptionist whose husband has Parkinson's. She owes me a small favor. I have asked her to confirm your active status this morning. She has done so."

"You have friends at TRW."

"Mr. Novak, I have friends everywhere. I have been in Cleveland since 1969."

I looked at Frankie.

Frankie said, "Dr. Hayes."

"Yes."

"Doyle knows TRW."

"Doyle has likely been surveilling the TRW parking garage for three days. Yes."

"So if Theo goes in —"

"Doyle will see him."

"— so this is a trap."

"It is a controlled exposure. We are going to draw Doyle forward with a specific piece of bait that is also functional, because we need the information for reasons that are operational and not merely misdirection. Mr. Novak will enter TRW. He will go directly to his office. He will retrieve the physical training records — two file boxes, I have been told, by the same receptionist. He will leave. If Doyle has been patient and is following protocol, he will follow Mr. Novak to a secondary location, which will not be here, and he will attempt to intercept. I have prepared a secondary location. Mr. Novak will not go to the secondary location. Mr. Novak will go home to the Forest Hill bungalow by a route that I will have drawn in advance. And we will use Doyle's movement during his pursuit as our final confirmation of his operational pattern, because by Sunday evening I intend to know his pattern well enough to predict his movements at the museum on Saturday next."

Frankie said, "Okay."

I said, "What about Rook."

"Rook is, at this point, an unknown quantity. He could be surveilling Doyle. He could have his own line on Mr. Novak. He is a professional. He is also, I believe, frustrated and operating under pressure from Moscow to deliver a resolution. Pressure makes professionals do things that are not in their training. That is the one thing in our favor."

"What do I do if I see him."

"You do not see him, Mr. Novak. If you see him, that means he has already closed the gap. If he has already closed the gap, you will not have time to execute a considered response. You will have time only to react. Your reaction should be to move at speed, in a direction that is not home, on a vehicle he cannot follow."

"The Ninja."

"The Ninja."

"I haven't ridden it in two weeks."

"It is probably still where you left it, at the half-double on Cedar."

"I assume they've been watching the half-double."

"I assume they have. But not the garage behind the half-double, because the garage is detached and shared with Dr. Anselmi's unit, and Dr. Anselmi's side of the structure looks unoccupied. You will approach the garage from the alley. You will retrieve the Ninja. You will ride to TRW on a route that I have drawn for you. You will leave TRW on a route that I have drawn for you. You will not take either route at any point other than your first traverse, so that nobody who is surveilling a single point can predict the full path. Is this clear."

"Yes."

"Good. We leave here at four PM. Until then, Miss Russo, a word?"

She took Frankie into the front room.

I sat at the kitchen table with the list in front of me.

I read Larry Acheson's name again.

Then I turned the page face down, and I put my hands flat on the table, and I thought about my career, and about the people I had taught, and about how many times in the last three years I had walked into a conference room in Lyndhurst and done my job and come out, not knowing what any of them had been.

Then I put it away.

Dr. Hayes was right. I had to put it away.

I sat in the kitchen of the bungalow and I put it away.

EIGHTEEN: *The Plan Locks*

The morning ran its course. The courier arrived at 3:18 PM.

He was a small, serious man in his sixties, in a brown uniform and a brown cap, riding a bicycle. He came up Dr. Hayes's walk with three envelopes in a canvas satchel, rang the doorbell, and waited with his hands clasped behind his back until Dr. Hayes opened the door.

"Dr. Hayes."

"Gustav."

"For you."

"Thank you."

"Is Kiri well."

"She is well. Thank you."

"Tell her I still make the tea."

"I will."

She took the satchel. He nodded and got back on the bicycle and rode away.

She closed the door.

"Who is that," I said.

"Gustav has been my courier for thirty-one years."

"Your what."

"Mr. Novak, there are several hundred couriers in the city of Cleveland. Most of them work for FedEx or UPS, and most of their work is trackable. A small number of them do not work for either of those companies. They operate out of their homes. They keep handwritten ledgers. They do not use fax machines. They do not use pagers. They take a package from one address to another in exchange for twenty dollars in cash. They have been doing this in Cleveland since before the First World War. Gustav is one of them. He is also, as of three minutes ago, no longer relevant to this conversation. Please do not ask me about him again."

"Okay."

She opened the satchel.

Three cream-colored envelopes. Heavy paper. Black engraved script on the front. Each one addressed by hand.

The Cleveland Museum of Art cordially invites you to a private preview of THE STARRY NIGHT AND BEYOND: VAN GOGH IN THE NORTHERN LIGHT. Saturday, September Seventh, Nineteen Ninety-Six. Six forty-five in the evening. Cocktail attire.

She fanned them out on the coffee table.

"These are real," she said. "Each represents a donor seat at the actual preview. Each is expected to be used on the evening of September seventh. Each is addressed to a name that is, in fact, a member of the CMA Donor Council, each of whom has agreed, at my specific request, not to attend the preview in person on September seventh, and to have agreed to the loan of their invitations in exchange for three additional dinners at Nighttown with me at my expense over the next two years."

"Three dinners at Nighttown."

"That is the favor I owed."

"Okay."

She set the envelopes down.

"Miss Russo, you will attend in a long sleeveless navy dress, which I will lend you — I have not worn it since 1984, but it is your size and it is in a garment bag on my hall closet rod. Mr. Novak, you will rent a tuxedo on Monday from the place on Shaker Square. You will try it on. You will have it altered. The place on Shaker Square can alter a tuxedo in forty-eight hours if the gentleman asks politely and pays a small additional fee. You will be wearing it to a specific standard. We cannot, unfortunately, avoid the fact that the tuxedo will be a visible size too tight in the midsection, because the only alternative is to have it so loose that you look like a teenager at prom, and we do not want that either. Do you accept this."

"I accept this."

"You will not eat large meals between Monday and Saturday. You will wear a belt."

"I will wear a belt."

"Good."

She sat down.

"Now," she said. "Tonight."

She walked me through tonight.

She had, at some point during the Wednesday-to-Thursday overnight, drawn a detailed map of Lyndhurst on a large sheet of butcher paper. The map was on her kitchen table. On the map were routes — three separate ingress routes, four separate egress routes, and what she called a *bail point* at each one of seven intersections. Each bail point was a specific maneuver I could execute if I noticed a particular kind of pursuit. She walked me through all of them. She used a pencil. She asked me to repeat each one back to her before she moved on. I repeated each one.

Then she handed me a key.

"This is a key to Dr. Anselmi's garage."

"How did you —"

"The garage is rented from the same landlord as your apartment. I procured a copy of the key two days ago from a source who owed me a favor. Dr. Anselmi is aware that you are not at the apartment and has been told, via a third party, that his garage may be used without question. He is also aware that he should not ask a question about this. Is that clear."

"Yes."

"Good. The Ninja is in the garage as you left it. I had the same source inspect it yesterday for any — unusual — features. It is clean."

"Define *unusual features.*"

"I mean that nobody has attached a tracking device to your motorcycle."

"Oh."

"You will enter the garage from the alley. You will leave with the Ninja. You will ride to TRW. You will enter TRW via the south employee entrance. You will use your badge. You will go directly to your office. You will retrieve two boxes of training records from the file cabinet adjacent to your desk. You will exit the building the same way you entered. You will not make eye contact with anyone in the building. You will not speak to the security guard at the front desk unless she speaks to you first. You will be in the building, total, less than ten minutes. Can you do this."

"Yes."

"Once you leave the building, you will ride the Ninja west on Richmond. You will not take Mayfield. You will not take Cedar. You will take a route I have drawn here" — she pointed at the butcher paper — "which will take you through Lyndhurst to South Euclid to Cleveland Heights to University Circle. You will pass within two blocks of Dr. Hayes's house but you will not stop here. You will continue to Forest Hill. Frankie and I will be at Forest Hill by the time you arrive. We will meet you there. Do you understand."

"Yes."

"If you are followed — if you *know* you are followed — you will execute this route." She pointed at a second line, which ran south of the first, through Beachwood, through Pepper Pike, looping south and coming back up through Shaker. "This route will add forty minutes and will put you through enough urban density that any surveiller will have to commit to either staying with you or abandoning the pursuit. It is a route designed to force a decision."

"Okay."

"If you are *actively pursued* — if a vehicle is trying to physically close a gap — this route." She pointed at a third line. "This route takes you to the Flats."

"The Flats."

"Yes."

"Why the Flats."

"Because a motorcycle can do things in the Flats that a car cannot, and because there is a specific geographic feature in the Flats that I want you to remember. On the east bank of the Cuyahoga, approximately half a mile south of the Main Avenue Bridge, there is a small industrial access road that runs along the railroad tracks between two specific warehouses — I have drawn them here. The road dead-ends at a grade crossing. The grade crossing is active. Freight trains cross it approximately four times per hour, at slightly varying intervals. If you are being pursued and you can reach this crossing and cross the tracks *just before* a train arrives, you will leave your pursuer stuck at the crossing for approximately fourteen minutes. That is enough time to get yourself across the Cuyahoga on the Main Avenue Bridge onramp and disappear into the Warehouse District."

"How do I know a train is coming."

"The crossing gates drop thirty seconds before. You will know."

"And if I miss the gap."

"Then you will have to turn around, Mr. Novak, and you will be — in essence — in a trap."

"Got it."

"I do not anticipate that this will be necessary. I anticipate that you will be followed, not actively pursued. I anticipate that Doyle will trail at distance, confirm the direction of travel, and hand off to a secondary surveillance unit — possibly Rook, possibly not — who will attempt to identify your destination. You will not give them a destination. You will circle and return."

"Okay."

"Are you ready for this."

"I don't know."

"That is an acceptable answer. Frankie."

"Yes."

"You will be in the Jeep on Richmond Road at the moment Mr. Novak leaves the TRW campus. You will be ahead of him, a quarter mile. You will confirm the identity of any vehicle following him by a specific set of criteria that we have discussed. You will not engage. You will return to the Forest Hill bungalow. You will meet him there. You will not at any point follow him; any vehicle doing both is too identifiable a pattern. Is this clear."

"Yes."

"Good."

Dr. Hayes looked at her watch.

"It is five fourteen. You have forty-six minutes to eat, to use the bathroom, and to clear your head. Mr. Novak, Miss Russo, go."

We went.

NINETEEN: *Frankie*

Dr. Hayes's forty-six minutes found us at the Forest Hill bungalow.

We were supposed to be eating. Instead we sat in what would have been the dining room if the room had contained anything other than a compound miter saw and a stack of baseboard trim. Frankie had set up two folding chairs by the kitchen threshold. She had a thermos of coffee from Dr. Hayes's kitchen, and she had brought bagels from the same Dunkin we had eaten at since Monday, which I would never, in later life, be able to walk into again without a specific involuntary recall of this particular week.

She set the thermos down.

"Theo," she said.

"Yeah."

"I need to tell you something."

"Okay."

"I'm going to tell you the whole thing. Not the outline. The whole thing. And I need you to not interrupt, because if I stop I don't know if I'll start again. Is that okay."

"Yes."

"Okay."

She sat in the folding chair opposite mine. She pulled her legs up, crossed them under her. She wrapped her hands around the coffee cup. She did not look at me. She looked at the floor between us.

"I was a corporal," she said. "Army Security Agency, attached to a SIGINT team at Lindsey Air Station in Wiesbaden, West Germany. I was there from December 1988 to May 1990. The team I was on worked East German border intercepts. We listened to phone lines. We listened to radio traffic. We translated what we could, and we wrote up what we called *takes* — which is the technical word for the little summary reports that go up the chain. We listened to everything. Commanders cheating on their wives. Factory managers embezzling. Junior party officials talking on the phone to their mothers. We built files on people. Most of the files were never used. Some of them were used later. Some of them got people killed. We did not know, most of the time, what happened to the files after we sent them up."

She took a drink.

"I was nineteen when I shipped. I was twenty when the Wall came down. I watched it happen on television in the day room of the barracks with fourteen other girls from my unit and a bottle of something that I think had been *intended* to be schnapps and had probably come from a German grocery store. Everybody was crying. I was crying. I thought — I genuinely thought that night — that we were going to go home. Because we had done it. We had won. The mission of my unit had been, broadly speaking, to help collapse the Soviet system, and the Soviet system had collapsed, and I thought we were going to — we were going to be reassigned, or I was going to be let out of my contract, or I was going to get to fly to Paris for a weekend. I don't know what I thought. I was twenty."

I did not say anything.

"We were not reassigned. We were given a new mission. The new mission was called Operation NIGHT CLERK. It was a joke name — the men in my unit thought it was hilarious because a night clerk is a person who sits at a desk and files paperwork that nobody is going to read, and we had, in effect, been doing that for two years, and now we were going to keep doing it, just with new paperwork. The paperwork was files on East German officials who our side thought might be useful to us in a unified Germany. Politicians. Mid-ranking ministry people. Academics. Diplomats. We were compiling dossiers. Not to use against them. To use *with* them. The idea

— or the idea that was explained to us — was that a unified Germany was coming, and that the West would want to have useful relationships with as many of the reasonable East German figures as we could identify, and that the dossiers would help the State Department and the West Germans figure out who those people were."

She took another drink.

"One of the files," she said, "was on a man named Martin Kowalczyk."

She paused.

"Martin Kowalczyk," she said, "was a twenty-eight-year-old junior officer at the East German Foreign Ministry. He was — he was gay, which was still a professional problem in East Germany at that point, and he had been working with West German intelligence as an asset for eighteen months. He was one of ours. Not technically ours — the West Germans ran him — but he was in our network. His name was in everybody's files. Including mine. I had, over the course of a four-month window in late 1989 and early 1990, compiled approximately seventy pages of material on him. Most of it was intercepted phone calls with his sister in Leipzig, in which he spoke about his boyfriend in deliberately ambiguous language, and in which he complained about his boss at the ministry. Nothing actionable. Just — him. Him living his life. Him being a twenty-eight-year-old gay man on the phone with his sister."

She took a breath.

"I finished the file in February of 1990. I handed it up the chain. I moved on to the next one.

"In early March of 1990, Martin Kowalczyk was found dead in a canal in East Berlin. The official East German report said he had slipped on ice while drunk. He was not drunk. He did not drink. He was pulled out of the canal with marks on his arms consistent with being held under. The West

Germans knew within twenty-four hours what had happened. So did our people. Nobody did anything about it, because the Wall had fallen and there was no good diplomatic path for us to raise the question without complicating ongoing negotiations.

"Six weeks later — this was April — I was going through an intercept log from a *different* operation, a comms maintenance log I had been tasked with reviewing, and I found a transmission from December 1989 in which a senior American officer at the Berlin station — a man I did not know — had given Kowalczyk's name, his real name, to a Stasi handler. As part of what the transcript described as *a good faith information exchange in the interest of transitional stability.*

"He had been traded.

"Kowalczyk had been traded to the Stasi. In December. By us. As a gesture. In exchange for — I have no idea what. Some access. Some goodwill. Something. And the file I had compiled was one of the files the American officer had been working from when he made the trade.

"I took the log to my direct supervisor. I sat in his office and I showed him the transmission and I said — I said *this man is dead because of something we did.* My supervisor read the log. He was — I'm not going to tell you his name. He was a good man. He had been good to me. He had taught me most of what I knew about the work. He read the log, and he looked up at me, and he said, very gently: *Corporal, you are going to walk out of this office and you are going to put this out of your mind, and you are going to keep doing your job. Because if you do anything else — if you write a letter, if you make a phone call, if you take this to the Inspector General — your career options in this specialty are going to narrow very quickly, and you will spend the next several years being quietly useless, and you will not help a single person who is still alive, and you will not bring Martin Kowalczyk back.*

"He said it exactly like that. Word for word. I have heard him say it in my head every day for six years."

She wiped her eyes.

"I walked out of his office. I did not write a letter. I did not make a phone call. I did not take it to the IG. I went back to my desk and I finished my shift and I went back to my bunk and I cried for three hours. And then I went to the base chapel and I sat in a pew for an hour and I tried to pray and I could not pray. And then I went to my company commander the next morning and I asked for early release on the basis of a family emergency I did not have. He knew I was lying. He signed the paperwork.

"I flew home to Cleveland in May of 1990. I went to trade school at Cuyahoga Community College in September. I bought a set of tools at the Sears at Southgate Mall with the money I had saved on deployment. My grandfather was still alive then. He showed me how to use the circular saw. He had not known I was coming home. He had not known I had been in the Army. I had not told my family where I had been for two years, because what I had been doing was classified, and my family did not ask.

"I started restoring houses.

"I have not said Martin Kowalczyk's name out loud in six years."

She stopped.

She took a sip of coffee.

I did not say anything.

She was not crying. She was tired. She had the specific exhaustion of a person who had been carrying something for a very long time and had just been allowed to set it down for a minute, and who was going to have to pick it back up in a minute, because setting it down was temporary.

I moved my chair closer to hers. I put my hand on her knee.

She did not look at me.

"I never told you," she said, "because I wanted to wake up every morning and be a handywoman from Collinwood, not a signals analyst who had helped identify a gay dissident to the Stasi in exchange for nothing. I wanted that to be the person you loved. I wanted it to be true. And most of the time, for two years — for two *actual* years — it was true. I was a handywoman. That was what I did. That was who I was. I can be that person again, someday. I'm not sure I can be her in August of 1996. But I can be her again."

"You can."

"Yeah."

"You're her now, Frankie."

"I'm not, Theo."

"You are. You're also other things. But you're her."

She did not answer.

"You're letting me lead this," I said, finally. "Why."

She looked up at me for the first time since she had started talking.

"Because you're smarter than I am," she said. "You always have been. I can shoot. I can walk a ransacked room and tell you what was taken without touching a thing. I can follow a handler in a two-car pattern through six cities in two countries, and I can do three other things I am never going to tell you about. But I cannot sit down at Dr. Hayes's kitchen table and read a microfiche of forty-seven names and understand what the names are going to do next. That's what you do. You watch. You notice. You know what people are going to do before they do it, because you spent ten years watching them learn. We need both of us to be good at what we're good at right now. I don't need us both to be me. We need you to be you."

She took my hand off her knee. She held it between both of hers.

"Different jobs," she said.

"Different jobs."

"I love you."

"I love you, Frankie."

I stood up. I leaned down toward her in the chair. She was still sitting, and she was still taller than me sitting, and I reached up — three inches, maybe more — to kiss her on the forehead. Her skin was warm. Her hair smelled like the shampoo from Dr. Hayes's guest bathroom, which was a smell I would associate, for years afterward, with a specific phase in my life in which a lot of things that were true about other people had first become visible to me.

I pressed my forehead against hers for a second.

"Come on," I said. "Let's go to bed for an hour."

We went upstairs.

We did not sleep.

We lay on the mattress with Ramona between us, and we held hands across the cat, and we did not talk. Through the window I could see the top branches of a silver maple moving in the wind. The sun was on them. They were the color, for a minute, of something that I will not try to describe, because I have been trying to describe them for thirty years and I have never gotten it right.

At seven we got up.

We had work to do.

TWENTY: *The Flats*

I left Dr. Anselmi's garage at 7:52 PM.

The Ninja started on the first try. It had been sitting for two weeks and it had not had the grace to die on me. The headlight came on in the specific way a Kawasaki headlight comes on — a half-second delay, then a low warm yellow. I walked it out of the garage and down the alley by hand. I did not start it until I was a block south on Euclid Heights Boulevard. When I started it the engine sounded exactly the way I remembered it sounding, which was the only thing in the preceding sixteen days that had.

I rode south on Coventry, then west on Mayfield, then north on Taylor, then east on Cedar, which was backwards from every route I normally took, which was the point. The construction on Cedar had, thankfully, been cleared since Memorial Day. I made it to Lyndhurst in nineteen minutes.

I passed the TRW front gate and kept going for half a mile. I looped back. I pulled into the south employee lot at 8:11.

The lot was mostly empty. It was Friday night. I parked near the south entrance. I did not dismount for a moment — I sat on the Ninja and I looked in both directions and I counted. There were four other cars in the south lot. All four of them were parked straight. All four of them were cold — no rumble of an engine idling, no breath of exhaust from a tailpipe. I could see three of them clearly. The fourth was partially behind a pillar. I could see its hood. The hood was not warm, not cold — the metal did not have the specific gleam of a hood that had just been driven.

I dismounted. I walked to the south entrance. I swiped my badge. The light went green. The door unlocked.

I went in.

The building was dim and quiet. The lights on the ground floor were on motion sensors. They came up as I walked. I took the service stairs to the eighth floor. The service stairs smelled like the concrete of every university basement I had ever been in. My footsteps did not sound like anything in particular.

The eighth floor was empty. Doreen was not at her desk. Her cinnamon roll plate was not on her desk. The desk had been tidied, which meant Friday had ended and Doreen had gone home like a normal human being with a normal life.

I walked down the hall to my cubicle.

My desk was exactly as I had left it. The postcard of the Cedar Point Gemini. The calendar from the Cleveland Museum of Natural History. The Polaroid of Frankie on the porch in Euclid. My monitor, which I had turned off two weeks ago.

The file cabinet was next to my desk. It was locked. I had the key on my key ring. I unlocked it.

Two boxes of training records, bottom drawer, as the receptionist had described. Each one was a file box sealed with a rubber band. I pulled them out. I set them on my desk. I opened the top one.

Rosters. Organization charts. Attendance logs. Certificates. Names and names and names, in my own typing, on my own letterhead. Three hundred pages per box, conservatively. The receptionist had been specific: *bottom drawer, two boxes, 1993 forward.* Everything I had done.

I closed the boxes. I retaped them. I put one under each arm. They were heavy, but not heavy-heavy — maybe fifteen pounds each. I walked back down the hallway. I took the stairs. I exited through the south entrance. I was outside the building at 8:18.

I walked back to the Ninja. I had a small leather saddlebag strapped to the back — the only storage on the bike. One box went into the saddlebag. The other box I had to hold in my left arm against the gas tank, which was going to be — not ideal — while I rode, but I was not going to leave it.

I put the helmet on. I started the Ninja.

I pulled out of the south lot at 8:22.

The grey Taurus picked me up on Richmond.

I saw it in the mirror. It was three hundred yards back. It had emerged from a parking lot on the east side of Richmond — not TRW's; a smaller lot belonging to an office building I had always assumed was insurance of some kind. The Taurus was the specific grey of Doyle's Taurus. The driver was silhouetted.

I kept to Dr. Hayes's primary route: west on Richmond, south briefly on Brainard, west on Cedar.

The Taurus stayed at three hundred yards.

At the light on Cedar and Fairmount, which turned red as I approached it, I pulled up. The Taurus did not pull up directly behind me. It stopped a car back, behind a late-model Camry that had been between us on Cedar for the last block.

I kept my eyes on the mirror.

It was then that I saw the Crown Vic.

It was black. It was four cars behind the Taurus, in the right lane. It had been there since Brainard. It had the posture of a car that was specifically not catching up. The driver was a man I could not see clearly at this distance, but who was alone, and who was wearing a grey jacket over a grey shirt.

I understood, in that moment, that I was in a different situation than Dr. Hayes had anticipated.

I was being surveilled by Doyle. Doyle was being surveilled by Rook. Rook had been tracking Doyle, and Doyle had led Rook to me. And Rook, having now seen me, was going to decide — in the next thirty to sixty seconds — what he was going to do with the situation.

I did not wait for his decision.

The light turned green.

I did not continue west on Cedar. I cut right, hard, across two lanes of southbound traffic on Fairmount. A Buick honked at me. I took Fairmount south, hard, down the hill toward Cleveland Heights.

In the mirror I saw the Taurus try to follow. It could not make the right turn across traffic without committing to a wider maneuver. It fell back. The Crown Vic, four cars back, had more room. The Crown Vic cut a diagonal across two lanes and took the right.

The Crown Vic closed.

I was on Fairmount going forty-five in a thirty-five zone with a file box against my gas tank and my helmet strap digging into my jaw. The Crown Vic was closing at sixty. I had maybe ninety seconds before it caught me.

I went through Dr. Hayes's routes in my head.

Primary — cancelled. I had already broken it.

Secondary — too gentle. The Crown Vic would stay with me.

Tertiary — the Flats. The grade crossing. The train.

I took the tertiary.

I cut east on Euclid Heights Boulevard to get around the back of University Circle. I took Euclid west through the Cleveland Clinic complex. I took Carnegie west into downtown. I took West 9th south to Front Street. I took Front across the Superior Viaduct.

The Crown Vic stayed with me.

He was good. He drove the way somebody who had learned to drive in a different country drives, with a specific aggressive smoothness that Americans did not do because Americans did not need to. He did not tailgate. He did not brake late. He moved through traffic the way a professional closer moves — a little ahead of where you would expect him to be, always. I could not put a car between us for more than ten seconds at a time.

I took Front to Canal Road. Canal Road took me along the east bank of the Cuyahoga, into the Flats.

The Flats at 8:38 PM on a Friday night in August 1996 were the Flats at 8:38 PM on a Friday night in August 1996. There were bars. There were warehouses being converted into nightclubs. There were music venues. There were tourists. There were also, because we had been sliding into the off-peak hours of a summer Friday, fewer cars than there would have been at ten. I took a series of short cuts I had not planned on — down an access road behind a seafood restaurant, along a service alley behind a concrete plant — and I lost the Crown Vic for eleven seconds at one point.

He picked me up again. Of course he did.

I was a block from the grade crossing when the gates started to drop.

I heard the warning bell before I saw the arms come down.

It was a specific two-note bell, spaced about four seconds apart, from a signal box at the edge of the crossing. The bell had started to sound. The striped arms were starting to drop. A freight train was approaching the crossing from the north. I could see the headlight of the lead engine through the trees along the tracks. It was close. It was coming fast.

I had maybe six seconds.

I opened the throttle.

The Ninja was not a fast bike by modern sportbike standards, but it was fast enough — a 1993 ZX-6 with 92 horsepower and a curb weight of 437 pounds, one of which was me and about thirty of which was a file box pressed against the tank. I accelerated down the last block of the access road. I could see the tracks. I could see the gates coming down on both sides. I could see, on the far side of the crossing, the curved onramp that led up to the Main Avenue Bridge.

I hit the crossing at forty-four miles an hour.

The gate on my side was at about five feet of drop — I had to duck. I ducked. The gate on the far side was almost all the way down. It caught my left elbow. It did not stop me. I went through it. I heard it snap back up behind me. I heard the bell continuing. I heard, then, a second bell — the warning at the next crossing — and underneath all of it I heard the specific growl of a freight engine at full load, and I felt the ground shake, and I did not look back.

I took the base of the onramp at forty-eight.

The onramp to the Main Avenue Bridge was an elevated curved structure that rose eighty feet in half a block and then straightened out onto the deck of the bridge itself. At forty-eight miles an hour, in the dark, with one arm on the handlebar and the other arm clutching a file box against my tank, with a cracked helmet strap and a growing awareness that somebody in a Crown Vic was fourteen minutes behind me, I did not have the balance for the curve.

I made it about two-thirds of the way up.

The back tire slipped on a patch of gravel — I found out later it was not gravel, it was the sandy residue of a load of concrete that had been hauled up the ramp earlier in the day, and it sat in a thin line down the inside of the curve like a signature. The rear tire lost traction. The bike went sideways. I went with it. We traveled together, sliding, across the pavement, for about forty feet.

The file box flew open. Three years of training records — three hundred rosters, fifty thousand names — scattered across the two inside lanes of an empty onramp to an empty bridge on a Friday night in Cleveland.

I hit a guardrail.

I do not remember the exact moment of impact. I remember the specific sound, which was a soft *crump* that I understood at the time to be my ribs. I remember the specific feeling of having my helmet slam back against the asphalt, which was not the helmet hurting, but something behind the helmet — the specific feeling of a bruise to come.

Then I was lying on the road.

The bike was five feet from me. The engine was still running. The back wheel was spinning.

I could hear the freight train.

I could not hear the Crown Vic.

I did not get up right away.

For maybe fifteen seconds I lay on the pavement of the Main Avenue Bridge onramp and I watched the night sky, which was that specific color city skies get in late August — dark blue with a wash of orange from the sodium lights downtown. I took one breath. It hurt. I took a second breath. It hurt less. I took a third breath. I understood that something on my left side was cracked but not broken. A rib, probably. Two ribs, possibly.

I rolled onto my side.

The file box had emptied. Papers were everywhere. I could see, from where I was, that they were being blown south by a small breeze off the lake, across the lanes of the onramp, toward the east guardrail. Some of them were going over the edge, into the dark of the Flats below.

It was, in the specific way a person can notice something useless in a moment when everything useful is inaccessible to them, almost funny.

I pushed myself up.

I got to one knee.

I stood.

I walked to the bike. I killed the engine. I lifted it upright — it took everything I had on a left side that was not working — and I set it on its kickstand. The fairing was scraped but the bike was intact. The front brake lever was bent. The left mirror was gone.

I gathered the papers. Not all of them. Maybe a third of them. The ones that had gone over the guardrail were gone. The ones that were still on the pavement I stuffed, in fistfuls, into the second file box, which had stayed in the saddlebag. I did not try to sort them. I picked up anything I could see that had a roster header on it. I left what I could not find.

I walked the bike down the onramp.

I could not ride it — not on that side, not yet, not with the ribs the way they were. I got to the base of the ramp. I turned left onto a service road that I vaguely remembered from a client project two years ago. I walked the bike west under the bridge, along the river, for what felt like a very long time and was, in fact, about half a mile.

I came out on West Twenty-Fifth Street.

Metro Health was half a mile further north.

I walked the bike the rest of the way.

I called Frankie from a payphone outside the ER, at 9:27 PM.

"Theo."

"I'm at Metro."

"Are you okay."

"I'm alive. I have — a rib. Maybe two."

"Stay there."

"Yeah."

"Don't go inside. Stay in the payphone vestibule. I'm coming."

"Yeah."

I did not go inside. I sat in the payphone vestibule. A nurse saw me and asked if I was all right and I said I was waiting for a ride, and she nodded and went back inside, because she had, in her own professional life, seen a thousand men sit in payphone vestibules who had decided that they would rather wait for a ride than go into the ER, and she had the wisdom not to force it.

Frankie arrived at 9:58.

She was driving the Jeep. I noticed immediately that the plates had been switched — they were Ohio, but they were not the plates I knew. She had the engine running. She got out. She walked straight to me. She looked at me.

"I'm going to hug you very carefully," she said.

"Please."

She hugged me very carefully.

Then she stepped back and she looked at my ribs and she said, "Which side."

"Left."

"Which ribs."

"Lower three, I think."

"We are going to get you to a private doctor tomorrow. Tonight you are going to take these." She handed me a bottle of ibuprofen. "Right now you are going to get in the passenger side. The Ninja stays here. The Ninja is officially lost. I will come back for it later. The files — where are the files."

"In the saddlebag. I lost about half."

"Okay."

"Frankie."

"Yeah."

"He was good. He was very good."

"Yeah."

"And Doyle was watching me. And Rook was watching Doyle. They both saw me, Frankie."

"I know."

"He was going to take me."

"I know, Theo."

"Where's Hayes."

"At home. Waiting."

She took the saddlebag off the Ninja. She walked the bike to a corner of the parking lot and locked it to a signpost with a chain she produced from the Jeep's back seat. She got back in the driver's seat. I got in the passenger side. I did not get in well. I winced through every inch of it. She watched. She did not hurry me.

"Change into these," she said. She handed me a bag. Clean shirt. Clean pants. A baseball cap. A pair of Carhartts that were, I realized, men's work clothes — borrowed from one of her job sites, maybe, or from her own stash. I changed, slowly, in the passenger seat. She turned her face away and watched the rearview mirror for the whole thing.

"Ready."

"Ready."

"We are not going to Forest Hill tonight. Hayes is moving us. New house. New neighborhood. She'll meet us there."

"Where."

"Parma."

"Parma."

"Parma."

"Okay."

She put the Jeep in drive. She checked the mirrors one more time.

"Theo," she said. "You made it."

"Yeah."

"Good job."

We drove south.

The lights of downtown faded behind us. The Jeep was quiet. Frankie was driving very carefully, very deliberately, with both hands on the wheel. She had switched the plates because, she said later, she had made a point of doing that when she picked up the Jeep at Forest Hill — because Dr. Hayes had, at 9:00 PM, made two phone calls, and the second one had been to Frankie, and the second one had been to tell Frankie that the Crown Vic Theo was being pursued by had just cleared a grade crossing on Canal Road, fourteen minutes later than it should have cleared it, and that its plate had been photographed at 9:14 by a Cuyahoga County sheriff's deputy who was not on the MEADOWLARK list and who had sent the photograph, at 9:17, via a friend of a friend, to an old Russian Studies colleague of Dr. Hayes at Case Western who had forwarded it, at 9:19, to Dr. Hayes's pager, which was the only form of incoming communication Dr. Hayes used on Fridays.

The car in the photograph was a 1995 Ford Crown Victoria, plate 1RVR-412, stolen from a long-term parking lot at Cleveland Hopkins International Airport on August 23rd.

Rook was still out there.

He was approximately nineteen minutes behind me.

I did not know any of this at the time.

At the time, I knew only that we were driving south in a Jeep with switched plates, that my ribs were screaming, that my tuxedo appointment on Monday was going to be very uncomfortable, and that my left elbow, which had hit the crossing gate, was going to bruise in the shape of a stripe for most of the next week.

Frankie held my hand on the console between us.

I held it back.

"I got most of the files," I said.

"Yeah."

"Not all of them."

"Yeah."

"Some of them went into the river."

"We'll tell Hayes."

"Okay."

"Theo."

"Yeah."

"Look at me."

I looked.

"You did a thing tonight that you didn't know you could do. And we are going to do a thing Saturday that neither of us knows we can do. And we are going to do that thing the same way."

"Different jobs."

"Different jobs."

She squeezed my hand.

I closed my eyes.

Cleveland passed around us.

TWENTY-ONE: *Frankie Taken*

Ramona did not travel well.

We had learned this on a four-hour drive to Hocking Hills in May of 1995, when Ramona had spent the entirety of the drive in her carrier, screaming the specific sustained scream of a cat who had decided that the entire operation was a personal betrayal. She had stopped screaming only when we pulled into the cabin driveway, at which point she had accepted her reality and, over the next forty-eight hours, had turned the cabin into a space she was willing to occupy. When we had driven home she had screamed again, for the full four hours, without intermission, and the next day Frankie had taken her to the vet and the vet had written a prescription for a low-dose feline anxiolytic and had said, in the specific tone of a veterinarian who had administered this conversation eight hundred times, *she is high-strung, she is not doing it on purpose, do not make her travel without the medication.*

The medication was in a small amber bottle in the medicine cabinet of the upstairs bathroom of the half-double on Cedar.

We had not retrieved it during the ransack flight. Ramona had not been showing symptoms at the time. Between Sunday and Friday, in the relative stability of the Forest Hill bungalow, she had been fine — Frankie had theorized that the Forest Hill house had enough residual Frankie-smell from the restoration work to register, in Ramona's nervous system, as home.

Parma did not have Frankie-smell.

Parma was Dr. Hayes's idea. A house in Parma owned by a friend of Dr. Hayes's named Vera, who was in Florida until October, who had left her key under a rock by the garage that was not actually a rock but a realistic rubber replica of a rock that had a small hinged door, and who had left us her landline, her basement freezer, and a note on the kitchen counter that said WELCOME LORRAINE'S FRIENDS HELP YOURSELVES in cheerful cursive with a smiley face.

We had pulled up to Vera's house at 10:48 PM on Friday night. Frankie had half-carried me up the walk. She had helped me out of the stained shirt and into bed. She had set Ramona up in the guest bedroom with her food and her water. She had gone out to the Jeep and carried in the file boxes, or what was left of them. She had locked the doors. She had checked the windows. She had sat by my bed until I fell asleep, which had taken a long time, because even with 800 milligrams of ibuprofen in my bloodstream, every breath was a small negotiation with the left side of my chest.

I had slept until ten on Saturday morning.

I had woken up to the specific sound of Ramona yowling from the guest bedroom.

She had started some time before I woke. Frankie was already up. She had already, she told me, picked Ramona up and carried her around the house for twenty minutes and had not been able to settle her. She had tried treats. She had tried a patch of sunlight. She had tried a closed bathroom, which was the move that usually worked. None of it was working.

Ramona was pacing. Ramona was yowling. Ramona was trying to hide under furniture and finding that the furniture in Vera's house was not the furniture that she knew how to hide under.

"She needs her pills, Theo."

"We don't have them."

"They're at the half-double."

"Okay. I'll go."

"You have cracked ribs, Theo."

"Two cracked ribs. I can drive."

"Drive with cracked ribs, sure. Enter an apartment that has been surveilled for ten days, climb the stairs, retrieve a small bottle, come back downstairs, and get back into a vehicle, all with cracked ribs and a bruised elbow the size and color of an eggplant. Less sure."

"Frankie."

"I'm going."

"Frankie."

"Theo. I am going. You are staying with the cat. I will drive the Jeep. I will be there and back inside forty minutes. I will call you from a payphone twenty minutes in as a proof of life. I will park two blocks away. I will go in through the back. The back stairs were not where they came in last time — they came through the front. If anyone is still surveilling the apartment — which I doubt, because they now know we don't have it there — I will see them before they see me. I will leave if anything is wrong. I will not engage. Is that clear."

"I can —"

"It is clear."

"Yes."

"Good."

She kissed the top of my head. She picked up her tool bag. She opened the front door. She looked back at me one time. She was framed in the doorway of Vera's front hall, five-nine, in jeans and a dark green work shirt, with her hair in its apocalyptic-orange bandana, and I would remember her exactly that way for a long time afterward — not because it was the last time I saw her, because it was not, but because it was the last time, for a specific compressed period of my life, that I saw her free.

"Forty minutes," she said.

"Forty minutes."

She left.

She called at 11:21. I was sitting on the floor of the guest bedroom with Ramona half on my lap, half not, because Ramona was unwilling to commit to me fully in this unfamiliar house. My left side was on fire. I was holding the Nokia in my right hand.

"Proof of life."

"Proof of life."

"Where are you."

"In the truck at Cedar and Coventry. I went past the house. There's nothing on the block. No Buick. No Taurus. No Crown Vic. No pedestrians who don't belong. I'm going to park on Euclid Heights Boulevard and walk back."

"Frankie."

"Yeah."

"Be careful."

"Yeah."

"Twenty minutes."

"Twenty minutes."

She hung up.

I set the Nokia down on the floor next to me. Ramona yowled. I picked her up. I rocked her like a small bald miserable infant. My ribs screamed. She was not comforted. I put her down. She went under the bed.

I sat on the floor and watched the clock on the nightstand.

11:35. 11:40. 11:48.

11:55.

At noon I picked up the Nokia. I called the number she had called from.

It rang. Nobody answered.

12:05. 12:10.

At 12:13 I called Dr. Hayes.

I would learn what happened at the half-double much later, and I will tell it now, though I did not see it, because Frankie told me every detail of it six days later when we were sitting in an FBI safe house in Rocky River with the sun coming up over Lake Erie and a mug of tea cooling in her hand.

She parked on Euclid Heights Boulevard at 11:24.

She walked south toward Cedar. She did not take the most direct route. She took a residential street that paralleled Cedar for two blocks and then cut through an alley that ran behind the row of half-doubles on our block. She came up the back garden of the Marcinkus family — a Lithuanian couple in their eighties who did not lock their gate and who had a small vegetable plot that Frankie had helped them expand in 1994 in exchange for pierogi, two dozen of which Mrs. Marcinkus had given her in a Tupperware container the following Sunday. The Marcinkus house was two doors down from ours. Frankie came through their garden, over a low wire fence, through the narrow side yard between their house and the Beckers', and up the back stairs of our half-double.

She did not see the Taurus. The Taurus was not there. She was right about that.

She did not see the Crown Vic either. The Crown Vic was not there.

The back stairs let out onto our second-floor kitchen porch, which was shared with Dr. Anselmi. The porch door was locked, as Frankie had locked it two weeks ago. She opened it with her key.

She stepped into the kitchen.

The kitchen was as we had left it, which was to say, trashed. Nobody had tidied the ransack. The silverware was still on the counter. The refrigerator had been emptied; the contents had spoiled over the course of the ten days since.

Frankie walked through the kitchen, through the living room where the pothos plant had died on its shelf, down the hall to the bathroom. She opened the medicine cabinet. The amber bottle was there, on the bottom shelf, behind a tube of cortisone. She picked it up. She shook it. It was full. She slipped it into her tool bag.

She turned around.

The man in the bathroom doorway was the man from the Buick Century. The man from the olive stall. The man I had last seen in my mirror on the Main Avenue Bridge onramp, fourteen minutes from the grade crossing.

Rook.

He was in a grey windbreaker. His hands were at his sides. His posture was the posture of a man who had been standing very still in a dark hallway for some period of time and who was not, at this moment, surprised to see her.

He said, in clear English: "Put your hands out in front of you."

Frankie did not.

Frankie threw the tube of cortisone at his eyes.

Rook flinched. In the quarter-second he was flinching, Frankie came at him at full speed, which — at five-foot-nine of Collinwood Russo carpentry muscle, moving through a narrow bathroom doorway — was the speed of a train. She drove her right shoulder into his sternum. He hit the hallway wall behind him. She heard the specific sound of a man having the wind forced out of him against drywall, and she moved past him into the hall.

There were two more men in the hall.

The first one reached for her as she came through. She caught his wrist, turned it, rotated her body under his arm, and bent him forward over a position that brought his head against the banister. He went down. He did not get up.

The second one had a Taser.

He was at the top of the front stairs. He had the Taser in his right hand, aimed. He had been waiting for her to come through the hall. She saw, in the half-second she had to evaluate, that he was standing exactly where a person would stand if they had been told *cover the front stairs while we take her in the bathroom, we'll push her to you.* Rook was not supposed to have made first contact. Rook had flanked.

She did not go toward the Taser.

She went for the back stairs.

She was four steps down when the third man, who was halfway up the back stairs with a second Taser, put her down with one clean shot to the right shoulder blade. The electrodes hit at approximately the angle and location Army Signals had been taught, in 1988, was the most efficient neutralization point on a target moving downward. The shock cycled for five seconds. She went down the last three stairs in a way that was, in her description of it to me later, "not graceful." She broke her left pinky on the landing. She did not go unconscious. She was, in technical Taser terms, neuromuscularly overwhelmed, and for the eighteen seconds between the end of the shock cycle and the moment the man caught up with her on the landing and administered a second shock, she was aware of the sound of her own breathing in a way she had never previously been aware of it.

The second shock sent her into full unconsciousness.

At 12:13 I called Dr. Hayes from the Nokia in the guest bedroom of Vera's house in Parma.

"Mr. Novak."

"Frankie hasn't called back."

"Tell me."

"She called twenty-two minutes into her run. It was a proof of life call. She was going to park on Euclid Heights Boulevard and walk in. She was going to be twenty minutes. It's been forty-five."

"Where are you."

"Parma."

"Get in the Jeep."

"I can't drive, my ribs —"

"Get in the Jeep, Mr. Novak. Drive to the Cedar-Fairmount half-double. Do not enter the house.

Park one block south. I am leaving Lee Road now. We will meet at Tommy's on Coventry. Thirty-five minutes."

She hung up.

I stood up, which was a mistake. My ribs sang. I took three ibuprofen, which was too many ibuprofen. I grabbed the Jeep keys off the kitchen counter. I shut Ramona in the guest bedroom with food and water. I locked the house.

I drove to Cleveland Heights.

I drove slowly because every lane change hurt in a specific way and every pothole hurt in a different specific way. I kept both hands on the wheel. I did not listen to the radio. I was at Tommy's, the deli on Coventry, at 1:14 PM. Dr. Hayes was already there, in a booth by the window, with a cup of tea and a worry line on her forehead that I had not seen before.

I sat down across from her.

"I went past the house," she said. "There is nobody on the block."

"Where's Frankie's truck."

"Parked on Euclid Heights Boulevard. I walked past it. There is nothing wrong with it."

"And the apartment —"

"I did not go into the apartment. I do not intend to go into the apartment. The apartment is almost certainly empty at this point. Whatever happened inside happened some time ago. I am interested, at this point, in finding out what happened and in — Mr. Novak."

"Yes."

"I need you to stay with me."

"Yes."

"I need you to not go to the apartment. I need you to sit in this booth and drink a glass of water that I am going to order for you, and I need you to breathe. Because Frankie needs you to breathe right now. She needs you intact. She needs you here. She needs you at Vera's in Parma at some point in the next several hours, because the thing that is about to happen is going to require you to do something there, and you will not be able to do it if you are panicking. Is that clear."

"Yes."

"Drink this water."

I drank.

"I am going to make some phone calls. You will sit here for twenty minutes. Do not leave the booth. Do not order food you will not eat. Do not talk to the waitress about anything other than the weather and the Indians."

"Yes."

She got up. She went to the payphone at the back of the deli. She made three phone calls. I could not hear the conversations. I watched her hands. She was holding the receiver in a specific way — the same specific way she had held the receiver when she had called Ruth, which I now knew was the handling of a phone that was about to carry a piece of news the listener was not expecting.

She came back at 1:41.

"We are going to Vera's," she said.

"Why."

"Because if they have Frankie — if they have Miss Russo — they are going to make contact. They are going to make contact at a location we consider ours. The half-double is a location that is ours but that is not currently inhabited. It is a possibility. Vera's is a location that is inhabited. It is a higher-probability possibility. If they know about Vera's — which they will if they broke Miss Russo — they will reach us there. We are going to be there when they do."

"If they broke her —"

"Mr. Novak. Miss Russo is not a person who can be *broken* in the hour and a half that has elapsed since her last phone call. She is, however, a person who can have her tool bag searched. Her tool bag is likely to contain a receipt from the Parma public library that I encouraged her to use on Wednesday to generate a paper trail locating her in a neighborhood that was not her actual base of operations. The library is three blocks from Vera's house. A professional would, in forty-five minutes, connect the two. I believe that is what has happened.

"It was not Doyle's people," she said.

"How do you know."

"Because Martin Doyle does not have a kidnapping operation in Cleveland. He is a CIA station officer. His instruments are paperwork, institutional leverage, and official channels. What happened in that apartment was a three-man field entry with Tasers — that is Yegorov's contractor network. Bratva-adjacent, locally sourced. Doyle may know about it. Given what we established last night, he almost certainly does. But he did not order it." She paused. "They are running parallel tracks to the same object. Yegorov simply moved first."

"We are going to Vera's. Let's go."

We got to Vera's at 2:32.

The front door was locked. I unlocked it. I went in. I checked on Ramona. Ramona was fine — miserable, yowling, under the bed — but she was alone in the house, which was what mattered. Dr. Hayes was walking through the rooms with her head slightly tilted, the way a person listens when they are not sure whether they are about to hear something.

She came back to me in the guest bedroom.

"Check the bedroom," she said. "The master. Look on the pillow."

I went to the master bedroom.

There was a Nokia 2110 on the pillow on Frankie's side of the bed.

It was not my Nokia. It was not Frankie's. It was not Dr. Hayes's. It was a fourth Nokia — black, identical model, slightly newer, sitting upright on the pillow in the specific position of an object that had been placed.

It rang.

I looked at Dr. Hayes.

She nodded.

I picked it up.

"Hello."

"Mr. Novak."

The voice was male. Accented — Russian, specifically, but refined, not heavy. A voice that had learned English at an institution with standards. The voice of a man who had been sent, years ago, to a specific school, and who had been drilled on specific sounds until the wrong ones stopped coming out.

I said, "Yes."

"Your girlfriend is safe. She has some discomfort. She is otherwise unhurt. She will continue to be unhurt until next Saturday, at which point she will either be returned to you or she will not be, depending on a decision you are about to make."

I closed my eyes. I said nothing.

"You will bring the real microfiche to the Cleveland Museum of Art on the evening of Saturday, September seventh, during the donor preview for the Van Gogh exhibit. You will come alone, or you will come with Dr. Hayes. You will not come with federal agents. You will hand the real microfiche to me inside the museum. You will leave. Your girlfriend will be returned to you within four hours of the handoff. If you bring a decoy, your girlfriend will be killed. If you bring agents, your girlfriend will be killed. If you fail to appear, your girlfriend will be killed. You know which Saturday. She has until then."

There was a pause.

"Do you understand, Mr. Novak."
"Yes."
"Good."
He hung up.
I stood in Vera's master bedroom with the Nokia in my hand, staring at the pillow.
Dr. Hayes was in the doorway.
She said, "He said 'the real microfiche.'"
"Yes."
"Which means he knows there is a decoy."
"Yes."
"Which means."
She did not finish the sentence.
She did not need to.
Which meant Doyle had told him.
Which meant Doyle, after his visit Tuesday, had not simply gone back to his hotel to plan. He had gone back to his hotel and made a phone call.
Which meant the call had contained a specific warning — not *there is a decoy,* because Doyle had not seen Hayes's cedar closet, had not seen the blank film or the light box or the Selectric II. But he had known Lorraine Hayes for twenty-one years, which was long enough to know what she would do with a night and a reason. He had told Rook to assume one.
Which meant Doyle and Rook were, at this specific moment, working together.
Which meant the museum on Saturday was not going to be what we had planned.
Which meant Frankie had a week.

TWENTY-TWO: *The Counter-Plan*

I did not take it well.

I will spare you the twenty-three minutes of my life between the end of Rook's phone call and the beginning of the conversation that followed, because those twenty-three minutes were not my finest twenty-three minutes. I will say only that Dr. Hayes sat in Vera's master bedroom with me, on the edge of Vera's bed, with her hand flat on the back of my hand, and she did not speak, and she did not rush me, and she did not, at any point, suggest that my reaction was unreasonable. When I was ready to hear her she let me be ready, and she let me start the conversation.

I started it by saying, "We give them the real microfiche."

"No."

"Dr. Hayes."

"No."

"I'm not — this is not a negotiation. Frankie — I'm going to give them —"

"Mr. Novak. Listen to me. I am going to say this one time. You are going to hear it. Then we are going to move on to the plan."

"Okay."

"If we give them the real microfiche, Miss Russo will be killed. You will be killed. I will be killed. Every person named on that microfiche will live — most of them to comfortable retirements, a few to high federal pensions. The man on the phone — Pavel Yegorov, Rook — will return to Moscow. Martin Doyle will return to Langley. Next year and the year after and the year after that, Russian intelligence will continue to run the forty-seven networks named on that microfiche, and they will run them for a generation, and the Americans they damage will never know who damaged them. That is the outcome if we give them the real microfiche. That is also the outcome *if we give them the decoy* and they retain Miss Russo as leverage to force a second exchange. The man who called you just now is not an honorable man. He is also not an honorable man who is under pressure from Moscow to close this operation, which means he is not going to release Miss Russo at all, not with the real, not with the decoy, not under any scenario in which we negotiate directly with him."

"Then what —"

"We do not negotiate directly with him. We extract Miss Russo. In parallel with the museum event. By a third party who is not going to be negotiating."

"Mwangi."

"Mwangi."

"You can't reach her."

"I could not reach her through any of the channels Doyle was watching. I am going to reach her through a channel he does not know exists. I am going to do that today. Now. Once I have reached her, she is going to come to Cleveland, and she is going to bring resources, and she is going to find Miss Russo, and she is going to get her out. What you and I are going to do is the same thing we were planning to do, with the same microfiche, in the same museum, on the same night. The parts that change are Mwangi's parts. The extraction. The parallel operation."

"Okay."

"Do you trust me, Mr. Novak."

"Yes."

"I am going to need you to trust me in a specific way over the next week. I am going to need you to accept that I do not always know whether the person we are trying to keep alive is going to live. I am going to need you to accept that I will try with everything I have, and that everyone I can put on the effort will be put on the effort, and that even so, there is a nonzero chance that on Saturday evening at 8 PM, when the operation is concluded, I will have to tell you that we did not get her out. I need you to know that in advance, because if I do not tell you now, and if it then happens, you will never forgive me. And I want you to be able to forgive me if it happens."

"You're saying she might die."

"I am saying she might die. I am also saying she might live. I am saying that the probability of her living goes up with every hour between now and Saturday in which we execute the plan properly. I am saying the probability of her living goes to zero if we negotiate directly with Yegorov. I am saying I am going to do everything I can. I am saying nobody on this earth is going to work harder to keep Francesca Russo alive for the next seven days than I am going to work. Do you understand."

"Yes."

"Say the other thing."

"What."

"Say you know she might die."

"I know she might die."

"Say you can forgive me if she does."

"I — Dr. Hayes —"

"Say it, Mr. Novak. For me. Out loud. Now."

"I can forgive you if she dies."

"Thank you."

She squeezed my hand. She took her hand away.

"Now. Let's go to work."

She made the phone call at 3:17 PM from Vera's landline.

The line, she had confirmed with Vera before accepting the safe house, was unmonitored — it was a simple residential line attached to a forty-year-old handset and a monthly statement from Ameritech that Vera paid in cash at a storefront on Ridge Road. Dr. Hayes dialed a number from memory. She did not consult a notebook.

It rang four times.

A woman answered.

"Hello."

"Ruth," Dr. Hayes said.

There was a beat of silence.

Then Ruth — I did not know her last name at the time; I would learn later that it was Halpern — said, "Oh my God. Lorraine."

"Yes."

"How long has it been."

"Eleven years."

"Eleven years."

"I need a favor, Ruth. I need it tonight."

"Tell me."

"Your daughter is still in touch with Claire Mwangi."

A small pause.

"Yes."

"I need Claire. I need her now. I need her on a secure line. I do not have one to call her on. Doyle has been intercepting every channel I have. I do not have the ability to make a secure call to Langley or the Bureau through any route that will not be seen. I need Claire to call me at this number, from a line that is not hers, within the next thirty minutes."

"Lorraine, is this —"

"It is the thing. It is the thing we talked about in 1985."

Ruth was silent for three beats.

Then she said, "Tell me the number."

Dr. Hayes read out Vera's landline number. She said it twice. Ruth said, "I'll have her call you within the hour."

"Thank you, Ruth."

"Lorraine."

"Yes."

"Is Kiri —"

"Kiri is fine. I still have not gotten around to the pierogies. I am very sorry."

Ruth laughed. It was a short laugh and it had something old in it.

"You are a terrible friend," she said. "You always have been. Go save somebody."

She hung up.

Mwangi called at 3:48.

Dr. Hayes picked up. She said, "Agent Mwangi."

"Lorraine."

"Claire."

"What the hell is going on."

"Are you on a secure line."

"I am in a pay phone at a Sunoco on North Michigan Avenue. I am not on a secure line but I am on a line that is not mine and that was not mine before fourteen minutes ago."

"That is sufficient. I will be brief. You have been the target of an internal manipulation for eleven days. Martin Doyle, CIA Cleveland station, pulled you onto a manufactured joint task force in Chicago on the morning of August twenty-second. The manipulation was designed to intercept a specific piece of contact I was attempting to make with you in connection with material of very high classification. Doyle intended to receive the material himself, on the presumption that delivering it to you would have exposed his name on it."

Mwangi said, slowly, "His name."

"Yes."

"Doyle is on —"

"Yes."

There was a pause. I could, standing next to Dr. Hayes in Vera's kitchen, hear Mwangi breathing on the other end of the line.

"Lorraine. Tell me what you need."

"I need you in Cleveland by midnight. I need the material authenticated and processed by an FBI team that reports outside the CIA chain. I need a hostage rescue package assembled around an extraction I cannot yet give you coordinates for but believe I can locate within forty-eight hours. I need the whole thing synchronized to an event at the Cleveland Museum of Art next Saturday evening, which will function as a coordinated operation. I need you to fly into Burke Lakefront, not Hopkins, to avoid the possibility of observation. I need you to come directly to a location I will give you when you land."

"What's the hostage situation."

"A civilian. Francesca Russo. She was taken today by a Russian-national operator — Pavel Yegorov, who has been Doyle's handler for the last six years — working with two to three local contractors. I believe she is being held at a warehouse somewhere on the east side of the Cuyahoga, probably in the Euclid corridor. I do not yet have the precise location."

"Is she alive."

"As of ninety minutes ago, yes. I have no reason to believe she is not still alive. The hostage-taker has promised to release her Saturday evening contingent on a material exchange that, in my professional view, he does not intend to honor."

"Fuck."

"Yes."

"Okay. Lorraine, I need to — I need to move. I'm going to be on a private charter at O'Hare in ninety minutes. I will be at Burke at nine. Where am I going after that."

Dr. Hayes gave her the Lee Road address.

"Lee Road."

"Yes."

"I know that address."

"Then you know the way."

"Give me twelve hours and I am there."

"Fly safe."

"You too."

Mwangi hung up.

Dr. Hayes set the receiver back in the cradle. She stood for a second with her hand on it. Then she turned to me.

"Now," she said, "we wait."

"Dr. Hayes."

"Yes."

"Ruth said *is this the thing we talked about in 1985.*"

Dr. Hayes looked at me for a beat.

"Mr. Novak, that is a conversation for a day that is not today."

"Okay."

"Pack a bag. We are going back to Lee Road. I gave Mwangi my address, not Vera's — I am not going to be the person who exposes this house to federal surveillance, even friendly federal surveillance. Vera has lent me this safe house twice in sixteen years, and I am going to give it back to her tonight the way I borrowed it."

"Okay."

I packed Ramona into her carrier. She did not yowl. She had, I think, yowled herself out.

We drove back to Lee Road.

TWENTY-THREE: *The Briefing*

Claire Mwangi arrived at 11:42 PM on Saturday night.

She came in a silver Ford Escort from the Burke Lakefront rental counter, which she had selected specifically because, as she explained later, a silver Ford Escort rental is the least-memorable vehicle in the Cleveland metropolitan area and she had been trained, in her first year at the Bureau, to select the least-memorable vehicle in whatever the applicable metropolitan area was. She parked three blocks east of Dr. Hayes's bungalow. She walked the rest. She arrived at the front door in a dark blue suit, a white blouse, low-heeled shoes, and a leather briefcase that was older than the suit by at least a decade.

She was five-foot-ten. She had her hair pulled back in a low bun. She had the specific posture of a person who had been a competitive swimmer in college and had retained the body for it. Her face, when she saw Dr. Hayes, did something I had not seen a federal agent's face do — it registered relief. Actual relief. The kind of relief that was not professional, that was personal, that came out of a specific relationship I did not yet know the shape of.

She said, "Lorraine."

"Claire."

They did not hug. They did something instead that was, in its way, more intimate — they took each other by the upper arms, briefly, and they looked at each other, and they nodded once, and they let go. I understood, watching it, that these were two women who had spent a very specific kind of time together in 1988 at a ski resort in Colorado and that whatever had happened there had bound them in a way they were still honoring eight years later.

Mwangi turned to me.

"You must be Theo Novak."

"Yes."

"Claire Mwangi."

Her handshake was firm and brief. She did not waste it on niceties.

"Lorraine says you have been remarkable. I will take her word for that. We will see how remarkable you are in the next seven days. May I see the material."

"Yes."

"Where."

"The kitchen table."

"Lead the way."

She read the microfiche for forty minutes.

Dr. Hayes threaded the film onto her reader in the kitchen — she had moved the reader out of the cedar closet and onto the kitchen table for this meeting — and Mwangi sat down in front of it. She brought her own loupe out of her briefcase. She set a legal pad beside her. She did not speak for the forty minutes. She read, frame by frame. She took notes. She did not use shorthand. Her handwriting was large and clean and all capital letters, and I could read it over her shoulder without meaning to.

At frame thirty-one she stopped.

She stared at the frame.

She said, "Oh my *God*."

It was the specific curse of a woman who almost never cursed.

She kept reading.

At frame thirty-seven she stopped again.

She said, "No. No, no, no."

I looked at Dr. Hayes. Dr. Hayes shook her head — *not yet,* the shake said. I did not ask.

Mwangi got to frame forty-seven. She wound the film off the reader. She put it back in the Mylar envelope. She put the envelope in an interior pocket of her briefcase. She locked the briefcase with a small key that she wore on a chain inside her blouse.

She looked at Dr. Hayes.

"Doyle's on this."

"Yes."

"Number twenty-nine."

"I had not confirmed which number. Twenty-nine fits."

"Twenty-nine fits."

"How long have you suspected him."

"Since 1991. I could never prove it. I could never get anyone to listen to me."

"I know."

"How long have *you* suspected him."

"I have not suspected him specifically. I have suspected *someone* in that office for the same period. I did not have a name."

"Now we both have a name."

"Yes."

"How complete is the TRW section."

"Fourteen names confirmed. We were missing three — I could not place them from open sources. Novak's training records closed the gap. All fourteen are now placed with department, clearance level, and facility location."

Mwangi wrote something on the legal pad. "That narrows the pre-arrest scope considerably."

"Yes."

"Smart."

"It was a risk. He took it."

Mwangi closed her eyes for a second. When she opened them she was a different person — not warmer, not colder, but focused in a way she had not been at the door. She picked up Dr. Hayes's kitchen phone.

"I need to make some calls."

"Please."

"Lorraine, I need to tell five people about this in the next hour. Three of them are colleagues. Two of them are not. I am going to tell all five of them in ways they will recognize. None of the calls will be long. All of them will be routed through the bureau of records exchange, which is Doyle-blind. Is your phone line clean."

"Yes."

"How do you know."

"I have someone walk it every two weeks."

"Who."

"A retired lineman from Ohio Bell. His wife bakes me zucchini bread."

"Of course she does."

She dialed.

She made five calls between 12:21 AM and 1:47 AM.

The first was to a man in Washington named Howard. She said four sentences. She did not use her name. Howard asked one question. Mwangi answered it in three words. Howard said, "Twenty minutes," and hung up.

The second was to a woman in Alexandria named Patrice. Same pattern. Same cadence. Same quick hang-up.

The third was to a man named Greg, in Arlington, who — based on the tone of Mwangi's voice — was either her boss or her boss's boss. This call was longer. Mwangi gave him the full shape of the situation in about four minutes. Greg said something that made Mwangi say, "That's not going to work, Greg, no. That is not what we are going to do. I am briefing you. I am not asking for permission. I am *briefing* you. Do you understand the distinction." There was a pause. Then Mwangi said, "Thank you, Greg. Good night." She did not sound thankful.

The fourth call was to Cleveland HRT.

HRT was the FBI Hostage Rescue Team. Mwangi did not call them by that name. She called them by a code I did not recognize. She spoke to a man whose name I did not catch. She gave him three specific pieces of information: the make and approximate plate partial of a Crown Victoria (1RVR-something — which she had gotten from Dr. Hayes, who had gotten it from the Cuyahoga sheriff's deputy), the name of the hostage, and a time window (Saturday, 6 PM to 11 PM, September seventh). She asked for a preliminary deployment team assembled by Tuesday, full asset readiness by Friday noon, active surveillance starting tomorrow morning. The man on the other end said, "Copy. Cleveland division?" Mwangi said, "Cleveland division. Report directly to me. Not to field office management. Do you understand."

"Copy."

She hung up.

The fifth call was to a woman named Terese in the Cleveland field office — a woman who was, Mwangi explained to us afterward, the one FBI agent in Cleveland whom Mwangi trusted absolutely, who had been excluded from Doyle's manipulation because Doyle did not believe Terese was important enough to bother with. Terese was going to be the Cleveland coordinator. Terese was going to be the one to receive Mwangi's morning reports. Terese was going to be the person who actually ran the parallel operation at street level, on Mwangi's instruction.

That call took seventeen minutes. At the end of it, Mwangi hung up the phone and looked at Dr. Hayes and said, "We have a team."

At 3:12 AM we had a warehouse.

The cell-tower triangulation had taken, Mwangi explained to me later, about ninety minutes of work by an FBI technical analyst in Washington. The Nokia phone Rook had used to call me had connected to a specific cell tower in East Cleveland at 2:24 PM on Saturday afternoon. The tower had also received contact from the same Nokia at 2:57 PM, at 3:04 PM, at 3:31 PM, and at 4:12 PM. The phone had remained within the cell radius for the full period. The cell radius covered approximately

1.4 square miles of industrial real estate on the east bank of the Cuyahoga — a triangle bounded, roughly, by East 55th on the west, Euclid Avenue on the north, and Superior on the south.

The FBI had, within the triangle, seven warehouses with plausible Bratva associations.

By 3:12, surveillance teams were rolling.

By 3:36, the pool had been narrowed to three.

By 4:50 AM — the sun was not up yet, but the sky over Lake Erie was starting to lighten — a surveillance team had photographed a Crown Victoria with plate 1RVR-412 parked at the rear loading bay of a warehouse at 6342 Euclid, owned on paper by a shell company headquartered in Boca Raton and in practice by a man named Grigory Kostenko, who was known to the Cleveland FBI field office by a first-name-only file marker and who had, on three previous occasions, been photographed in the company of a man whose name appeared on the MEADOWLARK list at number nineteen.

They had found her.

They did not move on the warehouse. Not yet. Moving too soon would tip Rook, and tipping Rook would get Frankie killed. The surveillance team held at a distance. Rotated every four hours. Logged every movement in and out of the warehouse. They saw Frankie twice over the next six days, at brief intervals, being moved between a back office and a bathroom — always alert, always watching, looking, as Mwangi later said, *like a woman who had not given up on us.*

I did not see any of this. I was at Dr. Hayes's bungalow. I was drinking coffee I did not taste. I was counting days.

But I knew.

Mwangi had said to me, at 3:42 AM, across the kitchen table, "Mr. Novak. We are going to get her out."

She had said it with the specific flatness of a woman who was telling me a thing that was true, not a thing that was comforting.

"Yes," I had said.

"We are going to get her out by 8 PM next Saturday."

"Yes."

"I need you to be at the museum at 6:45. I need you to do what Lorraine has planned for you to do. I need you to do it the way she planned it. If you do that, Miss Russo is going to come home. If you don't, she isn't. Is that clear."

"Yes."

"Good."

She had stood up.

"Lorraine. I need a guest bed."

"Upstairs. The second room on the left."

"Thank you."

"Claire."

"Yes."

"It is good to see you."

Mwangi had paused at the bottom of the stairs.

"You too, Lorraine," she had said. "You look — you look well."

"I look old."

"You look old and well."

She had gone upstairs.

Dr. Hayes had looked at me across the kitchen.

"Sleep, Mr. Novak. You have a week of waiting to do, and nobody does waiting well on three hours."

I had gone upstairs.

I had lain on the guest bed with Ramona at my feet.

I had not slept.

TWENTY-FOUR: *The Night Before*

The week was a specific kind of bad.

I will not describe it in detail, because a week of waiting for one thing, in a house that is not your house, with two other people whose primary task is also to wait for the same thing, is a kind of experience that does not benefit from being described in detail. I will say that Ramona eventually settled. I will say that Dr. Hayes's kitchen had a clock with a loud second hand that I began to hate. I will say that I finished a novel — a Dick Francis, from Dr. Hayes's shelf, the last one I would ever read in my life — and that I cannot now, thirty years later, remember a single thing about it.

Mwangi did not stay at Dr. Hayes's. She stayed at a Holiday Inn in Independence, where she could rotate through hotel rooms every forty-eight hours and where the FBI team could, if needed, surveil her own location as a fallback. She came to the bungalow once a day for briefing updates. She did not mince words. She did not offer comfort. She offered progress reports, structured in a format I came to understand was her standard briefing pattern: positions, movements, timeline, next steps.

On Wednesday afternoon at 2:14 PM, Dr. Hayes's landline rang.

Mwangi answered it, which was a thing we had all agreed on — any incoming call went through her. She listened for fifteen seconds. She said, "Hold." She handed the receiver to me.

"Proof of life."

I took the phone.

"Theo."

It was Frankie.

Her voice was tired. It was not hurt. It was her voice, in the specific way your person's voice is your person's voice no matter what, and I closed my eyes and I sat down on the floor of Dr. Hayes's hallway.

"Frankie."

"I only have about ten seconds."

"Are you okay."

"Yeah. I'm okay. They have not — I'm okay."

"Where —"

"Hey. Listen. Tell Dr. Hayes — tell her Mrs. Nabokov is still biting."

"What."

"Tell her. You'll remember. She'll understand."

There was a sound on the other end — something scraping, a voice, a shift.

Frankie said, "I love you, Theo."

"I love you, Frankie."

The line went dead.

I stayed on the floor of the hallway for a full minute.

Mwangi squatted down beside me. She did not speak. She was not, I would realize later, trying to comfort me. She was letting me sit.

After a minute I said, "She said Mrs. Nabokov is still biting."

Dr. Hayes was at the top of the stairs.

"She did," Dr. Hayes said. "Good. She's still her."

"What does it mean."

"It means she is undamaged, Mr. Novak. It means she wants us to know she is undamaged in a way that is not a thing she could say directly. It means, in the specific code of our household, that she has not been medicated and that she is not being coerced into saying anything she does not mean. Mrs. Nabokov is a cat who bites. If I were drugged, and somebody were feeding me specific sentences to say, I would not spontaneously remember Mrs. Nabokov. Frankie did. She is fine. She is herself. She is waiting."

"Okay."

"Good."

Mwangi stood up. She walked back to the kitchen. She said something into another phone — a call to Terese, I assumed, though I did not hear it clearly. The FBI team would now, I knew, be logging the timestamp of the Frankie call against their surveillance records of the warehouse. They would see, in retrospect, a movement that matched: a guard coming to a specific door at a specific time, carrying a phone. They would confirm that she was in the back office. They would refine the extraction plan.

I stayed on the floor of the hallway for a while longer.

Ramona came and sat next to me. She did not try to get on my lap. She just sat next to me, the way cats do when they know you are alone and they have decided to be the thing that you are not, by proximity, alone with.

I stroked her back with one hand.

I thought about the fact that my girlfriend had managed, in a kidnapping, in a warehouse, under duress, to construct a nine-word sentence that signaled both life and freedom.

I thought about how much I loved her.

I thought about the fact that I was not going to lose her.

I got up.

On Thursday evening Dr. Hayes took me to the tuxedo rental.

The shop was on Shaker Square, as she had specified, and the man who ran it — an Armenian named Harout, who had, Dr. Hayes informed me, altered her husband's one and only tuxedo in 1974 — was willing to turn around a fitted tuxedo by Saturday afternoon if I paid fifty dollars extra in cash. I did. He measured me. He made notes on a piece of paper. He did not ask why I was wearing it. He handed me a rental form and a receipt and he said, "Saturday, three PM." He did not take a deposit. He had been taking Dr. Hayes at her word since 1974, and he continued to.

On Friday afternoon Dr. Hayes went over the museum map with me for the seventh time.

She had sketched it from memory on butcher paper. She had marked the entrance, the coat check, the first gallery, the Armor Court, the Pharaoh gallery, the docent's office where I would likely end up with Doyle, the rotunda, the bench where I would leave the pamphlet. She had marked the approximate position Mwangi would take. She had marked my path through the museum — where I would walk, where I would stop, where I would put my hand in my pocket, where I would take my hand out.

She had also marked the position of the decoy swap. Doyle did not know, in advance, that I would hand him a decoy. Doyle thought I was going to hand him the real thing, under duress, because Rook had him on a parallel leash and Rook had Frankie. The plan, as Doyle understood it, was: I hand Doyle the decoy *labeled as the real one.* He reads it. He discovers, in three or four frames, that it is old and outdated. He realizes he has been given a decoy. He tries to grab me — at which point, Mwangi and two FBI agents emerge from the second door.

In other words: Doyle was going to take the decoy, discover it was a decoy, draw his weapon, and be arrested at the draw.

Rook was a different problem.

Rook was going to be watching from somewhere in the building. Rook was going to be waiting for Doyle to hand off the microfiche. Rook was going to realize something was wrong when Doyle did not exit the docent's office. Rook was going to move. Rook was going to go for the envelope — which Mwangi, or rather Mwangi's pamphlet pickup, would have already taken. Rook was going to go for me. Rook was going to escape.

"And Frankie," I said for the seventh time.

"Frankie gets extracted at 7:48 PM from the warehouse, while Rook is in the museum watching Doyle. Her primary guard — the Taser operator from Saturday — will be outside on the warehouse's east-side loading dock, waiting for Rook's confirmation call. HRT will neutralize him at 7:46. The other two guards will be inside. HRT takes them silently. Miss Russo will be out of the building by 7:55. She will be in an FBI vehicle on the way to a Rocky River safe house by 8:00."

"And you're sure."

"Mr. Novak."

"Yes."

"We have done this before. Not with these exact people, not in this exact city, not on this exact night. But HRT has done operations of this profile forty-one times in the last eighteen months, with a success rate on hostage survival of ninety-two percent."

"Ninety-two percent."

"Yes."

"That's — eight percent."

"Eight percent, yes."

I looked at the map.

"She is going to be in the high ninety-two percent," Dr. Hayes said.

"Yeah."

"She is in the high ninety-two percent because HRT has had six days of live surveillance on the warehouse, detailed floor plans, guard rotation patterns, and a full profile of the hostage, who is an Army-trained signals operator capable of making herself useful during an extraction rather than passive in it."

"Yeah."

"Yes?"

"Yes."

"Good."

She put the butcher paper down.

"Go to bed," she said. "Three AM tomorrow is going to come whether we sit up for it or not."

"Yeah."

Three AM came at three AM.

I had been asleep for maybe two hours. I woke up in the guest bedroom at Dr. Hayes's house — which was now my bedroom, which had been my bedroom for a week — and I could not go back to sleep, and after ten minutes of lying in the dark, I got up.

Ramona was on the foot of the bed. She lifted her head. I picked her up. I carried her downstairs.

The kitchen light was on.

Dr. Hayes was sitting at the kitchen table in her bathrobe. She had a mug of something in front of her. The kettle was on, and it whistled about ten seconds after I came in, and she got up without looking at me and poured a second mug and brought it to me. It was chamomile.

She sat back down.

"Couldn't sleep."

"No."

"Me neither."

We drank tea in silence for a while.

At the second sip I said, "Dr. Hayes."

"Yes."

"What happens if tomorrow goes wrong."

"In what sense."

"I mean — if I hand Doyle the decoy and he shoots me before Mwangi can enter the room. Or if Rook figures out the museum is a trap before he goes in. Or if HRT's breach is delayed. Or if any of the fifteen things that could go wrong go wrong. What happens."

"Then tomorrow goes wrong."

"Yeah."

"Mr. Novak, I am not going to lie to you. If tomorrow goes wrong in the specific way you just described — if, for instance, Doyle shoots you before Mwangi can enter the docent's office — then Martin Doyle leaves the Cleveland Museum of Art alive, the decoy is discovered later in a CIA safe in Langley, Mr. Yegorov makes a phone call about five minutes later and Miss Russo dies in the warehouse on Euclid, and Agent Mwangi and I spend the next seven years of our lives undoing the damage to the American intelligence community that is caused by the death of a civilian in a CMA docent's office. That is what happens."

"Okay."

"If, on the other hand, Doyle reads two frames of the decoy, understands what he has, draws his weapon, and Agent Mwangi is two seconds later than her protocol — then, Mr. Novak, what matters most, operationally, is where you have positioned your body in the eight seconds between the moment you hand Doyle the decoy and the moment Agent Mwangi opens the second door. I have walked you through this. The floor is tile. Tile is slick. If Doyle draws, you drop. You do not try to get out of the room. You do not try to get to Mwangi. You drop. The table is between you and him. You drop behind the table. You are a small man. You are capable of getting behind a table quickly."

"Yes."

"What matters after you drop is not under your control. What matters before you drop is. Clear."

"Yes."

"Good."

I drank the tea.

"Dr. Hayes."

"Yes."

"What are you willing to do, if tomorrow goes wrong."

She looked at me for a long time.

"Mr. Novak. What are *you* willing to do?"

"I asked you first."

"I know you did. I am not going to answer you first, because I do not want to influence your answer. I need to know where you are, not where you think I want you to be. What are you willing to do if tomorrow goes wrong."

I thought about it.

I thought about Frankie on the phone on Wednesday. I thought about the specific cadence of *Mrs. Nabokov is still biting,* which I now understood was a sentence Frankie had been composing, in her head, in a warehouse, in a back office, over the course of four days, waiting for a moment when she might be allowed ten seconds on a phone. She had engineered a nine-word sentence to tell us she was undamaged. She had rehearsed it. She had held it, ready.

I thought about a man named Martin Kowalczyk who had been pulled out of a canal in East Berlin in 1990 because a file had moved through a building.

I thought about my girlfriend.

I thought about the sculpture I had pulled off a tree lawn in Shaker Heights twenty-one days ago, and the small stamp on the base of it, and the man whose initials those were, and the fact that the man had died on a Friday in April before he had gotten to pass the object forward.

I thought about what was owed to a person when you inherited their unfinished work.

"Whatever I have to," I said.

Dr. Hayes looked at me.

She reached across the kitchen table. She put her hand over mine. Her hand was small, and warm, and marked with the specific brown age spots of a woman who had spent seventy years using her hands for difficult things.

"Good answer," she said.

"Yeah."

"Only answer."

"Yeah."

She patted my hand once. She took her hand back. She picked up her mug.

"Drink your tea," she said. "I am going to go back to bed. I will see you at seven. We have, by my count, about thirteen hours to get through before you put on a tuxedo that does not fit you. Try to get some sleep."

"Okay."

She stood. She looked at me for a beat.

"Mr. Novak."

"Yes."

"I am glad it was you."

"What."

"Who picked it up. Who picked up the sculpture. I am glad it was you."

"Why."

"Because most of the people I have worked with in my life who have done what you are about to do tomorrow have been professionals. And professionals are a specific kind of person. They are a kind of person who has been trained out of some of the things a person should have. You are not a professional. You are still a person."

"Okay."

"That is important."

"Okay."

"Good night, Mr. Novak."

"Good night, Dr. Hayes."

She went upstairs.

I sat at the kitchen table for a long time.

Ramona was still on my lap. She had been on my lap for the entire conversation. At some point during the conversation I had started scratching the base of her ears without noticing, and she had, sometime during Dr. Hayes's speech about the tile floor in the docent's office, begun to purr. I had not noticed that either. She was still purring now. She was warm. She was small.

She was, I realized, the only thing in the kitchen that had no sense of what the next day was going to bring, and she was, for that reason, the only thing in the kitchen that was genuinely at peace.

I sat with her while she purred.

Outside, through the kitchen window, I could see the very first grey edge of dawn beginning to come up over the maple trees on Lee Road.

September seventh.

Saturday.

I stayed up until the light was full.

TWENTY-FIVE: *CMA Exterior*

Harout finished the alterations at 3:12 PM on Saturday.

He said 3:00, and he was twelve minutes late, which for Harout was the equivalent of, for any other tailor in the greater Cleveland area, being four hours late. He took it seriously. He apologized twice. He pressed the jacket a third time while I was already in the changing room. He adjusted the cuff half an inch while I stood in front of the three-way mirror and practiced not looking terrified.

The tuxedo was black, single-breasted, with a satin shawl collar. It was the tuxedo of a man at a gala in 1996. It was also, across the midsection, a tuxedo that had been ordered by a taller thinner man and let out as much as a rental tuxedo could be let out. The jacket button strained. The trouser waistband, when I did not suck in, created a small shelf above the belt.

Harout stepped back. He looked at me. He nodded, without enthusiasm.

"Good."

"Good."

"Belt, under."

"Belt under."

"You are not eating tonight."

"No."

"Good."

I paid in cash. I walked out in the tuxedo with my street clothes in a garment bag. I got in the Jeep. I drove north up Shaker Boulevard toward Dr. Hayes's house in a tuxedo at 3:40 PM on a Saturday in September, and I understood that I had now entered a phase of my life that was genuinely absurd.

Dr. Hayes was in a stunning black dress.

I do not often use words like *stunning,* and I understand the risk of using them about a seventy-one-year-old woman to whom I was, in no meaningful way, related. I use the word deliberately. Dr. Hayes had, at some point between my departure for Shaker Square and my return, transformed herself from the person who had sat across the kitchen table from me at 3 AM into a specific woman at a specific event, and the transformation was the kind of thing you only got to witness, in your life, a few times. The dress was black silk, long-sleeved, knee-length. Simple. It had hung, she later told me, in a garment bag in her hall closet since 1977, when she had bought it in Vienna during a conference she should not have been at. She was wearing small pearl earrings and a pearl brooch at her throat that had been her mother's. Her hair was the same steel-wool cut it had been every day I had known her, but she had brushed it carefully, and she had put on a small amount of lipstick that was the same red color her pearl brooch's pin-back catch had, a detail I would not have noticed without having once designed a training module on color theory, and that I noticed now because I noticed everything now.

She looked up when I came in.

"Mr. Novak."

"Dr. Hayes."

"You look appropriate."

"You look beautiful."

She paused.

Then she said, quietly, "Thank you."

We left Lee Road at 6:15 PM.

She drove. I sat in the passenger seat. The Jeep — which was by that point the most-driven vehicle in the operation, having been through Parma, Lakewood, Cleveland Heights, and University Circle in the preceding nine days with two different sets of plates — seemed to me, that evening, like a different kind of vehicle than the one I had bought used in

1991. It felt more formal. It did not want to be treated poorly on the short drive to the museum. I adjusted my posture against the seat and I held the dashboard grab-bar with my right hand in a way that did not aggravate my ribs, and I watched the streets of University Circle go by.

The Cleveland Museum of Art had been built in 1916 out of white Georgia marble, on the north edge of Wade Oval, facing south across the reflecting pond toward the lagoon and, beyond it, the rest of the Circle. It was, on a summer evening, probably the most beautiful building in the state of Ohio, and I did not dispute this, but I had never thought of the building as anything other than a building until 6:34 PM on September seventh, 1996, when we pulled up to the valet circle off East Boulevard and I understood that for the rest of my life the white marble of the CMA would be, in my particular synesthesia, the color of the night I had stepped out of a Jeep in a tight rented tuxedo to walk into what was going to be the defining hour of my existence.

I gave the valet the keys.

I did not tip him. Dr. Hayes tipped him. I was not ready to perform casual currency transactions.

We walked up the south steps.

A docent in a green sash checked our invitations at the main entrance.

She was a small white-haired woman in her seventies, who I realized after a few seconds of her looking at our invitations was a friend of Dr. Hayes — she was reading them with a kind of performative slowness, pretending to verify them while actually giving Dr. Hayes a specific silent greeting that I could read only because I had spent three weeks learning to read Dr. Hayes's specific silent greetings. She nodded. She handed the invitations back. She said, "Welcome, Mrs. Wycoff," to Dr. Hayes — Mrs. Wycoff was the real name on Dr. Hayes's borrowed invitation — and, "Welcome, Mr. Wycoff," to me, and she moved us along with a practiced gesture.

We stepped into the rotunda.

The rotunda of the Cleveland Museum of Art is a domed circular space about seventy feet across, with a large bronze of Rodin's *The Age of Bronze* — not *The Thinker,* which is outside, but his younger brother — standing in the center. The dome's coffered ceiling rises maybe ninety feet above the marble floor. The acoustics are the acoustics of a secular cathedral. At 6:45 PM on a September Saturday, filled with one hundred and twenty-three donors in cocktail attire, holding flutes of champagne, talking quietly about art and about money, it felt exactly like what it was — a room in which very wealthy people spent a small part of their evening looking at things their grandchildren would one day inherit.

Dr. Hayes took a champagne flute off a passing silver tray. She handed me one too. I took it.

"We do not drink these," she said, quietly. "But we hold them. A man without a champagne flute at this event is a man with nothing to do with his hands, and a man with nothing to do with his hands is, in a room like this, a man who is being watched."

"Okay."

She took a small ceremonial sip of hers. I did the same. The champagne was good. It tasted like the specific absence of budget. I set it carefully on the edge of a tray as a passing waiter moved by.

"Not on a tray."

"No?"

"No. It creates a moment of dead champagne that the staff has to deal with. Keep holding it."

"Yes."

I picked it back up.

I had been scanning the room since we stepped through the entrance. Three weeks of Hayes had built the habit in me — I did not yet have her ease with it, but I had the reflex. Clockwise from the south door. Postures first. What people were facing. What they were not facing.

At the east pillar, near the archway to the Armor Court: a man in a dark grey tuxedo with silver hair cut with surgical precision. He was looking at the Rodin. He had not moved to a second angle.

I had sat six feet from this man on a couch on Lee Road twelve days ago.

I said, quietly, to a point in the middle distance that was not him: "East pillar."

Dr. Hayes did not look.

"Yes," she said. "Twelve minutes early."

“Where is Mwangi.”

“Mwangi will be here at seven-oh-five, entering as a guest of Mrs. Petersen, a Cleveland Donor Council member who Mwangi is *not* pretending to be tonight. She will be in burgundy. She will be holding a small beaded clutch that contains her badge. She will not acknowledge us. She will be on her usual circuit by seven-twelve, which is when you will begin yours.”

“Rook.”

“I do not see Rook. I do not expect to see Rook in the rotunda. I expect to see Rook somewhere between the Armor Court and the Pharaoh Gallery within fifteen minutes of the doors closing. He will be in a plain dark suit. He will be carrying a catalogue rather than a champagne flute. He will look like a slightly distracted art historian from Cleveland State who has been invited in a secondary capacity. He will move through the galleries alone. He is the only person tonight who will be working alone.”

“Will he recognize me.”

“He has seen your photograph. He has seen you at a pierogi counter. He has seen you on a motorcycle in the Flats. Yes. He will recognize you.”

“Will he approach me.”

"No. He will watch. He will not move until Doyle moves."

"Okay."

"Are you all right, Mr. Novak."

"No."

"That is an acceptable answer."

"Okay."

"Breathe."

"Okay."

At 6:58 the lights in the rotunda dimmed by about a third.

A woman in a cream dress — the CMA's director, I would learn later — stepped onto a small dais by the southern archway and spoke briefly into a microphone. She welcomed the donors. She thanked the exhibition's corporate sponsors. She told us that the galleries on the second floor and the west wing had been opened for the preview. She said, "Please, go see the Van Gogh. We are so honored to have it here with us in Cleveland. And thank you, always, for making this museum what it is." She smiled. She stepped down. The crowd made the polite noise a crowd makes when a speech has been appropriately short.

People began to move.

The first wave headed for the Van Gogh galleries in the west wing. The second wave, perhaps forty donors, drifted into the Armor Court, which was closer to the rotunda and was, for anyone who had seen the Van Gogh on loan before in another city, the more novel destination.

Dr. Hayes and I moved into the Armor Court.

The Armor Court of the Cleveland Museum of Art was a long, double-height gallery lined with fifteenth-century arms and armor, with stained-glass windows along the east wall and a mounted knight in full plate at the far end. It was, and had been since the museum's opening, a room that functioned partly as a display and partly as a theater. Schoolchildren loved it. Adults, who were often somewhat embarrassed to love it, loved it also. Wooden benches ran down the center — three of them, long, with slatted backs — and on each bench was, among other things, a stack of the night's commemorative pamphlets: glossy, trifold, featuring a reproduction of Van Gogh's *Starry Night Over the Rhône* on the cover.

The bench I wanted was the middle bench.

It was seven feet long. It faced a glass case containing a sixteenth-century suit of Italian parade armor. Nobody was sitting on it.

I walked to it. I sat. Dr. Hayes sat beside me.

She did not speak.

I reached into my jacket pocket. I took out the envelope I had been carrying since 6:00 PM. It was thin — the Mylar cover, folded, containing a small slip of microfiche. On the outside of the Mylar, I had, at Dr. Hayes's direction, taped a small label that read *Exhibition Preview Program — supplemental.* The label was not necessary; nobody would see it before Mwangi picked it up. But Dr. Hayes had wanted it there, because Dr. Hayes believed in belts and suspenders.

I slipped the envelope between pages 12 and 13 of a commemorative pamphlet I had picked up off the bench. I closed the pamphlet. I set the pamphlet, casually, on the bench between me and Dr. Hayes.

I sat with the pamphlet beside me for approximately forty-five seconds.

Then I stood up.

I moved to the glass case. I looked at the Italian parade armor. I did not look back at the bench. Dr. Hayes stood up a beat after me. She also moved to the case. We stood, together, in front of the sixteenth-century suit of armor, as a couple might. I said, for the benefit of any listener, "It's beautiful."

"It is. I have always thought the shoulder articulation was extraordinary."

"How did they —"

"Hinges. Tiny leather-backed hinges. Easier to manufacture than they look."

"Huh."

We were making conversation. It sounded real. It was real. At the edge of my peripheral vision, without looking directly at it, I watched the bench.

A woman passed.

She was in burgundy.

She paused at the bench, as if to fix the strap of her shoe. She reached down. She lifted the pamphlet. She opened it, pretended to read the first page — the one with Van Gogh's *Starry Night Over the Rhône* — made a small, contemplative face, and closed it again. She tucked the pamphlet into her small beaded clutch. She straightened up. She moved on into the next gallery.

It had taken approximately four seconds.

Dr. Hayes did not look at me.

She said, "Good."

"Good."

"Now Doyle."

"Now Doyle."

TWENTY-SIX: *The Pharaoh Gallery*

I moved west through the Armor Court, through the archway, into the gallery of medieval liturgical objects.

I paused in front of a twelfth-century reliquary chest that had, at some point in its life, contained what a docent card informed me was *the finger of a saint, identity uncertain.* I stood there for a respectable interval. I had done this before, earlier in the week, in my head. I knew the galleries. Dr. Hayes had made me memorize them.

I moved on.

Three other donors in the liturgical gallery: an older couple holding hands, a woman of about forty-five studying a crucifix with a frown, and a man in a navy blazer I had not seen in the rotunda. I did not make eye contact with any of them. I was, I hoped, looking like a man who had taken too much champagne on an empty stomach and was walking the galleries slowly to let it settle.

I was not drinking.

The champagne flute in my hand was still the first one I had taken. Still three-quarters full, the bubbles almost gone — a small clock I was carrying without meaning to.

I moved into the gallery of medieval Italian panel painting, which was smaller, and which had, as planned, almost no donors in it. The Van Gogh in the west wing was pulling everyone in the other direction. I stopped in front of a Duccio di Buoninsegna. I did not look at it. I looked at the reflection of the gallery behind me in the glass of the display case.

Doyle was in the gallery behind me.

He had followed me through two rooms, holding a distance of about ten meters. Dark grey tuxedo. Silver pocket square. He was pretending to study a fifteenth-century Venetian oil. He was not pretending very well. I took one step sideways to examine the adjacent panel. In the reflection, Doyle took one step in the same direction.

I moved into the small corridor connecting the Italian gallery to the Pharaoh Gallery.

I entered the Pharaoh Gallery at 7:24 PM.

The gallery occupied a wing on the north side of the building's second floor — long, narrow, dimly lit to protect the pigments. Cleveland's Egyptian collection: a few funerary stelae, a sandstone shawabti, a wooden Third Intermediate Period coffin with painted hieroglyphics on the lid, and the pride of the room, a basalt bust of a Twenty-Fifth Dynasty pharaoh whose name Dr. Hayes had tested me on three times and that I had committed to memory with the specific desperation of a man who understood that arriving at the right spot at the right time required knowing what to pretend to be interested in. Three doors: one from the corridor behind me, one to the west galleries, and one marked STAFF ONLY off the east wall between two display cases.

The STAFF ONLY door was the door Dr. Hayes had walked me through on a sheet of butcher paper on Wednesday afternoon.

The room behind it was the room I would, in the next three minutes, be standing in.

I walked slowly past the shawabti. I stopped at the basalt bust. I looked at it.

I waited.

Doyle came up beside me.

He did not speak at first. He stopped at my left shoulder, half a step behind — close enough for conversation with a stranger at a gallery, not so close as to be conspicuous. The distance of a man who had done this before.

"It's a beautiful piece," he said, quietly.

"Yes."

"Twenty-fifth Dynasty."

"Yes."

"Mr. Novak."

"Yes."

"Walk with me, please."

His voice was pleasant. The voice of a colleague at a networking event. Not the voice of a man with a weapon inside his jacket.

I turned. He smiled at me — the same smile he had given me in Hayes's front doorway two Tuesdays ago, warm and correctly calibrated, the smile of a man who had learned, a long time ago, which facial expressions opened doors. Something about seeing it here, in a dark Egyptian gallery, in a tuxedo, at the end of twenty-one days, made it specifically repellent.

"Where," I said.

"Just through this door." He nodded at the STAFF ONLY sign.

"I'd prefer —"

"I'm sure you would, Mr. Novak. But we're going to walk through this door together, and we're going to have a brief conversation, and then you're going to rejoin your party, and nothing unpleasant is going to happen to anyone tonight. Walk with me."

"Okay."

He put his hand on my upper arm. The smallest possible physical coercion — the kind that looked, to any observer, like two men who were friends. Not painful. But firm. My cracked ribs understood, without being consulted, that pulling away was not going to work.

He opened the STAFF ONLY door with his free hand.

We went through.

The docent's office was ten feet by twelve, painted a specific institutional green I had encountered in conference rooms at three different corporate clients and had always diagnosed as the color of a 1980s budget cut. A desk against the far wall, cluttered with pamphlets, name tags, and a small stack of educational handouts on Egyptian funerary practices. An office chair behind the desk. Two wooden guest chairs in front of it. A corkboard on the left wall with the docents' September schedule. And a second door in the right wall, closed, marked CUSTODIAL.

Doyle closed the first door behind us.

He did not lock it.

I noticed this. I filed it without understanding it.

He gestured at one of the guest chairs.

"Sit."

I sat. My ribs screamed. I did not show it.

He leaned against the front of the desk and crossed his arms.

"Mr. Novak."

"Yes."

"Let's begin."

"Okay."

"The microfiche, please."

I reached into my inner jacket pocket. I took out the Mylar envelope — the decoy, the one Dr. Hayes had built over ten hours in her cedar closet, the one she had held up to the lamp at 11:15 PM and said was better than anything the Agency had ever produced. I held it out.

Doyle did not take it.

"Put it on the desk."

I put it on the desk.

He looked at me. He did not pick it up.

"Have a seat, Mr. Novak."

"I'm sitting."

"I meant metaphorically. Settle in. We are going to be here for a few minutes."

He walked around the desk, sat in the docent's chair, and opened the middle drawer. From it he removed an object I had seen described on a Wednesday-night kitchen table with a salt shaker standing in for the reader and a pepper grinder standing in for Doyle, but had never seen in person.

A handheld microfiche reader. Soviet-era, Czechoslovakian originally. Approximately the size of a large paperback, matte black, with a viewing lens on top and a film slot on the side. Designed, Dr. Hayes had said, in roughly 1978, and never updated, because it did not need to be — it was the only handheld reader that existed in that period which could reliably read the specific format the MEADOWLARK cache used. He had carried it into the Cleveland Museum of Art in a catalogue bag. He had been carrying it all evening, in a room full of a hundred and twenty donors, and nobody had known.

She had been right about this too.

He opened the battery compartment, checked the batteries, closed it. He picked up the Mylar. He opened it with a small tool from the drawer. He threaded the film onto the reader. He turned it on.

A small amber light came on at the top.

He began to read.

I watched his face.

The first frame: the header, date-stamped *22 JANUARY 1987*. Dr. Hayes had matched it to the original in every detail — typeface, compression marks, the specific spacing the Agency had used in that period. If you knew what you were looking for, it was perfect. If you didn't, it was still perfect.

The second frame: the cover letter, typed on a Royal typewriter Dr. Hayes had sourced this week from a vintage equipment shop in Parma, using a replacement head with key-strike wear patterns that matched the original. Only a specialist in a full lab would catch it.

The third frame: *ANDERSEN, K. R.* The first name on the real list, and the first name on the decoy — listed here with an obsolete handler designation and drop locations at a Brunswick train station surveilled and closed in 1992. Andersen had died of a stroke in March 1995. His obituary was in the *Plain Dealer.* A field officer reading fast would not notice the handler discrepancy. Doyle, in a ten-by-twelve room under time pressure, would not notice it on a first pass.

Fourth frame: *BAUER, H. G.* Also dead. Heart attack, October 1995.

Fifth frame: *CARMODY, W. L.* Dead. Car accident, February 1996.

The first three names in the decoy were the same as the first three names in the real list, and they were dead, and they were verifiable, and Doyle could not verify them in this room, and so he read them as confirmation. He was nodding slightly, the faint acknowledgment of a man seeing what he expected to see.

The sixth frame was *DOOLIN, R. P.*

Doyle was on the fourth name for maybe six seconds.

His face changed.

It did not go grey. It did not crumple. What it did was more precise and therefore more frightening: it went *still.* All the small constant motions of a face processing information — the micro-adjustments of the eyes, the almost-invisible movement of the jaw — stopped. He became, in those six seconds, a photograph of himself. I understood that he was making a decision, and that the decision was: *does my reaction matter.* He arrived at *no.*

He reached up. He turned the reader off. He set it on the desk.

He looked at me.

"Mr. Novak."

"Yes."

"This is a decoy."

"I don't — I don't know what you mean."

"Mr. Novak." His voice had not changed. This was the thing. His voice was still pleasant, still modulated, still the voice of the man with the well-made smile. "This is a decoy. I understand that you understand what a decoy is. I understand that you also understand that bringing one to this meeting was a very serious decision. I want you to think carefully, in the next ten seconds, about the decisions that are going to follow from that one."

I said nothing.

He reached inside his jacket.

I had rehearsed this moment on a kitchen table with coffee cups and butcher paper. Doyle's hand comes out with a weapon. I have eight seconds. The floor is tile. Tile is slick. A small man can drop fast. I drop. I get behind the desk. I stay down until I hear the door.

His hand came out of his jacket.

I watched it happen. That was the specific failure — not fear, not freezing, but watching. My legs knew the instruction. My legs had the instruction. And for the quarter-second between his hand moving and my legs receiving the message, my entire nervous system was busy processing the specific wrongness of seeing a weapon come out of a jacket in a ten-by-twelve room, and the tile floor stayed where it was, and I stayed in the chair, and the quarter-second went.

The door opened.

It was the wrong door.

It was the CUSTODIAL door, on the right wall — the door Doyle had not locked, the door I had noticed and filed and had not understood, because the not-locking I had been watching was the first door, and the door that mattered was this one.

The man who came through it was Rook.

Plain dark suit. A catalogue in his left hand. Moving fast, with a low balanced center of gravity, his right hand already inside his jacket. He was not pointing a weapon yet. He didn't need to be. The room understood immediately that he was a different order of problem from the one that had been in it thirty seconds ago.

He said, in Russian, a word that I would later be told translated roughly as *what the fuck.*

Doyle's hand stopped halfway out of his jacket. He turned — slowly, carefully, with the specific deliberateness of a man whose gun was partially drawn — to look at Rook.

He said something back in Russian.

Rook said, in English, "Nobody. I have been in the next room for twelve minutes."

Doyle answered in Russian, at length, and I could hear in the pitch of it the specific sound of a man improvising a cover story over a parallel operation that was now, catastrophically, adjacent to the real one. I did not speak Russian. I did not need to. I had spent a decade listening to people say things they did not mean, and underneath whatever Doyle was saying, the signal was unmistakable: *I have been doing something you were not supposed to know about, and I am now explaining it as something else.*

Rook stepped fully into the room. He closed the CUSTODIAL door behind him with his left foot. The door clicked.

"You have tried to take the list, *Martin,*" he said, in English now, because we were past the point of hiding the conversation from me. "So that it would not be read. Your name is on the list. I have known for six years your name is on the list. I have *looked after* you for six years. You were not going to take it from me tonight."

"Pavel —"

"*Do not speak.*"

"Pavel, listen to me, I was going to —"

"*Do not speak.*"

Doyle did not speak.

Rook's hand came out of his jacket.

He was holding a Makarov. It was pointed at Doyle's chest.

I should describe what I was doing during this.

I was against the back wall. When the CUSTODIAL door opened I had taken two steps backward without deciding to, and my back was now against the corkboard — the September schedule pressing into my shoulder blades — and I was positioned directly between the two men and the STAFF ONLY door, roughly five feet from Doyle and seven from Rook. I was not behind cover. I was a third body in a room with two guns. I was five foot six, soft in the middle, with cracked ribs and a tuxedo jacket a size too small across the chest, and I was breathing as quietly as I had ever breathed in my life.

Rook said, in English, "You will place your gun on the desk."

Doyle did not.

"Martin." Rook took one step forward. The Makarov was now three feet from Doyle's chest. "You will place your gun on the desk, or I will shoot you now, and I will go to the woman in burgundy who is leaving the museum by the south entrance in four minutes with a pamphlet in her purse, and I will take the pamphlet from her."

Doyle's face did the smallest thing.

He had, in that moment, understood something. Rook had been surveilling Mwangi. Not tonight — before. Over the preceding six days. Rook had watched the woman whose name Doyle himself had given him two Tuesdays ago. He had identified her. He had followed her hotel rotations. He knew her dress. He knew her purse. He knew the exit plan.

Rook was not reacting to tonight. Rook had been planning for it.

The first door opened.

I had been positioned, for the last twenty-two seconds, between the two men and the STAFF ONLY door. When the door opened and Mwangi and two FBI agents came through it, I was in their line of fire.

They held.

Mwangi was in burgundy. She was holding a Glock 19 with both hands, pointed at Rook. The two agents behind her had their own Glocks up: one on Rook, one on Doyle. A triangle of aimed weapons in a ten-by-twelve room with one man pressed against the schedule board and the ambient sound of Debussy coming through two walls.

Rook did not move.

Doyle did not move.

I did not move.

Mwangi said, "Pavel Antonovich Yegorov, you are under arrest."

Rook did not lower the Makarov. His eyes stayed on Doyle.

"Pavel. Lower the weapon."

"If I lower the weapon," Rook said, without turning his head, "I am dead in six months in a prison in West Virginia."

"That may be. But in ten seconds you will be dead here on the carpet, if you do not lower the weapon, and that will be a worse death."

Rook said, "Probably."

Then Doyle spoke.

I had not expected this. I do not think anyone in the room had.

"Pavel." He said it in Russian first, then in English. "If you lower your weapon, I will lower mine. We will both go with them. I will testify. I will testify that I was the handler. I will testify that you were my asset. I will testify that I coerced you. You will go to West Virginia, but you will be out in eighteen months. You have my word. Do not take the shot."

Rook's eyes shifted to Doyle for the first time.

"Your word, Martin."

"My word, Pavel."

Rook said, very quietly, "Your word is why we are here."

Then he shifted his grip.

He did not shoot Doyle.

He shifted the Makarov a quarter-inch — a small, conspicuous shift, designed to be read — and began to lower the barrel toward the floor. He did it slowly. He did it in the specific way a man lowers a weapon when he wants the agents aiming at him to understand that he is complying.

Mwangi said, "Good. Now set the weapon on the desk."

Rook took a step toward the desk.

He was closer to me than to Doyle now. He was also — I realized, one full second too late — closer to the CUSTODIAL door than he had been when he entered the room, which was the door he had come through, which was the door that was still unlatched, still not fully closed.

He set the Makarov on the desk.

He put his hands up.

"I am unarmed."

"Move to the east wall, Pavel. Face the wall. Put your hands on the wall."

Rook began to move.

He took three steps.

On the third step he pivoted and went through the CUSTODIAL door in one motion — it swung open at a touch, still unlatched — and he was gone before either of the two FBI agents had finished cycling their trigger fingers.

Mwangi said, "*Fuck.*"

She turned to the agent on her left: "Go. CUSTODIAL door. Thirty feet at most."

The agent went through. I heard it on the other side — footsteps on concrete, fast, then a door slam, then a second door, further, and then nothing for a long time. Mwangi processed the arrest scene without asking. She had Doyle, the decoy in the reader, the room. She worked.

Ninety seconds later the door opened again. The agent stood in the frame.

"He's gone. Service corridor to the loading dock. Fire exit to East Boulevard. He had a car on the street."

"Plates."

"Running them now."

She nodded once. The agent moved back to the room.

Doyle — still holding his weapon at his hip, pointed at the floor — was looking at the CUSTODIAL door. His face had, over the preceding twenty seconds, done a number of things I would spend a long time afterward trying to fully decode. What it had arrived at now was a specific kind of stillness. Not calm. Not resignation. The stillness of a man who had understood, with precision, that his best remaining option was a federal prison, and who was in the process of deciding to accept this.

Mwangi turned her Glock toward him.

"Martin."

"Yes, Claire."

"Put the weapon on the desk."

After a beat, he lifted his pistol slowly to the desk and set it down.

"On your knees. Hands behind your head."

He went to his knees. He put his hands behind his head. His silver pocket square was still in his breast pocket, still precisely folded. Somehow this was the detail that lodged.

The agent moved to cuff him.

Mwangi turned to me.

"Mr. Novak. Are you hit."

"No."

"Are you hurt."

"My ribs. From before. Not from this."

"Sit down."

I sat in the guest chair. It was the first thing I had done under my own direction in forty seconds and it required specific effort.

Mwangi looked at the microfiche reader on the desk. She looked at the Mylar. She looked at Doyle.

"Martin. You are under arrest for violations of the Espionage Act of 1917, under specific statutory authorities I will read to you when I have time. You will be arraigned in Cleveland federal court on Monday morning. If you cooperate between now and Monday, the U.S. Attorney will take that into consideration. If you do not, they will not. Do you understand."

Doyle — on his knees, cuffed, looking up at her — said, "Claire."

"Yes."

"I underestimated you."

"Most people do."

"I am sorry."

"No, you aren't."

"I am."

Mwangi did not answer.

The agent finished with the cuffs.

Mwangi turned to me again.

"Mr. Novak. Miss Russo."

"Yes."

"HRT breached the warehouse at 7:46 PM. Miss Russo was extracted at 7:51. She is unharmed. She was, at the time of the extraction, holding a belt she had taken off one of the guards and demonstrating a specific knot to Agent Valdez."

I put my face in my hands.

Mwangi said nothing for ten seconds. Then:

"Mr. Novak."

"Yes."

"She is in a vehicle on Euclid Avenue right now. She will be at a safe house in Rocky River in fourteen minutes. I will personally drive you there as soon as we have processed this scene."

"Yes."

"Good."

I looked up.

Doyle was being walked out through the STAFF ONLY door by the remaining agent. He did not look at me as he passed. His hands were cuffed behind him. His pocket square was still in place.

Rook was gone. Somewhere across East Boulevard by now, moving south through the Fine Arts Garden toward a car on a side street, toward a highway, toward an airport, toward a sequence of flights and aliases and backstop infrastructure that had been constituted for exactly this night, because Rook had been preparing for exactly this night, and because preparation was the one thing about Pavel Yegorov that nobody on our side had fully accounted for. We would not see him again. We understood this, in the docent's office, without saying it.

Mwangi holstered her Glock.

She turned to me.

"Mr. Novak, you did well."

"Okay."

"I am going to ask you to sit here for ten minutes while we finish processing. Then we go to Rocky River. Is that all right."

"Yes."

"Do you want Dr. Hayes."

"Yes."

"I will get her."

She turned to leave. At the door she paused.

"Mr. Novak."

"Yes."

"You have, in the last twenty-one days, done something that roughly fifteen people in the history of American counterintelligence have done. I want you to know that. It matters to me that you know that."

"Okay."

"Breathe."

She left.

I sat in the guest chair of a docent's office on the second floor of the Cleveland Museum of Art, and I breathed, and I thought about my girlfriend on Euclid Avenue, alive, explaining a knot to an FBI agent. Through two closed doors, from the rotunda two galleries away, the sound of a string quartet playing Debussy arrived as a murmur, muffled and formal and perfectly indifferent to what had happened in this room.

I breathed.

The amber light on the microfiche reader had gone dark.

I breathed.

TWENTY-SEVEN: *Parallel: The Warehouse*

Most of this chapter belongs to Frankie.

I was not in the warehouse on Euclid during any of the preceding week, and I was not in the warehouse during the events I am about to describe, and I am therefore going to tell it the way she told it to me — in pieces, over ten days of debrief, with a final complete version she delivered, in a monotone, on a Tuesday morning in Rocky River with a cup of coffee in her hand and a bandage over her left temple. I have stitched her pieces together and put them in the order she put them in, and I have used, where possible, her words. What follows is hers. I am only the one retelling it.

Frankie woke up on concrete.

She did not know, at first, where she was. The lights were off. Her wrists were cuffed behind her. There was a rolled blanket under her head that had been put there by somebody who wanted her alive, which was — she thought immediately — useful information. Her shoulder hurt in a specific way she recognized as the after-pattern of a Taser shock. Her left pinky, when she tried to move it, was broken. She pulled the rest of her fingers. They moved. That was something.

She did not try to sit up. She listened.

She could hear two men talking in a room next to hers. Not close. Maybe fifteen feet. They were speaking Russian, and they were speaking the specific casual Russian of men who had been colleagues for a long time and who were not performing. She understood maybe one word in four — her Russian was weak, had always been weak, had not gotten better since 1990. But she picked up specific words. *Nokia. Lee Road. Ostrowski.* And, twice, the word *wife.*

They thought she was his wife.

This was, she thought, going to be useful later.

She kept her eyes closed.

After a while the voices moved further away. There were footsteps on concrete. A door opened somewhere. A door closed. The space outside her room went quiet, but not empty — there was still a presence, at least one man, walking the kind of short pacing patrol that a man on duty walked when he was bored.

She opened her eyes.

She was in a small office. No windows. A steel desk against one wall. A folding chair. A gooseneck lamp that was off. A fluorescent overhead fixture that was also off — the only light in the room was a thin yellow bar coming in under the door from whatever was on the other side. The floor was concrete painted grey. There was a drain in the middle of the floor, which she filed away as information.

Her tool bag was gone.

The pill bottle for Ramona was also gone, which she was, in that moment, specifically sad about.

She worked her wrists.

The cuffs were standard police cuffs — the kind you could pick with a bobby pin, if you had a bobby pin, which she did not. She did have, in her left hip pocket, a small brass wire from the porch lamp repair she had been doing at Vera's that morning, which she had folded over and dropped in her pocket before she had gone out the door. She worked it out with her fingers. It took nine minutes. She did not rush.

She folded the brass wire against the seam of her jeans. She bent the tip. She worked it into the cuff's keyhole.

She got the cuffs off in, she estimated, thirty-five seconds.

She did not take them off.

She reached her hands back behind her and she held the cuffs loosely in place, one wrist slightly rotated, so that a cursory inspection would show them still cuffed. She closed her eyes again.

She had, at that point, been in the warehouse approximately four hours.

She was going to be there six more days.

They came in to check on her at 6:02 PM on Saturday night, which was — she would learn later — approximately four hours before Theo heard the Nokia ring on the pillow at Vera's in Parma.

The man who came in was short, wide, and carried a Glock 17 at his hip in a paddle holster. He was in his mid-forties. He had a face Frankie had seen on the back stairs of the half-double, which meant he was the third man, the Taser man, the one who had actually put her down.

She would later learn his name was Grigory Kostenko. He was the warehouse's owner. He was also, in a very local and specific sense, the Cleveland Bratva's top officer. He had worked his way up through Rocky River and Brook Park scrap-metal rackets in the eighties. He had not been trained. He was not, in the professional sense, a spy. He was a man who had been paid, specifically, to keep Miss Russo alive and contained for approximately a week, and he intended to do that, and he did not intend to do anything more than that.

He did not speak to her.

He set a paper plate on the floor by her feet. On the plate was a pierogi, a small wedge of cheese, and a chunk of hard bread. Beside the plate he set a plastic bottle of water.

He turned around and walked out.

He closed the door. He locked it from outside.

Frankie did not move for two minutes.

Then she sat up slowly — her ribs did not hurt, but her shoulder did — and she ate the pierogi in four bites. She ate the cheese. She ate the bread.

She drank half the water. She set the other half of the water aside, on top of the desk, because she had been in exactly this kind of situation twice before, in training exercises at Fort Huachuca in 1989, and one of the things you had learned at Huachuca was that captivity was a long game and that the thing you had the most of was time, and the thing you had the least of was water, and that the specific ratio of those two things was what separated people who got out from people who did not.

She lay back down. She cuffed herself again. She made it look convincing. She closed her eyes.

She began to count her heartbeats. It was a trick she had been taught at Lindsey — counting heartbeats was a way of imposing a specific internal rhythm on an external situation you could not control. It was a way of keeping the mind, over time, from breaking.

She counted heartbeats for six days.

She noticed things.

She noticed that meals came at 7 AM, 1 PM, and 7 PM, and that between meals, one of three men was on patrol outside her door. She noticed that the patrol rotated every four hours. She noticed that the 3 AM to 7 AM shift was held down by the youngest of the three men, a thin tall nervous man who — she could tell by the sound of his footsteps — fell asleep in his chair around 5 AM almost every night.

She noticed the second guard — the middle-aged one who had, she thought, been the man with the Taser at the front stairs of the half-double — was the most dangerous of the three. He paced. He did not sleep. He checked on her every ninety minutes, opened the door, shined a flashlight at her, closed the door, locked it again.

She noticed that the third guard — Grigory, the boss — did the morning shift, and that he was generally not present between 11 AM and 4 PM, when he was, apparently, managing whatever legitimate or illegitimate business the warehouse was the cover for.

She noticed that her Nokia — the real one, her own, that had been in her tool bag — was now being used by a fourth man she had not seen, who was in an office two rooms over, and who made short calls in English from it at irregular intervals. She could not hear the words. She could hear the cadence. The cadence was the cadence of a man delivering status updates. She assumed that was Rook.

She was right.

On the third day Rook brought a fifth Nokia into her room.

He came in wearing a grey windbreaker. He was her height. He looked — in the low light of her small concrete room — exactly the way she remembered him from the hallway of the half-double, which was to say, like a tired, underfed, competent professional. He set the fifth Nokia on the desk.

He said, in English, "Miss Russo."

Frankie did not say anything. Her eyes were half-open. She was still, operationally, a woman who had been Tasered twice and cuffed for three days and who had no reason to be responsive.

"In a few minutes," Rook said, "you are going to have a telephone conversation with Mr. Novak. The conversation will last approximately ten seconds. You will tell him you are unhurt. You will not give him information about your location, your holding conditions, your physical state, the building, the men who are holding you, or any aspect of this situation. You will tell him you are alive and then you will say goodbye. If you deviate from this, you will be shot immediately, and Mr. Novak will listen to you being shot. Do you understand."

She nodded, slightly.

"Say it."

"I understand."

"Good."

He set the Nokia on the desk.

He dialed a number. He held the phone to his own ear. He spoke briefly in English. Then he held the phone down to her.

She was still on the floor. Her hands were still cuffed behind her, as far as he knew. He held the phone to her ear with his own hand.

She said, "Theo."

And then, with Rook's hand on the phone and his eyes on her face and his other hand on the grip of the Makarov at his hip, she composed a sentence — on the fly, in eight seconds — that was going to tell her boyfriend nine specific things at once, of which *she was alive* was the least important.

She said, "Hey. Listen. Tell Dr. Hayes — tell her Mrs. Nabokov is still biting."

She said it with exactly the intonation she had used to tell him on Tuesday of her first week at Dr. Hayes's that Mrs. Nabokov had bitten her twice that day. It was a rhythm he would know. It was a cat nobody outside Dr. Hayes's house had heard of. It was a private reference. It was a message.

I am not drugged. I am not coerced. I have my wits. I am able to plan my own sentences in advance and deliver them cleanly. I remember the cat. I remember who you are. I am alive. I love you. I am coming home.

She said all of it in nine words.

Rook pulled the phone away.

"You have thirty seconds."

"I love you, Theo."

"I love you, Frankie."

Rook ended the call.

He looked at her for a beat.

He said, "Mrs. Nabokov."

"A cat."

"A cat."

"Just a cat."

Rook held her eyes for another three seconds.

Then he turned around. He walked out. He closed the door. He locked it.

She exhaled.

She had not, she realized, been breathing for the full ten seconds.

She cuffed herself again.

On the morning of the sixth day — which was Saturday, which was the day of the museum — Frankie made her move.

She had, by that point, worn down a specific corner of the left cuff with the brass wire until the locking mechanism would release with a single upward pressure from her thumb. She could shed the cuffs in about a second and a half. She had been eating half her meals, to keep her stomach empty for exertion. She had been doing isometric exercises — tension against the cuffs, tension against the floor — for twenty minutes at a stretch, three times a day, when nobody was watching. Her shoulder was no longer on fire. Her pinky had set crookedly but was functional. She had, in her back pocket, a six-inch piece of metal shelf bracket that she had found under the desk on the second day and had worked loose and pocketed on the fourth.

At 6:47 PM — not coincidentally, the moment the Cleveland Museum of Art donor preview was officially opening its doors — Grigory opened her door to deliver her evening meal.

He was in the middle of the same routine he had performed twenty-two times in the preceding six days. Paper plate. Plastic water. Step in, crouch, set it on the floor. Step out. Close the door.

He crouched.

Frankie came off the floor in one motion.

She had been sitting, not lying, for the last ten minutes. She had oriented herself toward the door. She had rehearsed this in her head approximately four hundred times. She went up through her knees into her hips and into her shoulder, and she drove her shoulder into his sternum at the full extension of her legs. He was wider and heavier than she was, but he was crouching, and his weight was badly distributed, and she had all of her body's momentum and six days of anger behind her. He went backward. His head hit the concrete of the back office floor. He did not hit it hard enough to kill him. He did hit it hard enough to stop him from getting up for a while.

She took the Glock from his paddle holster. She knew the Glock. Her Army SIG had been built on the same basic principles. She checked the chamber. There was a round. She thumbed off the external safety that a Glock technically did not have but that the owner had added via an aftermarket modification, which was the kind of modification an amateur made. She crossed the room to the door. She stepped out.

The second guard — the middle-aged Taser man — was in the corridor, four feet from the door, turning toward her with his own Glock coming out of its holster. He was fast. He was not fast enough.

She did not shoot him.

She was five-nine and he was her height and he was mid-motion, and she had two things he did not have, which were a fully-drawn weapon and the specific element of surprise. She put the barrel of the Glock against the back of his right hand, hard, and she said, in clear English, "Let it go."

He did.

The Glock clattered on concrete.

She stepped into his chest. She took his right shoulder in her left hand and she rotated his body ninety degrees and she walked him backward into the wall.

The grip woke the pinky.

The crooked-set bone shifted against itself — not a snap, something worse than a snap, a grinding realignment that sent a specific white light from the knuckle up through her wrist and her forearm to her shoulder and did not stop. She registered it. She filed it. She did not stop.

She rotated his right arm up behind him, past the point of normal range, to the point the specific feature of the shoulder socket said *no, past here I will not go.* She went past there. She heard the specific sound of a dislocation. He made a sound she would later describe, to me, as *the exact sound I used to make when I would hit my thumb with a hammer, but longer.*

He slid down the wall.

He did not get up. He cried quietly. He was still crying when a third man came up the corridor at a run.

The third man — the thin tall nervous one, the 3 AM to 7 AM shift sleeper, who had been outside smoking and who had heard the commotion — arrived with a pistol half-drawn. Frankie held the Glock at her side. She did not raise it. She pointed with her left hand, which was empty and which she did not, at that moment, look at.

"Belt."

He looked at her.

"Off. Slowly."

He complied.

She had him tie his own wrists together with his belt, in a specific half-hitch she had taught a corporal at Lindsey in 1989. She had him kneel facing the wall. She took his wallet out of his back pocket. She held it open.

The name first. She committed it. Then she turned to the address — his actual address, a block number, an apartment —

The warehouse's east loading bay door exploded inward at 7:46 PM.

The first FBI Hostage Rescue Team agent through the door was Agent Valdez.

He was in full tactical kit. He had a Heckler & Koch MP5 raised. He was in the specific low, fast posture of a man who had entered a hundred buildings and had every expectation of engaging within three seconds.

He did not engage.

He stopped.

Behind him, four other HRT agents cleared through the door and fanned. All of them stopped.

In the corridor of the warehouse's main floor, the view they had was of one short wide unconscious man in a small back office, face down, blood on the concrete from a cut on his scalp; of one middle-aged man slumped against the corridor wall crying quietly with his right arm hanging in a way a human arm is not supposed to hang; and of one thin tall man in his thirties, kneeling, facing the wall, with his wrists secured behind him in a half-hitch with his own belt.

And one woman in her thirties, five-foot-nine, in dirty jeans and a green work shirt, with dark curly hair falling out of what had once been a red bandana, holding a Glock at her side and a wallet in her other hand.

She looked up.

She looked at Valdez.

Valdez did not lower the MP5 immediately. He took a beat. He was looking at the tableau. He was, he would later tell Mwangi, trying to figure out how to write this in his after-action report.

Frankie held up the Glock by its barrel. She turned the grip toward him.

"Agent Valdez?"

"Yes, ma'am."

"Francesca Russo."

"Ma'am."

"Took you long enough."

She handed him the Glock. She held up the wallet.

"The address on this driver's license. What's the street."

Valdez took the wallet. He read it.

"West 55th and Madison. Apartment 3B. Brick four-flat on the corner."

"West 55th." She nodded once. "The ringleader is in a green Caprice on that block, plate RVG-4082. His name is on that same card. The apartment will have Nokia intercept logs on him. You will find, also, photographs of what they considered a kidnapping operation worth taking photographs of, because they are, Agent Valdez, profoundly unprofessional people."

Valdez said, "Yes, ma'am."

"I would also like an ibuprofen. And a pair of shoes that are not these shoes. And a telephone."

"We can do all three."

"In that order."

"In that order, ma'am."

She walked past him. Out of the corridor. Toward the breached door. Toward Lake Erie, which was, at 7:51 PM on September seventh, 1996, a dark line just visible to the north over the top of the warehouse.

TWENTY-EIGHT: *Rocky River*

I sat in the guest chair of the docent's office for twenty-two minutes.

I know it was twenty-two because I watched the second hand of the clock on the wall above the corkboard make twenty-two full revolutions, and I watched it with the specific focused attention of a person who needs something to do with their eyes. The room had been cleared. Doyle was gone. The Makarov was gone. The microfiche reader was still on the desk, open, amber light extinguished, the empty Mylar envelope beside it. The docent's September schedule was still on the corkboard. Nobody had thought to take it down. It said, in a volunteer's careful handwriting, that Saturday nights were covered through the end of the month.

Dr. Hayes came to the doorway.

She had been, I learned later, standing in the corridor of the Pharaoh Gallery the entire time. She had held her position — which was the position Mwangi had asked her to hold, because having an unbadged civilian inside the docent's office during a federal arrest was, operationally, a problem. Dr. Hayes had compromised. She had stood eight feet from the STAFF ONLY door and she had not moved.

She came in now.

She looked at me. She looked at the reader on the desk. She looked at the spot on the floor where Doyle had gone to his knees. She took in the room in one slow circle of her head, the way she took in every room, cataloguing before speaking.

"Mr. Novak."

"Yes."

"Miss Russo is safe."

"Yes."

"You are going to see her in approximately forty minutes."

"Yes."

"Are you able to stand."

"Yes."

"Then stand. Agent Mwangi will drive us."

I stood. My ribs hurt. The tuxedo hurt. Everything hurt in the specific way that things hurt when the adrenaline has been metabolized and the body has decided it is now safe to file its complaints.

Dr. Hayes took my elbow — not to support me, which was Frankie's move; to steady me, which was Dr. Hayes's move. We walked together out of the docent's office, through the Pharaoh Gallery, through the Armor Court — where, I noticed, the three long benches had been emptied of pamphlets, the pamphlets having been collected by a docent ten minutes earlier as the evening's preview shifted toward the Van Gogh rooms and away from medieval armor. We moved through the rotunda. The preview was still going. A string quartet in the corner was still playing Debussy. A hundred and twenty donors were still holding champagne flutes and talking about art and about money. Nobody in the rotunda knew that anything had happened.

This had been the point.

The point had been that nobody would know.

We exited through a staff door on the west side of the building. Mwangi was waiting in the silver Ford Escort rental with the engine running and her badge already off her neck.

I got in the back. Dr. Hayes got in the front passenger seat.

Mwangi drove.

Rocky River was west of downtown, along the lake, in the shadow of the Clifton Boulevard trestle bridge — the kind of inner-ring suburb that had been wealthy in 1920 and was still wealthy, more quietly, in 1996. Big brick houses on narrow lots, mature maples over the sidewalks, lake frontage for the twelve or fifteen properties that could afford it.

The FBI safe house was one of these: a two-story colonial with pale green shutters, set back from the road behind a maple that was just beginning to turn, with a brick drive that curved around behind the house and opened into a small private parking court.

We pulled in at 9:03 PM.

Mwangi parked on the brick drive rather than in the court. Pointed out, engine accessible. I would later understand this as part of a specific discipline — in a safe house, the vehicle was always positioned for fast egress. I filed it without asking.

She killed the engine. She turned in the driver's seat.

"Mr. Novak. The Bureau physician will arrive in approximately twenty minutes. Miss Russo has agreed to be seen tonight. She has a broken finger, a bruised shoulder, and a mild concussion from the second Taser shock she sustained six days ago, and she received nothing in the warehouse beyond what she specifically requested, which was ibuprofen. You will see her before the physician does. Fifteen minutes. Then I will need you to step out of the room."

"Okay."

"After the physician, I will leave for the night. I will return at two AM. We will go to the field office for a full debrief. Get some sleep if you can. There is food inside."

"Okay."

She got out. Dr. Hayes got out. I got out, slowly.

We walked up to the back door. Mwangi knocked twice, a pause, twice more. A woman in tactical gear — not Valdez, a different agent, maybe forty, short grey bob, the specific unhurried alertness of somebody three hours into a four-hour shift — nodded and stepped aside. We went in.

Frankie was sitting on a green couch in the front parlor.

She was wearing a Cleveland Indians t-shirt that was four sizes too big for her — I would learn later that an HRT agent named Torres had offered it off his own back in the warehouse, which was either a gesture of operational courtesy or the kind of thing that happened when a woman handed you a Glock and said *took you long enough* — and a pair of men's jeans rolled up at the cuffs. She had a blanket over her shoulders. She had a bandaged left pinky. She had a fresh white bandage over her left temple where, I would also learn later, the first Taser electrode had caught skin on the way down the back stairs. She had a paper plate in her lap with a donut on it she was not eating, and a mug of coffee on the end table beside her, from which she was drinking.

Her dark hair was washed.

Her hair was washed.

I don't know why that registered first. Probably because I had spent six days carrying a mental image of her in a warehouse, and somebody at the safe house had given her ten minutes with a shower and a bar of soap, and her hair was washed. She looked — in her own specific way, with the bandages and the rolled cuffs and the oversized shirt — like herself. Not a version of herself. Not a diminished or frightened or recovered version. Herself.

She looked up when we came in.

She set the mug down.

She did not stand, and I was grateful, because I had been dreading the standing — the moment of recalibrating our heights and the familiar geometry of us — and it would have undone me. Instead she was on the couch and I was crossing the parlor toward her and then I was not walking anymore, I was dropping — not sitting, *dropping* — to my knees next to the couch, with my hands finding her hands, looking up at her face from below because she was above me and I didn't care, and I could not speak for a while because I was not going to be able to.

She put her hand on the back of my head.

"Hi."

"Hi."

"You're in a tuxedo."

"Yeah."

"It's very tight."

"Yeah."

"I like it."

"It was Harout."

"Harout came through."

"Yeah."

"I knew he would."

We didn't say anything else for a while after that.

Her thumb was moving in slow circles along my scalp. She had been doing this since the first time she had ever done it, which was in my apartment in 1994, the September I had carried a stress headache for nine days straight, and she had sat behind me on the couch and pressed her thumb against the base of my skull without asking and the headache had broken in about four minutes. Her thumb moved now the way it had moved then. I understood, feeling it, that whatever had happened in that warehouse had not reached her hands. Her hands remembered what they were. They remembered what I was.

She said, quietly, "Theo."

"Yeah."

"I want to sit on this couch with you for about five hours."

"Yeah."

"And then I want to eat a steak."

"Okay."

"And I want to take four weeks off from everything."

"Okay."

"And then I want to go to Hocking Hills again."

"Okay."

"And bring Ramona."

"Yeah."

"And not put her in the carrier the whole drive."

"Okay."

"She needs her medication, though."

"Yeah. We'll get it."

"Did you get it."

"No. We didn't have time."

"I had it," Frankie said. "In the tool bag. They threw it out."

"Okay."

"I'm sorry."

"It's okay. We'll get another prescription."

"Okay."

"Frankie."

"Yeah."

"You're okay."

"I'm okay, Theo. I'm really okay."

"Okay."

I put my face against her knee. She kept moving her thumb.

The Bureau physician was a quiet man named Dr. Ellison who worked with the specific economy of someone who had done this before — seen people in safe houses after operations, in borrowed clothes, with fresh bandages and old adrenaline — and who asked only what he needed to ask and said only what he needed to say. He confirmed the pinky, noted the mild concussion, gave the bruised shoulder thirty seconds of careful attention, and prescribed nothing beyond rest and the ibuprofen already on the end table. He was in and out in twenty minutes. He shook Frankie's good hand on his way out and said, with a formality that seemed genuine rather than clinical, *Very glad you're here, Miss Russo.* She said, *Thank you, Doctor.* The door closed. The agent with the grey bob was somewhere toward the back of the house. Mwangi had gone to make calls.

We were alone for the first time since the morning Frankie had left for Cedar-Fairmount with the cat's medication in her tool bag and had not come back.

She had moved to the wingback armchair in the corner. I had moved from the floor to the couch. The blanket had traveled with her, and then back to me in a loose compromise that left both of us partially covered and neither of us cold. The parlor was quiet. Through the front window the maple at the end of the drive was a dark shape against the slightly less dark sky.

"Tell me something that happened," she said.

I thought about it.

"The tuxedo was Harout's. He was twelve minutes late with the alterations."

"I know that part."

"The fern is alive."

She was quiet for a moment.

"Good," she said. "I always hated that pothos."

I laughed. It came out larger than I expected. She smiled — the first real one, the kind that reached her eyes — and I understood, watching it, that I had been waiting for it without telling myself I was waiting for it. The smile landed and something in my chest that had been held at a specific tension for twenty-seven days let go about a quarter of an inch.

We sat.

At 1:40 AM Mwangi knocked twice and came in.

The FBI Cleveland field office was on Lakeside Avenue, nine blocks from Mwangi's Escort at the Marriott Key Center — a fact I noted, in my current state of two hours of shallow sleep and cracked ribs, as specifically unfunny. The building was ugly in the way federal buildings from the 1970s were ugly: brick box, government furniture that had not been refreshed since the Carter administration, fluorescent lighting in tubes that hummed at a frequency just below conscious notice. The conference room had a long veneer table, ten chairs, one window looking out at the back of an adjacent office building, and the institutional smell of carpet that had been steam-cleaned too many times.

We were at the table at 2:14 AM. Dr. Hayes. Frankie. Me. Mwangi.

On the table: four cups of coffee. A box of donuts from a shop in Rocky River that had opened at midnight for Mwangi, who had called ahead. A folder two inches thick. A single Mylar envelope containing the MEADOWLARK microfiche in a clear plastic evidence sleeve. Dr. Hayes's *Plain Dealer.*

On the ride in, Dr. Hayes had asked Mwangi to stop somewhere that sold the Sunday paper, because she wanted to do the crossword. Mwangi had stopped at a twenty-four-hour Convenient on Cedar. Dr. Hayes had bought the paper, unfolded it to the back page, and had been working the puzzle ever since — in ink, with the mechanical pencil she apparently kept in her cardigan pocket at all times, which I recognized as the same pencil she had used to write twelve numbered items on a red notebook at her kitchen table on a Sunday morning that now felt like a different century.

She was halfway through.

Mwangi opened the folder.

"All right," she said. "Here is where we are."

Frankie reached for a donut. She had already eaten the one she had not eaten in Rocky River. She took a second, a jelly, and bit into it. A small smear of strawberry landed on the bandage over her temple. I would wipe it off two hours later with my own thumb, because she would have forgotten it was there.

"Forty-three of the forty-seven names on the MEADOWLARK list are currently in federal custody," Mwangi said. "Martin Doyle was transferred from Cleveland station lockup to Quantico four hours ago. He has asked for his attorney and has not been forthcoming since, which is consistent with his training and which is not, at this point, our problem."

She turned a page.

"Galen Brennan was arrested at his home in Euclid at nine-forty PM. He cooperated at the door. He did not resist. He asked to kiss his wife. He was permitted. His wife did not cry."

She said it plainly, without commentary.

I said nothing.

I had not known, when I was thinking about Galen's face at the Lucky Star Diner — the two expressions in one second, the decision not to save me that had lived in his eyes — what those expressions were going to cost him. I knew now. I did not speak. There was nothing useful to say about it.

"Three of the forty-seven are dead," Mwangi continued. "Larry Acheson at TRW was found at his home at seven-oh-two PM, a single gunshot to the temple. His wife was at a community-theater dress rehearsal. Timothy Winstead at Battelle in Columbus was found in his garage at six-twenty-eight. Also a gunshot. Carlos Menendez at NASA Glenn was found at seven-fifteen in a parking garage on Brookpark Road. Gunshot."

"Three cleanups," Frankie said.

"Three cleanups. Twelve-minute window. Rook was occupied this evening."

I said, "Where is Rook now."

Mwangi paused — not to collect her thoughts, I understood, but to give me a second to prepare for the answer.

"Rook is not in custody," she said. "We have confirmed that a 1995 Ford Crown Victoria with Ohio plate 1RVR-412 was abandoned at Hopkins airport long-term parking at eight-fifty-four PM. A man fitting his description purchased a cash ticket on a Southwest Airlines flight to Las Vegas at nine-eleven. The flight departed at nine-forty-eight. Las

Vegas is a transfer point. An individual fitting his description purchased, at one-seventeen AM local time, a ticket to Miami on a different carrier, under a different name. From Miami, we do not know. We lose him, at this point, in what we assume is a backstop infrastructure specifically constituted for this contingency."

"He's in Moscow by tomorrow night," Dr. Hayes said, without looking up from the crossword.

"That is my assessment also, Lorraine."

The room absorbed this.

Rook was gone. He had been in the docent's office two hours ago and now he was an airplane over the Gulf of Mexico and in twenty-four hours he would be in a city we could not reach him in, and the three men he had shot in a twelve-minute window were dead in their garages and their parking lots and their homes, and the specific mathematics of the evening added up to forty-three accounted for, three eliminated, one escaped, and one unknown.

"One missing," Dr. Hayes said.

"One missing, yes."

"Which name." She turned a page of the crossword without looking up. "On the list, I mean. Which of the forty-seven is the one we haven't accounted for."

Mwangi closed the folder.

"That, Lorraine, is the question I cannot answer tonight."

"Claire."

"I know. I was given very specific guidance at eleven-forty-two PM by a woman in Washington who I am, for the foreseeable future, not going to disobey. The identity of the remaining MEADOWLARK subject is redacted even from my eyes at this point. It is under investigation by a compartment constituted specifically for it. I will know when they decide to tell me. I will tell you when they tell me. That is all I have."

Dr. Hayes set the pencil down.

She had been doing the crossword in a way that had, I realized now, functioned as a kind of listening posture — the pen moving as a metronome for her attention, giving the rest of us space to speak while she processed. When she put it down she was no longer processing. She had arrived somewhere.

"It has to do with the daughter," she said.

Mwangi did not answer.

"Claire."

"I cannot comment, Lorraine."

"It has to do with the daughter."

"I cannot comment."

I had been told nothing about a daughter. I had not, in any conversation with Dr. Hayes in the preceding three weeks, heard the word in connection with the operation. Frankie was looking between them with an expression that was careful and asking.

Dr. Hayes looked at us. She made a small visible decision — the kind that involved a deliberate loosening of the set of her jaw.

"Mr. Novak," she said, "there is one thing I have kept from you. Not out of secrecy. Out of what I hoped was a kindness, and what I am no longer willing to pretend is a kindness. It has to do with an aspect of the Ostrowskis' life that is not on the microfiche. I am going to explain it to you next Saturday, when we drive together to Society National Bank on Public Square to retrieve the contents of safety deposit box one-one-four-seven. The key you found with the microfiche is that key. The box belongs to Mikael Ostrowski. I have obtained, through Agent Mwangi, the legal authorization to open it. It will be opened on Saturday, September fourteenth, at ten AM. You and I will go together. We will be the ones to examine what is inside."

"Okay."

"We will talk about the daughter then. Is that acceptable."

"Yes."

"Thank you."

She picked up the pencil. She resumed the crossword. She worked it for a minute in the silence that followed, the pencil moving in its small precise flicks, and the fluorescent lights hummed their one note, and Frankie finished the donut.

Mwangi said, after a moment, "Twenty-three across."

Dr. Hayes glanced up.

"Yes."

"Nine letters. *Wartime subterfuge.*"

Dr. Hayes said, "*Deception.*"

"*Deception* is nine letters."

"Yes."

"That fits."

"Yes, Claire."

"Thank you."

Mwangi wrote it in her own copy of the *Plain Dealer,* which she had also bought at the Convenient on Cedar, which I would not have expected, and which was a detail I would remember for years — the two women at opposite ends of a conference table, at three in the morning, in a room that smelled of old carpet and fresh coffee, working the same puzzle.

Frankie finished the second donut.

She looked at me.

"Can we go home now."

"Frankie, we don't —"

"I mean to Rocky River. The house."

"Yeah. Yeah, we can go home to Rocky River."

Mwangi said, "I'll drive you."

Dr. Hayes did not look up.

She said, "I am going to finish this crossword first."

"Take your time, Lorraine."

"I intend to."

Outside, on Lakeside Avenue, the first grey edge of Sunday was beginning to come up over the lake. It was not yet light. It was the color that precedes light — the specific dark that knows it is losing. The Terminal Tower was a shape against it, and somewhere west of it, along the water, a two-story colonial with pale green shutters was waiting for us with an unlocked back door and a Bureau cook named Theresa who would, in three hours, make a Midwest meatloaf that would become, for both of us, the taste of the specific year in which we learned that coming home was a thing you had to earn, and that the earning was not the worst part.

Dr. Hayes turned a page.

She kept writing.

We waited.

TWENTY-NINE: *Box 1147*

One week later, on Saturday morning the fourteenth of September, Dr. Hayes picked me up from the Rocky River safe house at nine-fifteen AM.

The week between had been — unreal is not the right word. It had been *thin*. The days had felt thin. Frankie and I had slept a great deal. We had watched bad television on a small color TV in the front parlor. We had eaten meals prepared by a Bureau cook named Theresa who had, we learned, been assigned to the safe house since 1992, and who did not inquire about the identities of her guests, and who made a very specific kind of Midwest meatloaf that would, for both Frankie and me, become thereafter the taste of recovery. Ramona had been brought to us from Vera's by Mwangi on Monday morning. She had not yowled. She had looked at the parlor of the Rocky River safe house with the exact expression she had given the living room of the half-double the first time she had seen it in 1994, which was the expression of a cat who had decided she could work with this.

Frankie had slept eleven hours a night for five nights.

I had slept seven.

I had spent the other four hours, most nights, sitting in the bay window of the guest bedroom with Ramona on my lap, looking out at Lake Erie, which at three in the morning was a matte black surface against a charcoal sky with the specific faint orange glow of Cleveland coming up over the east horizon.

On Saturday morning I was ready.

Dr. Hayes was in a navy cardigan and a pair of grey slacks. She had her hair brushed. She was not in the black silk dress; that dress had been retired, she had told me on Tuesday, and had been returned to its garment bag on her hall closet rod, and was not going to be brought out again in her lifetime. We drove in her Volvo, which I had not previously known she owned — she did not drive much, she explained, because Cleveland was a walking city if you lived in the right neighborhood, but she kept the Volvo for occasions that required her specifically.

This was, she said, one of those occasions.

We drove east along the lake. We took I-90. We exited at East Ninth and circled back to Public Square.

Public Square was, in 1996, in the middle of a long slow transition that it had been in for twenty years and would remain in for twenty more — a central civic space with bank buildings on three sides and the Terminal Tower on the fourth, and with a statue of Tom L. Johnson in the middle of it, and with a pigeon population that was specifically its own. Society National Bank occupied the building at the northwest corner, which was a 1929 limestone tower with an ornate vaulted lobby and a vault on the basement level that, Dr. Hayes explained to me, dated from the building's original construction and had not been meaningfully updated since.

The key from the felt compartment of the sculpture said *1147* on its brass side.

We went inside.

The assistant bank manager who took us down to the vault was a woman in her fifties named Patricia, who had been expecting us, and who had a specific set of legal documents that Mwangi had prepared ready on a clipboard. Patricia verified Dr. Hayes's identification, which was not Dr. Hayes's identification — it was a federal document that authorized Dr. Hayes to access Box 1147 as the designated executor of an estate I would not, in that moment, have been told the name of. I signed as a witness. Patricia signed. We descended in a brass-paneled elevator to the basement.

The vault was a circular chamber lined floor to ceiling with brass-fronted safety deposit boxes of varying sizes. Box 1147 was on the east wall, second row from the floor, the size of a small brick. Patricia retrieved a second key from her own ring. She inserted her key. Dr. Hayes inserted the brass key from the sculpture. They turned the two keys in the specific synchronized way bank keys are turned.

The small brass door swung open.

Patricia stepped back.

"Take as long as you need. I will be outside. Please signal when you are ready."

She left. The vault door stayed open — Patricia stood outside it, professionally far, turned slightly away.

Dr. Hayes and I were alone in front of box 1147.

Dr. Hayes said, "Mr. Novak."

"Yes."

"You may reach in."

I reached in.

I felt, inside the box, a single object. It was heavier than I expected. It was small. My fingers closed around it. I drew it out.

It was a bronze sculpture.

It was four inches tall, three inches wide, approximately an inch and a half deep. It was by the same artist as the larger one I had carried in my left arm on a Sunday in August three weeks ago. It had the same roughness-meeting-patina surface, the same quality of hand-modeling, the same signature abstraction. It was a smaller version of the same study — the same upper figure, the same reclining lower form, but smaller, tighter, compressed into a desktop size. A maquette. An artist's study.

I turned it over.

On the bottom was a disk of dense wool felt, identical in material to the felt on the larger one. Adjacent to the felt, on the bronze edge, were two small sans-serif letters.

M. O.

And next to them, in Beck's original hand, her own small stamp.

Two signatures on the base of a smaller bronze.

My hands started to shake.

Dr. Hayes said, "Sit down, Mr. Novak."

There was no chair.

I sat on the floor of the Society National Bank vault.

Dr. Hayes sat down next to me. She was seventy-one years old. She sat on the floor of a bank vault with me without any visible difficulty. We sat side by side on the cold marble. She reached over and she took the sculpture gently out of my hands. She set it in her own lap. She took from her cardigan pocket the small jeweler's loupe she had used at the Shaker Lakes bench twenty-seven days ago.

She did not use it.

She used her fingers instead. She worked the felt edge with her thumbnail. The adhesive was old. It came up easily.

Underneath the felt was a thin circle of black foam.

Underneath the foam was a cavity.

Inside the cavity was a single folded piece of paper.

Dr. Hayes lifted it out. She unfolded it.

It was a photograph.

The photograph was color, four by six, faded. The edge had the specific serration of a photograph that had been developed at a Fotomat in the late 1970s. The back of the photograph was date-stamped, in red ink, *JULY 1979.*

The front of the photograph showed a small girl, about seven years old, standing on a patch of grass in front of a blue house. She had dark curly hair — curly like Frankie's, actually, although not the same shape. She was in a red-and-blue plaid dress with a white collar. She was squinting at the sun. She had a front tooth missing. Her mouth was slightly open. Her right hand was partway raised, as if she had been waving at the camera but had already stopped waving by the time the shutter clicked.

The back of the photograph had two lines of handwriting, in a careful sloping Italian-inflected cursive I knew.

Katya — safe. Minneapolis.

Protect her.

Dr. Hayes set the photograph down on the floor between us.

She put her hand over her mouth.

She did not cry — Dr. Hayes did not, in my experience of her, cry — but she did something that was adjacent to crying. She sat for a long time with her hand over her mouth and she looked at the photograph, and I looked at it, and neither of us spoke.

After about three minutes she took her hand away from her mouth.

She said, quietly, "Mr. Novak."

"Yes."

"The Ostrowskis had a biological daughter."

"Yes."

"She was born in Cleveland in 1972. They realized, in 1978, that their operational cover was compromised to a sufficient extent that keeping her would endanger her life. They placed her with an adoptive family in Minneapolis in 1979, using a network of extrajudicial channels I was — on the periphery of helping them set up. She was six years old. The adoption was closed. The records were sealed at levels that nobody could unseal. She was told, over the course of her growing up, that she had been given up by a single mother who had not been able to keep her. The adoptive family was told that she was the daughter of a young Polish immigrant couple who had died. She was renamed. She was, as of 1979, a different person."

"Okay."

"She was, however, alive. And the Ostrowskis kept a single photograph of her, taken a month before the adoption, in a safety deposit box in Cleveland."

"Yes."

"Her adoptive name — this was on a piece of paper Elena showed me once in 1984, in Milan, in a hotel room, after a bottle of wine I should not have finished — her adoptive name was Kate Bauer. She is, as of this year, twenty-four years old. She lives in Minneapolis. I do not know what she does. I do not know if she looks like her mother. I do not know if she remembers her first six years. I believe, based on things Elena said to me over the years, that she does not."

"Why are you telling me."

"Because the person who was on the fourth name of Mikael's original MEADOWLARK list — the one I have not told you about, the one that Mwangi could not tell me about, the one that is redacted at compartment — was not at TRW, was not at NASA, was not at any of the facilities we have been working against. She was at the University of Minnesota Hospital's biomedical research division. Her name, in the MEADOWLARK compilation, is *BAUER, K.* Not Kate Bauer. Katarina Bauer. But Kate Bauer was also, in an administrative sense, Katarina on her birth certificate. She was baptized Katarina. The name rolled over when the Minnesota adoption placed her. That is the name that was entered, in 1994, when she applied for the position she now holds."

"You're saying —"

"I am saying, Mr. Novak, that one of the forty-seven names on that microfiche is the biological daughter of the man who compiled it. I do not know whether Mikael knew. I do not know whether he compiled the list knowing she was on it. I do not know whether the list is why he was killed three days before he could pass it forward. I do not know whether Elena knew. I do not know any of that."

"Who's her handler."

"Unknown to me. That is a revelation for another day."

"Another day."

"It's a mindset I have, Mr. Novak. Claire and I relied on it two weeks ago. It means: there will certainly come a time when we know the whole truth, just not right now. That coming day will involve Minneapolis. That coming day will involve Katarina Bauer, whose name is on her biological father's list of Russian assets, and who does not know she was adopted, and who does not know she is the daughter of two CIA case officers, and who does not know that the last person to carry her photograph has just died of potassium chloride, and who does not know that a retired cryptanalyst on Lee Road in Cleveland Heights is about to make her the central problem of the rest of her life."

"Why."

"Because, Mr. Novak. Because I promised her mother, in a hotel room in Milan in 1984, that I would protect the daughter if anything ever happened to them. And something has now happened to them. And the daughter is alive. And on the back of this photograph is a specific instruction in Elena's handwriting that I owe an Italian art gallery owner who fed me too well for twelve years."

"*Protect her,*" I said.

"*Protect her,*" Dr. Hayes said.

"Dr. Hayes."

"Yes."

"I want to help."

"I know you do, Mr. Novak."

"No. I mean — I want to *help.* Whatever you are going to do in Minneapolis. I want to be there."

"You have a girlfriend. You have a cat. You have a career. You have, by all rights, earned a long period of time in which nothing like any of this happens to you ever again."

"I know."

"Frankie will not want you to."

"She will, actually."

"Yes, Mr. Novak. You are probably right."

Dr. Hayes looked at the photograph for a moment longer.

Then she folded it carefully. She put it in the cavity of the small bronze. She pressed the felt back into place. She put the sculpture in her cardigan pocket.

She stood up.

She was spry in a way that embarrassed me.

She offered me a hand.

I took it. I got up off the floor of the Society National Bank vault, in a tuxedo that was not a tuxedo, with ribs that had mostly healed, with a girlfriend four miles away, with a cat across town, with forty-six of forty-seven names in federal custody and one still in Minneapolis, and I took the small dry brown hand of a seventy-one-year-old retired NSA cryptanalyst, and I let her pull me to my feet.

She signaled Patricia.

Patricia came back.

We signed the release. We left the vault. We took the elevator up.

We came out into the lobby of the 1929 limestone tower, and through the brass revolving door, and into Public Square, where it was noon on a Saturday in September in 1996, and where the pigeons had the specific unhurried quality pigeons have when nothing is at stake.

Dr. Hayes and I stood on the sidewalk for a moment.

She said, "I will drive you back to Rocky River."

"Yes."

"We will talk to Frankie together."

"Yes."

"And then next week we will have a great deal of work to do."

"Yes."

"Do you need anything before we get in the car."

I thought about it.

"No," I said.

"Good," she said.

She fished her keys out of her pocket.

We got in the Volvo.

She pulled out of the parking space. She signaled. She merged into westbound traffic on Superior Avenue. The Terminal Tower receded in the rearview. Lake Erie appeared in the windshield, at the end of Superior, dark blue under a sky that was, that day, very specifically the color of a late summer afternoon.

The sculpture was in her cardigan pocket.

The photograph was inside the sculpture.

The daughter was in Minneapolis.

THIRTY — EPILOGUE: The Photograph

Dr. Hayes set the small bronze on the kitchen table between the four of us.

Mwangi looked at it.

"I see," she said.

"Yes."

Dr. Hayes pressed her thumbnail under the felt. She worked it up. She removed the photograph. She placed it face-up on the table.

Mwangi picked it up. She looked at it. She turned it over. She read the back. She looked up.

"Katarina Bauer," she said.

"Yes."

"She is the name you could not tell us."

"The name I could not tell *you,* Lorraine. There were reasons. You know the reasons."

"I know the reasons."

"I can brief you now, because the briefing has, since Tuesday, been downgraded to need-to-know with you two specifically. I was not going to brief you last Saturday in the field office because I did not, on Saturday, know whether Mr. Novak and Miss Russo were going to want to continue or to exit. I know now."

She looked at Frankie and me.

"Before I say what I'm about to say, I need to ask — do you want to continue."

Frankie said, "Yes."

It was instantaneous. She did not look at me. She did not consult me. She did not even consider. She said *yes,* flatly, across the kitchen table, and Mwangi did not show any surprise, because Mwangi had known, I understood in that second, that Frankie was going to say yes the moment Frankie had handed Valdez a Glock by the barrel and said *took you long enough.*

Mwangi looked at me.

"Mr. Novak."

"I need — can I have a minute."

"You can have two weeks."

"I need a minute."

"A minute."

I stood up. I walked out of the kitchen. I walked down the hall to the front parlor. I sat on the green couch. Ramona was on the arm of the couch. She looked at me with the expression of a cat who understood that something was happening and had decided, for the length of the decision, to be patient.

I sat for five minutes.

I thought about what Dr. Hayes had said, in her kitchen at three in the morning a week ago, about the tile floor of the docent's office and about my being a small man.

I thought about Frankie on the couch in this house when I had come in from the CMA in a tuxedo that was tight across the chest, with her hand on the back of my head and her thumb moving in small slow circles.

I thought about a girl with a tooth missing in a plaid dress in 1979.

I thought about the specific way my life had, twenty-seven days ago, contained exactly two people — Frankie, and my boss Kevin — who were operationally important to me, and about how it now contained five, all of whom were in this house or on an airplane somewhere specifically because of a sculpture I had picked off a tree lawn on a Sunday afternoon.

I thought about my job. I thought about the module due September fifteenth. I thought about how, when I returned to TRW on the fifteenth, I was going to walk past Galen Brennan's empty cubicle, and past Larry Acheson's empty cubicle, and I was going to sit down at my desk, and I was going to open a compliance training module on the classified handling of sensitive documents, and I was not going to be able to take any of what I had just learned and type any of it into the module, ever.

I was not going to be able to, ever again, design training for an organization without thinking about who in the organization might be on somebody's list.

I thought about the fact that this had already happened to me. That I had already become a person who thought that way. That nothing Mwangi was about to offer me was going to change that. The offer was not a decision. The offer was a recognition.

I stood up.

Ramona jumped down and followed me.

I went back to the kitchen. I sat down. I said, "Yes."

Mwangi nodded once. She opened the folder.

There is a lot of what Mwangi told us that afternoon that I am not going to reproduce here, partly because some of it is still not mine to tell and partly because the important parts I already knew. The name on the fourth line of the MEADOWLARK list was *BAUER, K.* — not an asset, not a spy, but the Ostrowskis' biological daughter, placed with an adoptive family in Minneapolis in 1979 under a sealed federal compartment, when Mikael and Elena had understood that keeping her was going to get her killed. Her adoptive name was Kate Bauer. She was twenty-four years old. She did not know what she was. She did not know that the last person to carry her photograph had died of potassium chloride at the Cleveland Clinic on a Friday in April.

She did not know that the next door, for the people in this kitchen, was hers.

What Mwangi told us that I did not already know: a specific compartment had been constituted, in the preceding week, to work the problem of Kate Bauer. It would involve Mwangi, and Dr. Hayes, and an FBI colleague in the Minneapolis field office, and a

Bureau physician with clearance. And if we said yes — which we had — it would involve us.

"Not now," Mwangi said. "Not this month, and probably not this year. You are going to go back to your life. You are going to fix your apartment. You are going to return to TRW. Miss Russo is going to rebuild her clients' porches. You are going to be, in all respects, yourselves — because yourselves is the best cover you have, and because you have earned a period of time in which nothing else happens to you. But when the time comes, I will call. You will decide, then, whether you answer."

She paused. She looked at the photograph still on the table.

"She has a front tooth missing," she said. "You can see it in the photograph. She was six years old. She does not, as far as we can tell, remember being six."

Nobody said anything.

"Somebody should," Mwangi said, "before someone in Moscow decides she is no longer useful and acts accordingly."

She closed the folder.

"One last thing. The sculpture. The small one."

"Yes."

"It stays with you."

I looked up.

"It is evidence that will not be processed. It is — by a specific agreement I have just obtained, with the specific provision that I am willing to stake my federal career on — retained by the original finder. Which is Dr. Hayes, who is assigning it to the person who did the actual finding. Which is you."

"Dr. Hayes —"

Dr. Hayes said, "Mr. Novak. I believe the sculpture ought to be in your possession, because the original is in federal custody and will be in federal custody forever, and because this one is the one you found. Not the one I found. The one *you* found. The original one you brought to my kitchen table on a Sunday morning in August. It is, I think, yours."

"The photograph —"

"The photograph stays with the sculpture. When the time comes — and it will come, Mr. Novak, within months — it comes out. Until then, it lives where Mikael put it."

"Okay."

"Take it home, Mr. Novak."

I picked up the small bronze. It was cool. It was dense. It fit in the pocket of the Cleveland Indians sweatshirt I was wearing, borrowed from Frankie, which was five sizes too small for Frankie and perfect on me. I felt the photograph inside the cavity shift slightly as I put it in.

Frankie reached across the table and took my hand.

Mwangi stood. She said a few more things — travel plans, next calls, logistics I was not going to remember. She paused at the back door.

"Miss Russo."

"Yes."

"In case nobody has said it tonight."

"Yes."

"Welcome."

Frankie said, "Thank you, Agent Mwangi."

"Claire, please."

"Claire."

Mwangi nodded. She walked out. The silver Escort backed out and turned east toward Detroit Road and disappeared.

Dr. Hayes opened the refrigerator. She took out three beers. She set one in front of each of us.

"I am seventy-one years old," she said, sitting down. "I have earned, after a day like today, a beer. You are also entitled."

Frankie opened hers. She drank.

I did not open mine right away.

"Dr. Hayes."

"Yes."

"Ruth. She said 1985. And the thing you said to her — it is the thing we talked about in 1985. What was 1985."

Dr. Hayes took a sip of her beer. She looked out the kitchen window. She set the bottle down.

"Mr. Novak, 1985 is a story for a specific Tuesday two or three years from now when we are sitting on a deck somewhere and you have earned the version of me that tells that story. You have, already, in your short career, earned a great deal of me. You have not yet earned that particular piece. Give me a few years."

"Okay."

"Good."

I opened the beer.

I drank.

It tasted like a beer in the kitchen of an FBI safe house in Rocky River at one-twelve in the afternoon on a Saturday in September of 1996, after a morning that had contained the retrieval of a photograph of a seven-year-old girl in a plaid dress, and it tasted, in the specific way of the first sip of a Dortmunder after you had gone three weeks without one, the way coming home tasted.

Three weeks later, on the first Sunday of October, Frankie and I drove to Shaker Heights.

The half-double on Cedar was repaired. Dr. Anselmi had — a fact that somewhat startled me — helped me replace the cushions of the couch. He had arrived on a Tuesday afternoon in a cardigan, with a book of upholstery swatches, and said, in a voice I had not heard in six years of being his upstairs neighbor, *I heard there was an incident. I have connections. Please allow me.* He matched the cushions to the original fabric in four days. He never mentioned the matter again. He had also, during the cushion incident, looked at me with an expression that suggested he knew considerably more about the preceding month than he had any right to know. He had never asked. I had never told. A specific understanding had been reached and then ignored into existence, which was the Cleveland Heights way.

Frankie had moved back in on the twenty-eighth. We rebuilt the back porch that weekend — the project she had been halfway through when all of it had started. On the Friday, she went to her mother's house in Collinwood with a cake from the bakery on Mayfield, and she sat at the dining room table, and she told her mother approximately thirty percent of what had happened. Her mother cried. Her mother hugged her for a long time. Her mother made me a plate of food I did not want and ate anyway. The conversation had not been repeated. It did not need to be.

The motorcycle had been replaced. I had bought, with the insurance money from the Ninja, a used 1995 Honda CB750 Nighthawk — an upright standard, comfortable seat, moderate forward lean, a bike for a person with healed ribs who had made certain decisions about his relationship to speed. Frankie saw it for the first time and said, *That is a dad bike.* I said, *Yes.* She said, *Good. I like the dad bike. Please have the dad bike.*

We rode the dad bike to Shaker Heights that Sunday.

It was the first genuinely cool day of the fall.

The leaves on the Shaker Heights streets had begun to turn. South Park Boulevard under the early October sky had a specific quality of light — brassy, low, coming through the sugar maples and the red oaks in a way that made the houses look unreasonably expensive, which they were. We rode north on South Park. I was in front. Frankie was behind me with her arms around my waist. Her chin was on my shoulder.

We passed 2341 South Park at 2:34 PM.

There was a U-Haul in the driveway.

A different U-Haul. Smaller. A man, forty, in jeans and a fleece. A woman, also forty, in a Michigan Wolverines sweatshirt. They were unloading boxes. A small girl — maybe seven, maybe eight — was running across the front lawn in circles, laughing, with an empty plastic pumpkin bucket in one hand.

There was a free pile on the tree lawn.

I slowed the bike.

The free pile had a stepladder, a set of four chairs, a box of Christmas ornaments, and — on top of a wooden crate — a small bronze sculpture.

Frankie said, from behind me, "Don't stop."

"I wasn't going to."

"You were slowing down."

"I was looking."

"Looking is okay."

I looked.

The sculpture on the crate was not Ruthanne Beck. It was not modernist. It was a small cast-iron Disney character — a bronze-painted reproduction of Mickey Mouse in a sorcerer's apprentice hat, maybe six inches tall, the kind of thing you could buy at a gift shop at Disney World in 1992. The previous owner had either not loved it or had received three of them and had unloaded the extra. I could not tell which.

It was, if you looked at it at a glance while riding past on a motorcycle, approximately shaped like a sculpture.

I did not stop.

I kept riding north on South Park.

The little girl ran across the lawn again, in a circle, laughing.

Frankie said, in my ear, "Theo."

"Yeah."

"You are going to notice every single bronze sculpture in Northeast Ohio for the rest of your life, aren't you."

"Yes."

"Okay."

"Yeah."

"I just wanted to confirm."

"Confirmed."

"I can live with that."

"Okay."

"I love you."

"I love you."

We rode to the end of South Park. We turned east on Van Aken. We took the long way back to Cleveland Heights, across the Shaker Lakes, past Dr. Hayes's bungalow on Lee Road, past the Fine Arts librarian's apartment building on Cedar-Coventry, which I had not yet visited but which I had, at some point in the preceding three weeks, located on a mental map I was beginning to keep. We rode in the early-October sun, and the maples over our heads were red, and the half-double was waiting for us with Ramona on the windowsill, and my cracked ribs were fully healed, and Frankie's broken pinky was still a little crooked, and the small bronze sculpture was on the top shelf of my living-room built-in, behind a pothos plant that had finally, at the end of the summer, given up and died, and which I had replaced with a fern.

The fern was alive.

The bronze was behind it.

Inside the bronze had been a photograph of a seven-year-old in a red-and-blue plaid dress, squinting at the sun on a patch of grass in front of a blue house, in Minneapolis, in July of 1979.

At 3:17 PM, local time, in Minneapolis, in an apartment on the second floor of a brick four-flat in the Seward neighborhood, a twenty-four-year-old biomedical research coordinator named Kate Bauer came home from a Saturday shift at the University of Minnesota Hospital and picked her mail off the floor inside her front door.

There were four pieces.

A credit card statement. A promotional flyer from a restaurant down the street. An envelope from her landlord. And a plain manila envelope, eight by ten, addressed to her in handwriting she did not recognize, with no return address and a Minneapolis postmark.

She set the other mail on the counter. She opened the manila envelope.

Inside was a photograph.

The photograph was color, four by six, faded. It showed a small girl, about seven years old, standing on a patch of grass in front of a blue house. The girl was in a red-and-blue plaid dress with a white collar. She was squinting at the sun. She had a front tooth missing.

The girl in the photograph was her.

She did not know how she knew. She had no memory, that she could access, of being seven years old. She had few memories, she would later realize, of being much younger than ten. But she knew, in the specific way a body knows, that the girl in the photograph was her.

She turned the photograph over.

There were two lines of handwriting on the back, in a careful sloping cursive. The ink was faded. The words, in English, said:

Katya — safe. Minneapolis.

Protect her.

She did not, at first, understand the words.

She understood, instantly and in a way she could not have explained to anyone, the *handwriting.*

The handwriting had a quality. She did not have words for the quality. It looped in a specific way, and the lowercase *a*s opened at the top in a specific way, and the downstroke of the *f* in *safe* had a particular small flourish at the bottom, and she looked at the handwriting, and something in her chest —

Something in her chest —

She sat down on the hallway floor.

She was on the hallway floor for a long time.

She did not call her adoptive parents. She did not call her best friend. She did not call any of the people she might normally have called.

She sat on the hallway floor of her apartment in Minneapolis, with an envelope in her lap and a photograph in her hand, and she looked at the handwriting on the back of a photograph of herself at seven, and she felt a thing she had never felt before, which was the specific pressure of a memory that was not accessible to her but that was — for the first time in her adult life — genuinely present in her body.

Katya.

Nobody had ever called her Katya.

She knew, somehow, that somebody had.

Outside her apartment window, on Twenty-Ninth Street, a bus went past. The bus shook the window in its frame slightly. The light in the hallway was the specific light Minneapolis apartments had on the first Sunday of October in 1996, in the late afternoon, when the sun came through the curtains at a low western angle and turned everything the color of honey.

Kate Bauer sat on the floor of her hallway and held the photograph.

After a while she would get up.

After a while she would put the photograph on her kitchen table and make herself a cup of tea and call her mother in Saint Paul and say, in a voice that was a little odd, *Mom, I got a strange piece of mail today.*

But not yet.

For now she was sitting on the hallway floor of an apartment in Minneapolis, looking at a photograph of herself at seven, and she was feeling a thing she did not have words for, and somewhere across the country — in a half-double on Cedar-Fairmount in Cleveland Heights, Ohio, on a shelf above a television behind a small fern — a small bronze sculpture stood empty, with a felt-bottomed cavity that had, for seventeen years, contained her.

\- ***End of Book One*** -

www.ingramcontent.com/pod-product-compliance
Lightning Source LLC
LaVergne TN
LVHW031925090826
845145LV00018B/2834

* 9 7 8 1 9 6 6 7 0 3 3 6 5 *